REA

**DO NOT REMOVE
CARDS FROM POCKET**

Hazard Zones

a novel

Keith Maillard

HarperPerennial
HarperCollins*Publishers*Ltd

First edition

Background cover image © 1995 PhotoDisc, Inc.

Canadian Cataloguing in Publication Data

Maillard, Keith, 1942-
    Hazard zones

ISBN 0-00-224397-0

I. Title.

PS8576.A49H3 1995   C813'.54   C95-931375-3
PR9199.3.M35H3 1995

---

96 97 98 99 ❖ HC 10 9 8 7 6 5 4 3 2

Printed and bound in the United States

...you only learn *the* shape of the river; and you learn it with such absolute certainty that you can always steer by the shape that's *in your head*, and never mind the one that's before your eyes.

—riverboat pilot Horace Bixby's advice to the young Mark Twain

1

FOR A WHILE THERE'S NO SOUND but the sad hum of the car on the highway. Then, just as I'm starting to drift away inside myself and get lost, Cynthia says, laughing, "*Moon Run*, I don't believe it."

I'd forgotten the sign that marks the turn-off to Moon Run, and I'm pleased that she's noticed it. I'm pleased by her readiness to notice anything the least bit exotic.

I'm driving south toward the river with my wife in a car I rented at the Pittsburgh airport. We've left our kids in the care of Cynthia's parents, and we're feeling a bit of that giddy, guilty, naughty elation we get whenever we can manage to be alone together longer than ten minutes. Cynthia's heard plenty about the Ohio Valley, but she's never seen it, and this unexpected chance to show it to her makes me oddly happy. Now I can't remember why I've always been so reluctant to take her to Raysburg.

Like a kid, she keeps asking, "Are we in West Virginia yet?"

"Nope," I say, "you'll see the sign."

My wife and I are the kind of people American industrial workers would like to stand up in front of a wall and shoot—she drives a vintage Beetle inherited from her mom, and I drive a Honda—and so, to carry us into the heart of the rust belt in the most appropriate fashion, I've rented a Chrysler New Yorker. It's a talking car, speaks to us in a deep, persuasive voice ("Fasten your seat

1

belt"/"Your door is ajar"), and isolates me so much from any sense of the road that I might as well be piloting a boat. Only a few hours ago we hadn't been planning to go anywhere, and it's happened too fast—flying will do that to you—so where we are feels as improbable as Kathmandu. It's a lovely evening late in May, and I'm happier than I have any right to be. If I weren't so anxious, I could make myself believe we're off on a grand adventure.

"I wish my grandmother was still alive," I say to Cynthia. "You guys would have really liked each other."

"Yeah, we probably would. The matriarch."

"No, she wasn't exactly a matriarch. She was more like—I don't know—she was like the river. She was always there. She defined the boundaries. She connected everything."

My grandmother's family—her "people," she would have said—were river people. "We've got the river in our blood, Larry," she used to tell me. So if my wife can't meet my grandmother, at least I can show her the river. The Ohio River is, you understand, the center of the universe.

My training's in geography (although I'd hesitate to call myself a geographer), and I have the perfect job. I'm a senior editor at Plenart and Northcott, one of the oldest and most respected publishers of textbooks in the United States. We don't have a corner on the geography textbook market, but we come close to it. We publish—and have published for nearly thirty years—*the* standard introductory textbook in physical geography. We publish nearly all of the first-rate American texts in human geography, and we were the first to publish an authoritative introductory text in ecology. It's now in its sixth edition and continues to sell like popcorn.

In the seventies, we branched out and now have several quite respectable psychology texts, and (begun by my ex-lover Phyllis, who, thank God, has left us to teach at Brandeis) a line in women's studies that's proven to be a big money maker. We've just brought out a cross-disciplinary book of selected readings in environmental ethics (it was my baby), and it's moving quite well. P. an' N. has always been a solid company, and it looks like it's going to continue to be a solid company even in the problematical nineties. If you know what you're doing, publishing textbooks is pretty much recession-proof.

I enjoy talking to geographers, and I know most of the top geographers in the United States on a first name basis and take them to lunch when they're in Boston. I don't make an obscene amount of money, but I certainly can't complain about what I do make. I'm fascinated by recent developments in human geography, and it's a legitimate part of my job to keep up with the literature. I love going to work, and I feel guilty about that from time to time. Most people I know don't love going to work. Lots of people these days don't even have any work to go to.

I'm fifty years old, and I can't imagine any life I'd like better than the one I've got. I'm finally the right man in the right place, and what got me to that right place was years of random meandering, vast blocks of wasted time, innumerable wrong turns, fuck-ups, and humiliating failures, a perverse dedication to screwing myself up, and a colossal amount of sheer, pig-headed stupidity. (I am not, you understand, recommending that route to anybody else— although my wife sometimes thinks I am.) And the eeriest thing about it is that if you had asked me only a few years ago, I would have told you that working at Plenart and Northcott was the most dismal of dead-ends—a wretched little cul-de-sac perfectly suited to a loser who couldn't finish his Ph.D.

When I started the Ph.D. I would never finish, I was drawn immediately into the study of hazard zones, probably because I'd grown up in one, grown up hearing my grandmother's tales of the great, legendary floods—the '98 flood, the pumpkin flood, the '36 flood—and I'd lived through a few floods myself and thought

3

they were great fun. (Of course I wasn't the one who had to shovel the mud off the sidewalks or clean out the soggy basement.) Working on the thesis I would never finish, I interviewed residents of Raysburg Island where I'd lived for the first eighteen years of my life. I asked them to fill out a questionnaire about the advantages and disadvantages of living on Raysburg Island. I was interested in how these people perceived their environment—in particular, how they perceived floods, but I didn't tell them that.

The Ohio River floods Raysburg Island with monotonous— although not predictable—regularity. "Ohio" is, of course, an Indian word; no one any longer remembers what it means, but it has been suggested that it might refer to the white foam on the river when it's flooding. The local Indians warned the first whites about floods, but those land-hungry pioneers knew a good hunk of real estate when they saw it and settled on the Island anyway (flood plains have always been attractive). During the twenty years preceding the Civil War, Raysburg Island—despite repeated flooding—was considered fashionable by Raysburg's gentry; after the war, when the wealthy began building along the Cumberland Pike (as they persisted in calling the National Road), the Island became home for the sober, industrious, middle American, apple-pie families who were still living there when I was a kid. The floods didn't seem to bother them either.

A system of dams and locks has, in recent years, reduced the severity and number of floods on the Island but has certainly not eliminated them. And what I discovered—at least in my preliminary research—was quite similar to what other researchers have discovered about people who live in hazard zones. It appears that the longer you live on Raysburg Island—that is, the more you actually know from firsthand experience about floods—the less you consider flooding a disadvantage at all.

The most interesting group in my study were lifetime residents of Raysburg Island old enough to remember the disastrous flood of 1936 when the entire Island was evacuated. A record number of lives were lost; approximately 20,000 people were rendered temporarily homeless; the Ohio picked up many of the houses in the low-lying areas of the Island and ground them against each other into kindling. But when they listed the disadvantages to living on Raysburg Island, eighty-seven percent of my respondents who had lived through the '36 flood did not bother to mention flooding at all; the other thirteen percent ranked it extremely low—in some cases lower than things they'd written into the blank I'd labeled "other," such as "Route 70's cut the Island right in half," or "there's a different class of people moving over here now." When I was a young hotshot in graduate school at Harvard, I used to think I understood the significance of this—you know, the big, major, *human* significance—but the older I get, the more I realize I don't know shit from Shinola.

Our day started in an absolutely ordinary way. Patrick wouldn't get up, so I yanked the blanket off him, and he went stomping into the kitchen in a funk, and Cynthia yelled at me from Alison's room: "Larry. For God's sake." (Her period's due any minute, and she was not, this morning, the most placid of moms.) "Will you please explain something to *your daughter*. Tell her if it's cold and raining, she's got to wear pants to daycare."

The way I talk sometimes drives Cynthia nuts—the way (and the formulation is hers, not mine) it takes me forever to get to the point. She pretends to believe that this is a genetic flaw selectively bred into all West Virginians and offers our daughter as evidence. Alison loves digression just as much as her daddy, and she and I often have long conversations so lacking in any point whatsoever that my wife can't stand to be in the same room with us.

5

"Alison," I said to my daughter this morning, "have you considered owls?"

Alison stopped screaming, and I was delighted that my ploy had actually worked—although I couldn't resist giving Cynthia a triumphant look: see how easy it is.

"Owls?" Alison said, looking up at me expectantly. Her eyelashes were beaded with tiny tears, each as perfect as a dew drop, and, for a good second or two, I loved her so much I ached with it. Alison, although she has never set foot in the state of West Virginia, speaks with a West Virginia accent (another genetic flaw, Cynthia says); she pronounces her own name Owlison, and so believes that owls are related to her. "Have you considered," I asked her, "why owls are so well adapted to flying at night?"

"Oh, for Christ's sake," Cynthia said and walked out—but I got Alison into pants, and Cynthia got Patrick out the door and across to the neighbors' where he waits for the school bus, and Cynthia went shooting off with Alison in the car seat in the Beetle, and I made the train with five minutes to spare, and everything was absolutely ordinary.

But now we've just entered the state of West Virginia, and they've changed the sign; it no longer says "almost heaven," and I'm keenly disappointed that it no longer says that, and then suddenly, with a sickening, visceral lurch, I remember *car seat*—Cynthia's dad, Warren, has achieved the kind of loopy, golden-age goofiness that should be the lot of all old folks but rarely is; at eighty, he's as pleasant as can be but has long ago ceased to be useful for anything as focused as driving an automobile, and so Flossie will be driving, and *does she have a car seat?* No, of course she doesn't, and it's over by now anyway; she's already picked up Alison at daycare, and Patrick at the neighbors', and if she's driven off the road and killed both our kids, it's already happened.

"You okay?" Cynthia says, picking up on my silence.

"Sure," I lie to her.

"We'll call as soon as we get to Raysburg, okay?" she says, one jump ahead of me as she often is.

The reason we're driving to West Virginia on a Thursday night when we should be at home feeding our kids dinner in Sharon, Massachusetts, is that my mother is in the Raysburg General Hospital. She had a heart attack or a stroke—or some damn thing—last night. No one knew about it until this morning. I had just arrived at P. an' N. when I got the call. My mother was still unconscious, the doctor said. Critical, he said. "Should I come down?" I asked. "Let's put it this way," the doctor said, "if she was my mother, I'd be on the next plane." We were on the next plane. We still don't know anything more than that. For all we know, she may be dying.

I know perfectly well she isn't dying. She spent two weeks with us at Christmas, and by the time she left, I knew she was going to be around to bug me forever.

"Is everybody in this town Jewish?"

"Sure, Maw. We're the only non-Jews within a radius of five hundred miles."

"Oh, Larry, don't be that way. I was just asking. By the way, do you always keep your house this cold?"

Our house is an old colonial, and a bit drafty, but I'd already turned the thermostat up to seventy for her. She sat in the kitchen close to the stove—whether anything was cooking or not—and drank vodka. I'd never known my mother to drink vodka. She drank it mixed with orange juice or V8 juice or 7-Up; when none of those were available, she drank it with water. She started drinking at lunch and drank steadily all afternoon and all evening. We were buying her a fifth every other day. "Hey, Maw, don't you think you're a little heavy into the sauce?"

"So what if I am? I'm on vacation."

Before she came to visit, all she could talk about on the phone—
and she calls me every Sunday morning—was moving to Sharon.
"No, I don't want to live *with you*. I lived a good many years on my
own, and I like my independence. But if there was a nice little
apartment..." There are no nice little apartments in Sharon.

And when she was actually in Sharon, she said, "This seems like
a pleasant enough little town, *but...* I don't know... I don't like it
much. It seems kind of bleak somehow."

"It's the end of December, Maw. If you don't like snow, bleak's
the name of the game. And Sharon's a bedroom community, you
know. There really isn't anything here much to rent. But if you
wanted to come up, we could probably find you something over
in Norwood—"

"Well, you can just forget *that*."

All of my mother's statements had an enormous *but* quivering in
the center of them like a dying fish. Cynthia's a good wife, *but* did she
ever learn to cook? Patrick's a perfectly nice kid, *but* it's a shame how
he talks back to his mother. It sure is nice to see you settled down,
Larry, *but* don't you think you should get some of that weight off?
The only one who was not subjected to my mother's terrible *but* was
her granddaughter. Alison knew a sucker when she saw one. Alison
had never tasted chocolate before Granny came to visit. Now she asks
for it every day. "You have a good life here, Larry," my mother said as
she was leaving, *but* I think I'll just stay where I am—*until I die*."

The first phone call I got from my mother when she was back
in Raysburg, she said, "Well, have you been thinking about my
future?"

"Your future? What about it?"

"What am I supposed to do, live alone here the rest of my life?
Have you thought about a nice little apartment in Sharon?"

So I say to Cynthia what I'm sure we've both been thinking:
"We're probably going to have to bring her back with us."

"Yeah, that's right."

We ride along in silence for a while, and I know we're both adding up the dollars. "Where we going to put her?" I say.

"We're going to have to wait and see how sick she is."

I hate Route 70, so when I can, I get onto the National Road. The sense of adventure has ebbed away, and suddenly I feel as old as Methuselah. If Cynthia weren't with me, I'd be hating every minute of this.

I met Cynthia at—of all crazy things—a lawn party. It was one of those parties with themes where you're supposed to come in a costume, exactly the sort of party I hate; the invitation said HONEST-TO-GOD OLD-FASHIONED LAWN PARTY and had a picture lifted from an old magazine of men in tuxedos and women in hats strolling languidly over somebody's impossibly big lawn. The party was given by Steve and Becky Segal because Steve had just been promoted to senior editor at P. an' N. (I hadn't yet, although I'd been there just as long as he had.) I'd been to their house in Sharon a couple times, so I knew how to get there. It would never have occurred to me in a million years that I might end up married, with two kids, living in Sharon.

I was just coming out of a long period of being totally dry. The thing about being a middle-aged man standing around at a party with a glass of Perrier in your hand is that all the other recovering alcoholics—as we like to call ourselves—can spot you from a mile off, and pretty soon you're deep in conversation with somebody else who's waving around a glass of Perrier, and what you're talking about is *not drinking*. But I had just discovered that if I went for a good, long swim before a party, I could drink exactly two beers at the cocktail hour (I was careful that it never turned into three) and get wonderfully, gloriously blasted—and then have dinner and end up sober as a stone an hour later. No mess, no fuss, no hangover, and the best thing about it is that if you've got a glass of beer in your hand, nobody is going to come up and want to talk about dry-out clinics and AA meetings.

The other thing was that I'd been seeing a therapist for a couple years. When I'd been at my worst, nearly everyone who knew me had said, "Hey, Larry, why don't you *see somebody?*" A certain Dr. Jessie Wilson came highly recommended; what everybody said about him was that there was "no bullshit, no mumbo-jumbo, none of this touchy-feely crap," and I'd liked that. So I made an appointment and walked into his office, and said "Dr. Wilson?" and he stood up and offered me his hand and said, "Call me Jessie." My friends, in true liberal fashion, had not bothered to tell me that he was a black man.

There ensued one of those long, meaningful silences that can be so effective in European movies—a much longer and more meaningful silence than Hollywood would ever allow—until he said, in a very matter-of-fact voice, "So, Larry, do you think you would be more comfortable with somebody white?"

"Yes," I said, "I'm certain I'd be more comfortable with somebody white, but I think I'll stick with you."

Jessie was a good choice. He listens very carefully and takes notes (although, at first, I used to imagine he was writing things like "milk, eggs, and don't forget the dry cleaning"), and then he quotes you back to yourself. Unless you have actually undergone this process, you can't really understand the effect it has; the effect it had on me was to make me realize just how profoundly stupid I've often been in my life, and then, when I'm just on the point of being stupid again, to make me stop and think about it, and then—maybe—do something different from what I usually do.

So I was at the lawn party, not really in costume, but at least with a tie on, and I was halfway through my second beer on an empty stomach and fairly buzzed, and Becky Segal drifted over to me and said, "Well, do you want to meet her, or what?"

I guess I must have been staring at Cynthia. She was the cool, lovely, self-possessed young woman standing alone under a tree, holding a glass of white wine like a prop while she surveyed the rest of us with a bored and somewhat superior air. (She knew hardly anyone there, was worried that she was overdressed, and felt so nervous and shy that she had just been on the point of leaving.) She was wearing a white, Masterpiece Theatre dress that must have cost a bomb (a hand-me-down from her mom), white kid gloves (an excuse to cover up her ratty nails), and lots more makeup than I was used to seeing (she liked to wear makeup to piss off her PC friends from Radcliffe), and I took her for a pampered Sharon rich girl (she was a single mom living with her four-year-old son in a tiny apartment in Norwood, taking night classes in computers so she could get a better job). "She's too young for me," I said.

"She's thirty-three or -four, something like that," Becky said, "that's too young?"

"Well... no." I'd thought she was about twenty-five.

"So why not meet her? She's perfectly nice."

I had, within the month, squirmed my way though a horrible session with Jessie in which I'd tried to explain to him why I'd never in my life been involved with the kind of girl or woman I'd really wanted. My initial position had been that they wouldn't go out with me, but that hadn't proven to be the case.

"Let's see," he'd said, consulting his notes, "there was the girl you met at a dance in high school. She was a majorette, and you thought majorettes were really sexy, and you thought she was more than just sexy, she was, what? A kind of ideal girl?" (I nodded; it was a good summary of what I'd thought.) "And you had a nice chat with her, and she gave you her number, but then you never called her up. Why was that?" And starting with the majorette (Susie MacGregor was her name, I still remember it), he'd gone

through a fairly long list of girls and women I had not asked out—
or I'd slept with once but had not seen again—but whose names I
still remembered and somehow mysteriously managed to bring up
in his office years later. "Do you see a pattern?" he'd said.

"What pattern?" I'd said, although I saw the pattern perfectly
well.

"All right, introduce me," I said to Becky, and she led me over
to Cynthia and introduced us. "You guys have a lot in common,"
she said. "Neither one of you finished your Ph.D.s," and she left us
to fend for ourselves.

I can't imagine anything worse Becky could have said. I saw that
Cynthia was just as upset as I was—dismayed, I think is not too
strong a word—but I was drunk as a skunk on my second beer, and
I felt a sappy, adolescent rush (she was, up close, even more won-
derful than she'd been at a distance), so I said, "That's terrific.
Where didn't you finish your Ph.D.?"

She smiled; I saw her relax—slightly. "Oh, out in California. How
about you?"

"Harvard."

"That's a great place not to finish your Ph.D. What didn't you
get your Ph.D. in?"

"Geography. I didn't write about hazard zones on the Ohio
River. What didn't you write about?"

"I didn't write about Mrs. Clarissa Coltsworth Epping," she
said, "the best of the second-rate nineteenth-century American
women novelists."

We were both laughing by then, and off we went strolling over
Becky and Steve's freshly cut lawn in the lovely summer sunshine,
and I told her that I'd never finished my thesis because I couldn't
stop doing the research, and I kept piling up more and more stuff,
and it kept getting bigger and bigger, and somehow I forgot what
it was supposed to be about. And she said that was amazing,

because that was a lot like what had happened to her—and then there was the problem of approach. Everybody in grad school had been getting into Lacan and Barthes and Derrida and *all that bullshit*, and she'd tried, but she didn't understand it, and when she did understand it, she didn't believe a word of it.

At that point I was well into my third year of being involved with Dr. Phyllis Langford who was doing her best to deconstruct me. I'd had Lacan and Barthes and Derrida quoted at me interminably; I'd heard all about what Simone de Beauvoir had to say about "otherness"; according to Phyllis, my attitudes toward women—specifically, the things I liked about women—were totally fucked, and the only hope for me was if I *changed*. "I *am* changing," I used to yell at her from time to time—although I wasn't, at least not in what I liked about women.

I looked straight into Cynthia's big brown eyes, and I thought, *you're too good to be true*. And Cynthia looked straight back into my eyes and thought (as she told me after I had moved in with her and Patrick): oh, what a nice man; I just hope he's got a steady job, and he likes kids, and he isn't afraid of making a commitment—*and he isn't a total flake like all the rest of them*.

If she'd met me even a few months before, I would have turned out to be a total flake like all of the rest of them.

I'd hoped that Cynthia and Dr. Phyllis Langford would never cross paths, but given life's little ironies, I should have known they'd run into each other eventually. Phyllis is only four years older than Cynthia, which makes them roughly of the same generation; they both come from upper-middle-class families; they both were sixties-style rebels in high school, went to good universities, studied English literature, and graduated with honors. Yet I can't imagine any two women less likely to feel attraction or sympathy toward each other—and I don't just mean that one finished her Ph.D. and the other didn't. I'd hoped they could at least be civil. No such luck. For starters, each was wearing the wrong uniform.

We were at the annual P. an' N. Christmas party—the first one after Cynthia and I got married—and attendance at these things is, if you know what's good for you, mandatory. Cynthia has a solid grasp of office politics, and, from her point of view, the outfit she'd chosen should have offended absolutely nobody. It was a navy dress with a white lace collar (and the skirt was not too short), worn with navy-and-white pumps (and the heels were not too high). As she often does when she's dressed up, she had a demure, old-fashioned look, and it worked perfectly well on old Tom Northcott who beamed at her like Jehovah.

Dr. Phyllis Langford was wearing a baggy cotton exercise suit and Nikes. She'd made an effort too. The exercise suit was fairly new and a cheery apricot color.

"That's *her*, huh?" Cynthia said.

"Yep," I said.

"Why am I not surprised?" She'd heard as much about Phyllis as I'd heard about Patrick's father—which was not everything, but enough. "So, are you going to introduce me?"

"Sure," I said, but I didn't quite get around to it.

Later, I was chatting with Steve and Becky, and I looked across the room, and there were Cynthia and Phyllis deep in conversation. Oh, terrific, I thought. Cynthia has never told me what they said; all I know is that, as suddenly as if they were on a drill team and the commander had shouted, "About face, forward march," they turned and walked away from each other. Cynthia was so angry the blood had drained out of her face. "Jesus," she said, "what a bitch."

"What on earth did she say to you?"

"Shit. It's not worth repeating."

Phyllis always looks for the deep, subconscious motivations that make people do what they do (as opposed to what they *say* about it, which, she claims, is always bullshit); so what made her insult Cynthia? (If that's what happened—maybe she thinks Cynthia insulted her.) And—as long as we're going to contemplate these great imponderables—why were Phyllis and I lovers for nearly three years despite the fact that we fought like terriers? What attracted us to each other in the first place, and what did we fight about? Just what, in short, were we *doing* with each other? If we're talking deep, subconscious motivation here, I haven't the remotest idea.

"Jesus, Larry," Phyllis must have yelled at me four hundred and fifty-three million times, "I am *not* a lesbian separatist." But after we split up (if that's what we did; she would never admit that we had been "together"), she chopped her hair off, gained fifteen pounds, stopped wearing makeup (she never wore much to start with), and set up house with another woman—a jolly, steel-haired women's historian in her fifties who's never been anything but totally pleasant to me—a hell of a lot more pleasant than Phyllis, for that matter.

Phyllis is still a consultant at P. an' N., so we're forced to see each other whether we want to or not—but we go one step further and do lunch a couple times a year. Neither of us approves of the other; I'm sure we each think the other has sold out—but no, that isn't the jargon she'd use; she'd say I'd been "recuperated"—but we know each other so well that we can, grudgingly, let bygones be bygones— almost. "You're such an asshole, Larry," Phyllis says, but she's smiling when she says it, and I hear in her voice something I could take for affection.

I'm amazed—and I think Phyllis is too—that we could have been together at all, under any pretext, and lasted at it longer than the first night when obviously the only thing we had in common—at least on that particular occasion we had it in common— was a horniness that would have done justice to a couple polecats.

So we continue to do lunch just so we can continue to be amazed. And Phyllis has never mentioned Cynthia, has never acknowledged that she ever met her, has never once asked me the easy, polite, ritual question: "So how's Cynthia?" She's never even inquired about the health of my children.

During the three years Phyllis and I were seeing each other, we wasted—I can't think of a gentler word, so, yes, we *wasted*—huge blocks of time searching for just the right something or other while she made her usual wry and witty jokes about "commodity fetishism." There was, for instance, only one possible brand of shampoo (an alternative in the Body Shop would do, but only in an emergency), and only one possible bra, and only a handful of stores (miles apart) that sold anything at all that a self-respecting woman would consider for a moment putting on her back.

After hours of futile shopping, we'd eat in small, hard to find, emphatically smoke-free, and breathtakingly expensive restaurants that slowly served imported white wine and exquisite tidbits of some strange fish accompanied by a melon slice, a bit of kiwi fruit, and a cilantro leaf. I used an after-shave that cost twenty-five bucks a bottle, wore imported Italian underwear, and tried to convince myself that I enjoyed collecting videos of classic European movies. We always had a shower before we went to bed—and often another shower when we got up again.

Now I favor restaurants that specialize in delivering, at lightning speed, a cold beer and huge portions of basic grub including the essential large blob of starch (mashed potatoes are always a good bet) that I can shove into Alison before she starts screaming. Cynthia shops at Frugal Fanny's, and if she doesn't see something she wants in ten minutes, walks out. I use Mennen Skin Bracer in the economy size bottle, wear whatever underwear's on sale at Filene's, and about the only things I collect these days are Cynthia's parking tickets ("Not fair!" I hear her yell from offstage in mind).

Cynthia and I both shower on our lunch breaks (I swim, and she jumps up and down to music—as she calls her aerobics classes—at the Norwood community center). The most physical intimacy we can manage most nights is holding hands as we lie side by side like a pair of medieval sarcophagus carvings.

I'm not sure I would have chosen Sharon as a place to settle down, but, seeing as the choice was made for me, I like it just fine. It is—I don't know how else to put this—a nice little community. There's maybe a bit too much money around and certainly not quite enough for teenagers to do to keep them out of trouble, but it sure beats Sommerville. What it all comes down to in the end is simply a matter of living your life, and I like my current life just fine. Our buzz-word for this is "lifestyle," and *style* should be a matter of personal preference, although in this meat-headed age, nothing is any longer personal, and we fight about matters of style the way the morons of the Middle Ages fought about religion. And the best I can tell—again, we're talking deep, subconscious motivation here, or trying to—is that the happier you are with your own life, the more room you can allow other people to be happy with theirs, even if their lives don't look a thing like yours.

I'd like to drive straight to the Ohio River, but I can't do that. As soon as we're in the lobby of the RGH (do they call it a "lobby" in a hospital?), Cynthia calls her parents. "The kids are fine," she whispers to me, holding the phone away from her ear; on the other end, Flossie, my mother-in-law, is yattering away like a gnome about dinners, eaten and uneaten, and bedtimes, and clothes for school and day-care—an apparent infinity of details and loose ends.

When I get my turn with the kids, Patrick asks me right off the top, "Is Granny all right?" He's a gawky, inward boy (much the way I was at his age), and his question takes me by surprise. It wouldn't have occurred to me that he could have managed to see outside of himself enough to care one way or the other—or maybe Flossie's primed him. "Oh, she's going to be just fine," I boom at him in the authoritative dad voice I reserve for statements like, "Yes, I am absolutely certain that spider is not a black widow"— although I don't yet know anything about my mother's condition (and, for that matter, couldn't tell a black widow from a flamingo).

"Grandmaw has a apple doll," Alison informs me.

"Is that right?"

"I don't play with her," she says dubiously. "Dad?" she says, brightly, as though the thought has just occurred to her, "can *I* have a apple doll?"

"I don't know what a apple doll is, hon."

"Yes, you do, Daddy. A *apple* doll. It's big, it's, uh, uh... you know, it's big and little. A brown one."

"Oh, I see. Well, if you're a good girl for Grandmaw, I'll bring you back a treat."

Then she says what she always says when I try a bribe like that: "I *am* a good girl."

We say our nighty-nights, and Cynthia and I are left for a long, fat moment in a fragile, decompressed state like a couple loony divers who have popped up too fast. I hate hospitals.

"There's the information desk," she says, taking charge. She's still in her office clothes, and I walk a step or two behind her, admiring her I-work-for-a-living suit and brisk little heels. "Oh... Mrs. Armbruster," the woman behind the desk is saying, "Oh, yes, she's on the fourth floor, I think. Maybe I'd better call. Yes, let me call." Something about this makes my skin crawl. "I'm her son," I say, too loudly, and add, idiotically, "I just got here."

Cynthia gives me a quick look and squeezes my hand. The fourth floor it is. We're met by a tall woman, maybe in her late twenties, who's not wearing a nurse's uniform. She introduces herself, but everything she says goes right by me; she tells us her name and what her position is, and the moment it's out of her mouth, I've lost it. She leads us into a little side room with chairs in it. "Mr. Armbruster—" she says.

"No," I say, "Cameron. My name's Cameron."

There's a snarl of misconnections hanging in the air at that; the three of us have suddenly been turned to porcelain and are staring at each other with brittle, inquisitive, and infinitely polite faces. The woman is not what you would call pretty, but she has a big, forthright, country girl's look to her—it's quite appealing—and I'm not surprised to see a wedding ring. She's risen slightly onto her toes and looks as though she might tip forward.

"Yes, but that's my mother," I manage to say—and see at once that I haven't clarified a damn thing.

"Mrs. Armbruster married again," Cynthia says, neatly. She steps close to me and takes my hand again. I realize that I'm not thinking straight. There doesn't seem to be anything I can do about the fact that I'm not thinking straight.

"Oh," the woman says. "But Margaret Armbruster is your mother?"

"Yes."

"I'm sorry, but she passed away."

"That can't be right," I hear myself saying, "I just got here."

"I'm sorry, Mr.—"

"Cameron. Larry Cameron. There must be some mistake. Are we talking about the same person?"

"Mrs. Margaret Armbruster?"

"Yes, that's right."

"I'm sorry. She passed away about an hour ago."

"Look," I say, really angry, "that can't be right. I got here as fast as I could."

"I'm sorry, Mr. Cameron."

I turn and look at Cynthia. Her eyes have filled with tears, but she's not crying. "We got here as fast as we could," I tell her firmly, as though matters of great significance depend upon that.

"I know we did, hon."

I am, so far as I can tell, not feeling anything. I am also acutely aware that everything that's coming out of my mouth is totally idiotic. Before I can stop myself, the next thing I say is, "Are you sure she's really dead?"

The woman assigned to us is not enjoying this. She can't even speak. At my question, her mask has slipped off, and now she casts me a look so openly sorrowful, so hapless, so downright *terrified*, that I feel like offering her my condolences.

Suddenly I have to sit down. My hands are shaking. I haven't smoked in ten years, but I'd kill for a cigarette. "Oh, God," I say, "this isn't right."

"No," Cynthia says, "It's not right. It's terrible."

The woman is speaking again. She sounds like a telephone company message. "She never regained consciousness. We did everything we could. Would you like to see her?"

When I walk into the room, I feel something hit my chest like a fierce electric shock. My mother is lying on her back in a hospital bed. The sheet is tucked neatly around her. Her hands are folded and her eyes are shut. She is wearing neither her glasses nor her false teeth, so she doesn't look like herself. I feel dumb and stupid and slow. I put my hand on her forehead, and she's not as warm as a normal person, but she's not cold either. "Hi, Maw," I say.

Behind me, the woman is going on and on and on. It's all about my mother's medical condition and what they did about it. I can't concentrate on anything she's saying. I turn and look at Cynthia, and Cynthia says to the woman, "Will you please shut up."

I hear a gasp, but the woman shuts up. I pat my mother's hands. I don't know what else to do. I know I should be thinking serious and profound thoughts, but there's nothing but a stuck record that keeps saying, "We got here as fast as we could." I would like the woman to leave us alone, but I know she's not going to. "Oh, God," I say to Cynthia, "this is the shits."

Then, suddenly—wham—I'm crying. It hits me so fast and hard I'm doubled over with it, and some distant thing in my head is saying, hey, this is familiar; you've done this before.

We leave. We should eat, I suppose, but I don't feel like it. Cynthia offers to drive, but I want to drive. The car says, "Fasten your seat belt." I drive across the Suspension Bridge, follow Front Street up to Belle Isle (only the old folks still call it that) and park. I unlock the door to my mother's apartment, climb the stairs, step into the living room, light the lights, and my mother should be pushing herself up from the big chair in front of the TV to say, "Hi, honey," but she's not. Her cane is hooked over the arm of the chair, and that's what gets to me, and again I'm bawling like a baby.

"We can't stay here," I yell at Cynthia, push past her blindly and run down the stairs.

I'm standing on the bank of the Ohio River—the "front" river—on Raysburg Island looking over to downtown Raysburg. Nothing much has changed since I was a kid—except one big thing: the air's clean now because they no longer manufacture steel here. But the "Raysburg Stogie" sign is still here, and the hills still rise up steeply behind the buildings of downtown; above and behind them, the twilight sky is gray as slate. I hear a nighthawk, and his raw squawk starts me crying again. Turning to my right, I can see the splendid lines of the Suspension Bridge; they've strung it with lights since I was here last, and it's eerily beautiful in the twilight—but then, it's always been eerily beautiful, lights or no lights. This little pocket of the world—this little river valley with its lumpy green hills—has more solidity, reality, and truth than the entire goddamned state of Massachusetts.

"I'm sorry you have to—you know, your first time—see it like this," I say to Cynthia.

"Oh, Larry," she says, sadly, "that's the last thing in the world you should be worrying about now."

We've only been married seven years, but it feels by now like Cynthia and I have always been married. It's a good feeling—solid as a rock—and I've never been more thankful for it. We're in a Holiday Inn—or at least it strongly resembles a Holiday Inn—somewhere out Route 70, I'm not sure exactly where because Cynthia drove and I wasn't paying attention. We've eaten dinner, and I was hungry as a bear, and the restaurant was okay, but now I can't remember what I ate. We're lying side by side on the bed watching the late news on the Raysburg channel. "They all talk like you," Cynthia says.

"Yeah. But they're trying not to. They're trying to sound like real announcers."

Ever since we got off the plane in Pittsburgh, Cynthia's been complaining about the heat, although, from a West Virginia point of view, it's not hot at all. The Holiday Inn, or whatever it is, hasn't even bothered to turn the air-conditioning unit on. I tried to get it going and gave up, opened the windows instead. A faint breeze stirs the drapes. We're quite a way back from the highway, and outside in the distance Route 70 is humming dimly away to itself. I don't mind this, not really. Everything is neutral, and we could be anywhere, and that's okay with me.

Cynthia is lying on our bed in her bra and underpants. I'm pretty sure that where we are is not okay with her. "What are we going to do about the funeral arrangements?" she says.

"Christ, I don't know."

"Did she ever talk about what she wanted?"

"Yeah, but... well, like everything else, it was never consistent. I know she didn't want to spend much money. I've heard her say that a million times. I think she wanted to be cremated. She had *her* mother cremated."

I've flipped back into that unearthly place—like a tiresome hall of mirrors—in which I can't believe my mother's dead, in which I can't believe that *anybody's* dead. A dozen times I've caught myself thinking that she's probably worried about us and I should pick up the phone and give her a call. "Do you think it's really true that Mary Baker Eddy was buried with a telephone in her coffin?"

"I don't know. I've heard that too."

I'm thinking about my grandmother dying. It's been over ten years, and I can't believe she's dead either. *Both of them* should be sitting there in that damn little apartment waiting for me to get home. One of the things I learned in therapy was that whatever stability I've got probably comes from my grandmother. She always knew what was right and wrong, and she never changed her mind on any significant issue since about 1898, and I never agreed with her on anything, but I always counted on her. When she died, it really knocked the pins out from under me—I even quit smoking, it hit me that hard—and now they're both gone, and that's the end of my connection to Raysburg, West Virginia. When I leave this time, there will be no reason to come back. That thought feels like a mine shaft I could fall down.

Cynthia sighs, and it dawns on me finally that this must be hard as hell for her.

"You okay?" I ask her.

"Oh, yeah, it's just... Remember that horrible bumper sticker you used to see all the time? 'Life's a bitch and then you die.' I keep thinking about my dad. He's not going to be around that much longer."

"Warren? He's healthy as a horse."

"Yeah, but he's eighty. How many men do you know who live to be much over eighty. I've never lost anybody close to me—"

I open my arms for her, and she slides into them. "A really sad thing about dying," she says, "I mean about *us* dying, is that our kids will be so unhappy, and we won't be around to comfort them. Isn't that a dumb thought? Poor little Ally keeps saying, 'Don't die, Mom,' and I say, 'Oh, no, I'm not going to.' What could she be thinking about? She doesn't even know what dying is."

Cynthia and I are great worriers—on behalf of our children, you understand—and between us, we've probably got every base covered in the worry field. She worries about Prop Two-and-a-half and what it's done to the educational system, and about the recession and if she's going to hold onto her job (her job's in no danger, the best I can tell), and if, maybe, she wouldn't be a better mom if she stayed home (although we can't afford it), and about our kids behaving like we did when they hit adolescence and getting AIDS.

I, being trained in geography, worry about irreversible alterations in the natural landscape—the destruction of the ozone layer and the greenhouse effect for starters—and whether or not our kids will get to live on a vaguely habitable planet (we've already got the first kids in human history who really should not be allowed to play unprotected in sunshine). If Cynthia and I are both worried at the same time, and talk about it, a process of negative feedback sets in and we can sink into gloom together like two anvils into quicksand. I can't let this happen tonight—although I don't know what the hell I'm going to do about it.

Cynthia's crying. "Poor old lady," she says, "she was convinced there was a nice little apartment for her in Sharon somewhere." That one really gets to me, so we cry together.

Then I must have fallen deeply asleep, because I'm as suddenly wide awake again as one of Alison's owls, and what woke me up was a nasty dream. It was a version of a recurrent dream I've had all of my adult life, and it almost always wakes me, so I suppose I should say it's a nightmare.

The single consistent element of the dream is that I've killed somebody—a guy—and he's buried somewhere nearby, and I'm afraid people are going to find out. I never know who he is or how I came to kill him; it feels like something I did stupidly or by accident when I wasn't paying enough attention, and I have a horrible shifty, guilty feeling because I know if people find his body, they're going to blame me for it, and I'll have to be punished, usually by going to jail for life. In some versions of the dream I seem to be getting away with it, because nobody knows that he's buried right *there*—in the back yard or under the floor or wherever—but *I* know he's there, and I know I can never rest easy because the body could be found at any time. In other versions I've been caught and sent to jail and put in a little gray concrete cell with no windows, and what wakes me up is the sickening feeling of being trapped. Sometimes I've been in jail a long time and have made friends with the other prisoners, and I think, hey, it's not so bad in here. When I told Jessie about this dream, he asked me what part of myself I'd killed, but I never could find any satisfactory answer to that.

In the dream tonight they found the guy's body and locked me away in the little gray cell, and I stood there crying because I knew I'd never see my wife and children again and I couldn't bear it.

I lie there a while until the fear starts to drain away; then I sit up quietly and look at my watch, and it's a quarter of three. The first coherent thought in my head is: oh, Christ, my mother's really dead. Cynthia's eyes are wide open and look dark and blank. "Did you sleep?" I ask her.

"Yeah. I must have."

"What are you thinking about?"

"Oh, the same old shit. Are you all right?"

"Oh, yeah. I just had a bad dream, that's all... Did your period start?"

"Nope." Earlier we'd both said we were too tired to make love, but now it turns out that we're not.

2

ALL THE EARLY EUROPEAN TRAVELLERS went into rhapsodies about how beautiful the Ohio River was. "Placid, gentle, lovely, serene" are standard adjectives from their accounts (so maybe those old guys never saw the river at full flood or roaring with a fiercely destructive ice-gouge). "*La belle rivière*" the French explorers called it, and a German geographer said it was more beautiful than the Rhine—which is high praise indeed coming from a German geographer. I've always perceived the Ohio as beautiful too, although by the time I was a kid, it was so polluted with effluent from the mills that its normal color was baby-shit brown.

Oh, the names of the rivers, the wonderful, evocative names of the rivers—I grew up loving the names of the rivers, and I still love them. The Allegheny and Monongahela join at Pittsburgh to form the Ohio. Other rivers pour into it—from the south: the Little and the Great Kanawha, the Big Sandy, the Kentucky, the Green, and the Cumberland; from the north: the Muskingum, the Scioto, the Miami, and the Wabash—and the whole shooting match dumps itself into the Mississippi at Cairo, Illinois. A quarter of the water that flows into the Gulf of Mexico comes from the Ohio.

The Ohio's about a thousand miles long. When the early travelers floated down it, they passed high imposing cliffs and low, rich, alluvial bottom lands (the flood plains that always look like perfect sites for farms and towns), a falls (at Louisville), and over a hundred islands ranging in size from tiny nubbins fit for gnomes to big ones like the Raysburg Island where I grew up. When I was Alison's age, just tall enough to get my nose over the window sill, I used to stand on the sun porch and look out at the river. It was the first thing I ever saw as beautiful.

Cynthia and I are walking along the river. We've just spent a couple hours stuffing garbage bags with my mother's clothes and other "personal effects," as these painfully vivid objects are called—her brushes and combs and powder and makeup and prescription sunglasses and false teeth cleaner and God knows what all—the astonishing number of things you need to maintain yourself while you're alive that nobody will want when you're dead. We've stuffed it all into bags, and carried the bags down to the back alley, and it was one of the most painful things I've ever done in my life, but maybe, having done it, we can sleep in the apartment tonight. And we're walking along the river, by God, because we need a break.

"You never told me how green it is," Cynthia says, looking up at hills on the Ohio side.

"Didn't I? I guess it goes without saying."

Neither of us want to talk about my mother. We have, for the moment, had just about enough of my mother. Cynthia is smiling faintly, as though she's just told herself an amusing story, and the expression on her face is that of someone who's gone far far away.

"The Ohio," she says slowly, pronouncing it the way it's written, pronouncing it like someone who doesn't live around here (we say "Uh-hi-uh"). "Amazing. We're in Mrs. Epping's country—the big, fat American heartland."

Mrs. Epping hasn't been around for a while, but I'm not surprised that she's just joined us on the river bank. She's always popped up in our lives at odd moments. The last time was when we bought the house in Sharon.

27

We'd been renting in Norwood and saying, "Oh, well, maybe we'll never own a house," and trying to convince ourselves that there are wonderful advantages to renting (I can't now quite recall what they are), but then the interest rates started tumbling, and the real estate market in Sharon went into a slump, so Cynthia started looking "just for fun," and before I knew it we were mortgaged up to our eyeballs and moving to a seventy-year-old colonial that Cynthia said was her dream home.

It was the afternoon of moving day, and I'd gone off to the hardware store. I came back and found Cynthia sitting on the floor of her dream home crying. I'd never seen her like that before; she was crying in big, terrible, gasping, heartbroken sobs, and I thought, oh, my God, the kids. They were at her parents'—or at least they were supposed to be—but something dreadful must have happened. I knelt on the floor, took Cynthia's hands, and braced myself for the worst. She looked just like Alison does when she's worked herself into a state—tears and snot pouring down her face—and she looked up at me with big, tragic, inconsolable eyes and said, "I've lost Mrs. Epping."

I was so relieved I almost laughed, but, thank God, I didn't. "No, you haven't," I said. "She's got to be around here some-where." That was the first time I understood that Cynthia felt an attachment to her unfinished Ph.D. thesis (I feel very little attachment to mine).

"No, she's not," Cynthia sobbed. "I've looked for her *every-where*. She must have got thrown *away*. If you threw her away, Larry, I'll never forgive you. Oh, God, *she must have gone into the garbage.*"

Cynthia's thesis has been personified as long as I've known her; the four densely packed cartons have always been referred to as "Mrs. Epping." I couldn't imagine how four cartons could have been thrown away. "Come on," I said, "let's look for her."

We were in the midst of chaos, you understand; there were boxes everywhere, and I was sure that if we just started putting everything away, Mrs. Epping would eventually turn up on her own. But we didn't start putting everything away—we went through the house opening boxes. The movers had mixed up Mrs. Epping with the canned goods, and we found her at the back of the pantry.

When Cynthia had been finishing her undergrad degree at Radcliffe, she'd decided to specialize in nineteenth-century American literature, but in grad school in California there was not a hell of a lot of interest in the nineteenth century—or, for that matter, anything much older than last week. "Everybody was looking for the newest, the latest, the most radical, the most revolutionary," she says. "Critical theories went out of date faster than newspapers."

She wanted to do her thesis on Kate Chopin, but her thesis advisor pointed out to her that there seemed to be a run on Kate Chopin at the moment. Her advisor was a middle-aged specialist on Hart Crane who'd been radicalized in the sixties. He didn't have much hair left so he shaved his head like Mr. Clean; he dressed like a wrangler at the rodeo, taught a course on "erotica" in which he deconstructed such classics of the genre as *Deep Throat* and *Debbie Does Dallas*, and he honored his favorite students by inviting them over to his pad to do a little blow or munch peyote buttons. Cynthia was sleeping with him.

No one, he said, had written much of anything about Clarissa Coltsworth Epping since William Dean Howells had sung her praises in a superficial article at the turn of the century. With all the interest nowadays in neglected women writers, he said, it was only a matter of time before somebody rediscovered Mrs. Epping—dull as she was—and if Cynthia moved fast, she could be in on the ground floor. Cynthia read the only one of Mrs. Epping's books held by the university library (they had to dig it out of storage) and didn't find it the least bit dull. "Apply for a grant," he said. She did, and got it, and went to Massillon where Mrs. Epping had lived most of her life. She planned to spend, at the most, two weeks in Massillon, because that's the longest she could imagine staying in a little asshole town in Ohio. She stayed all summer.

I, of course, have heard all about Cynthia's thesis topic. Clarissa Coltsworth (who would later become Mrs. Epping) was born in the late 1840s, grew up near Boston. Her father was in the shipping business, and the Coltsworths were well off but far from rich. Cynthia has a good copy of a photograph taken of Mrs. Epping when she was eighteen and being introduced into society. To a modern eye, Clarissa Coltsworth was no raving beauty but certainly a very attractive young woman, if somewhat plump. She had bright, intelligent eyes; and even the static old photograph preserves an amused, impish expression, as though something wildly funny is going on behind the photographer and she's got to restrain herself from cracking up. Her pale, oval face is framed with tight ringlets that Cynthia says would have been considered a little old-fashioned by then.

Mrs. Epping had more education than you'd expect for a middle-class girl of the time, but not much more. She always had a literary bent, and was apparently encouraged in that direction by her family. In her mid-twenties, she published two short novels— "strongly influenced by Dickens," Cynthia says, "charming in their way, but quite minor." Several suitors appeared and departed, and Clarissa Coltsworth appeared to be well on her way into perpetual spinsterhood when she published her third novel, the one that changed her life. *Redemption, or the Story of Emily Compton*, was about a genteel girl whose family has fallen on such hard times that she has to go to work in a cotton mill. Emily undergoes a series of terrible trials and tribulations (including an encounter with a rich, dastardly cad who is bent on ruining her), but, through pluck, determination, sweetness of character, and reliance on the Lord, she overcomes all obstacles and is saved, in the end, by marrying the perfect young gentleman who has been conveniently waiting in the wings the entire time.

"As silly as all of this might sound to us now," Cynthia says, "*Redemption* shocked the pants off people in the 1870s." The treatment was far more realistic than readers were used to, and Clarissa Coltsworth apparently broke a number of taboos. Middle-class girls were not supposed to work in cotton mills—even in novels—and they certainly were not supposed to have sexual feelings. "The wording's as discreet and understated as possible, but Emily does, obviously, have sexual feelings." And Emily, from time to time, allows herself internal monologues about the plight of women, and even—good heavens!—considers the possibility that it might not be altogether a bad thing If they were accorded considerably more rights than they had.

Clarissa Coltsworth was dismayed to find herself at the center of a storm of controversy. A number of literary figures (including Hawthorne) praised *Redemption* to the skies, but sermons were preached against it, and in some places it was banned. The Coltsworth family felt a distinct social chill; old friends cut them dead on the street. Then something happened that was exactly like an event from one of her own novels—Clarissa got a fan letter from a merchant named George Epping who lived in the tiny town of Massillon far far away across the Ohio. He'd been so moved by *Redemption* that he'd felt impelled to put pen to paper to express his profound appreciation to the authoress. He and Clarissa exchanged letters for a year; then he came to Boston, and—to the considerable relief of the Coltsworths—married Clarissa and carried her away to Massillon where she lived the rest of her life.

Mrs. Epping had four children and wrote eleven more novels, a book of advice to young ladies, and her memoirs. For more than twenty years she wrote a weekly column in the *Massillon Register;* at the height of her popularity, it was syndicated and appeared in papers all over the midwest. Her column was addressed to women, but Mrs. Epping wrote about whatever crossed her mind and did not restrict herself to what would have been considered women's topics.

A fierce moderate, Mrs. Epping lampooned both the male chauvinist pigs of her day and the more wild-eyed of the feminists. She was always receiving visits from young women hoping to enlist her to their causes. Once, when one of them said to her, "We might yet succeed if we could only have three generations of single women," she replied, "Oh? How then would you propose that we have a second generation?" But she strongly supported the movement for women's suffrage, and she made sure that her son, the senator, supported it too. "She walked straight down the middle," Cynthia says, "and that's probably what endeared her to her female readers."

The height of Mrs. Epping's popularity was in the eighties and nineties; her readership was largely female. By the turn of the century, she had slipped out of vogue; by the teens, she was considered stodgy and old-fashioned; by the time she died in the early twenties, no one any longer remembered her books. Mrs. Epping's short obituary in the *New York Times* ran under the headline: SENATOR EPPING'S MOTHER DIES. It was mentioned, in passing, that she had written several books. "And that," Cynthia says, "was the farewell to Mrs. Epping, whom William Dean Howells had called 'the greatest American woman novelist of her generation.'"

Now, looking across the Ohio River, Cynthia says, "Are we far from Massillon?"

"It's only a couple hours drive," I say, "you want to go?"

"No. I just wondered how close we were."

"Well, why not, since we're down here? Wouldn't you like to see it again?"

"Huh-uh," she says and walks on ahead of me.

"*I've* never seen it." This is a lie; I have been through Massillon, but I have no memory of it whatsoever.

"It's not that different from Raysburg," Cynthia says, "a lot smaller...," and then, after a moment, gives me a single, quick look, as bright-eyed and uncommunicative as a cat's. "Oh, I know what you think," she says. "You think if I went back, I'd get all excited about Mrs. Epping again."

We've talked this to death. She knows what I think. "Fuck the thesis," she says, takes my hand, and we continue along the path in the little park they've put up by the river in Belle Isle.

A couple months ago Cynthia and I were going out for dinner and a movie in town. She'd left work early, settled the kids with the sitter, and driven in to meet me at work. We get our competitors' catalogues, and she was flipping through one while I finished up a few things on my desk. "Oh, Christ," she said, "are these really textbooks? '*Gender at War: Discourses on the Practice of Struggle and Resistance...* brilliant, state-of-the-art discourses'—yeah, that's what it says—'expose the covert strategies practiced by Western, male theorists to legitimize the continuing construction of a disempowering femininity...'"

My opinion of this stuff is pretty much the same as Cynthia's, so I laughed, but she wasn't laughing. She kept reading to me bits from the catalogue, and she was so mad she couldn't even smile.

"Wow, here's one that 'challenges the repressive assumption of binary sex opposition.' Great stuff, huh? 'Appropriating crucial texts of Barthes and Foucault... examines the sexual, gendered, and racial identities constructed in the densely textured world of poststructuralist discourse...' You like that one? How about this one? 'By the use of the transgressive critical practice of the fracturing of texts... systematically dismantles the narrative strategies of the patriarchal canon.' And here's one that 'insights'—yeah, it's used as a verb—'*insights* gender hierarchies. A dazzling new reading of Lacan, de Beauvoir, Saussure, Derrida, Freud, Marx, and Lukacs—'"

She threw the catalogue down like a dead rat. "Well, the girls have all finished their Ph.D.s and got them published. How nice for them."

I said the first thing that came into my head (and I still believe it, but I probably shouldn't have said it): "If you'd finished your Ph.D., you wouldn't give a shit."

She was so mad at me she couldn't say a word. Stupidly, I kept right on going. "Why don't you finish it? You've done all the research."

"Why the hell don't you finish *yours?*"

"I'm fifty, and you're forty—and I've already got the world's greatest job, but you're working at an insurance agency."

"Larry," she said, "I'd rather die."

Later, over dinner after she'd cooled off, she said, "I know you think I'm just being perverse or self-defeating or something. But you don't understand. They didn't leave me any ground to stand on."

Cynthia hasn't said a word in ten minutes. Despite her "fuck the thesis," she's probably thinking about it, but I know better than to mention it again. "What's the matter, hon?" I say.

She sighs. "I don't know, Larry."

We keep on walking. "It's like—you know—your mother," she says. "There's a life, and then it's gone, and so what? Like Mrs. Epping—she was a perfectly ordinary woman of her time. The only reason we remember her at all is because she wrote. Your mother was a perfectly ordinary woman of her time, but she didn't write, didn't distinguish herself in a way that, you know, in a way that would make anybody want to come around and collect information about her, and now she's gone, and there's an apartment full of stuff, and we're going to sort through it, and then it's... no record. Nothing. Gone. So what? It just seems a shame, you know. Nothing left."

I don't know what she's getting at. "Well, there's me," I say.

"Yeah, of course there's you. But isn't that what we've always said about women? There's the kids. *That's* the point. Jesus, I sound like a feminist, but—".

"What are you trying to say?"

She stops walking, turns, faces me, and says in a fierce voice: "Just that there ought to be some kind of record. You know, Larry. I mean, just some kind of *record*."

Yesterday, after our chat on the river bank, we drove over to the mall in Ohio, and Cynthia bought big manila envelopes, a plastic box of file cards, a couple pads of lined paper, and a box of Pilot pens. Now she's sitting cross-legged on the floor surrounded by piles of junk: old photographs, newspaper clippings, letters, postcards, birth and death announcements, wedding invitations, placemats from restaurants, matchbooks, God knows what all. Cynthia is wearing her turquoise aerobics shorts and favorite t-shirt (Patrick gave it to her on her last birthday, and it says, "Because I'm the mom, that's why!"), and she's sorting through my mother's junk, and my grandmother's junk, and—as Cynthia has just discovered to her unbounded delight—it goes back over a hundred years. "Who are the Atkinsons?" she says.

"I don't know. Some branch of my mother's family."

"What branch?"

"I don't know. I think it might have been my grandmother's maiden name."

The junk surrounding Cynthia came out of a half dozen dusty cartons; some of it, I'm sure, hasn't seen the light of day in fifty years, and Cynthia's in heaven. Just like the graduate student she used to be, she's cataloguing it all—for Alison, she keeps saying, so she'll know something about her grandmother and her grandmother's family, but it isn't, of course. It's for Cynthia.

"You mean to tell me you don't know your grandmother's maiden name?"

"I think it was Atkinson, but I couldn't swear to it."

"My God, Larry, you're hopeless."

Cynthia, as she says with a certain perverse pride, is getting to be more like her father the older she gets, and loopy old Warren—he's Dr. Warren Lewis, Ph.D., LL.D., Professor Emeritus—taught classics at Harvard for forty years. He gave all of his kids classical names (Cynthia was one of the moon goddesses they had kicking around back in the good old days), and he honestly believes that western civilization never amounted to much after people stopped doing all their serious writing in Latin. Since he retired, Warren has been living life, he will tell you, the way it ought to be lived, and when you drop in to visit, you'll find him reading Horace for pleasure.

Cynthia doesn't read Latin, but she does share her father's veneration for the past (our daughter is called Alison because it is one of the most ancient of Anglo-Saxon girls' names still in use—"*from alle wymmen mi love is lent and lyht on Alysoun*"), and I was not surprised that when I asked Cynthia what we should keep of my mother's, she said, "Oh, you know, Larry, anything *old*."

So, while she does her paperwork, I'm supposed to be going through the glassware, and I'm holding in my hands a piece of junk—it's a pale green bowl with a fluted edge—because I can't tell whether it's worthless junk that my mother bought in the

Ohio mall a year or two ago or highly valuable junk that, maybe, my great-grandmother got for a wedding present. "Hey, hon, do you want to look at this?"

She takes the bowl from me and studies it reverently. "What a wonderful piece. It's got to be from before the First World War."

I have no idea how she knows that, but I believe her and wrap the bowl in newspaper and pack it in plastic chips along with the other pieces of ancient junk that we're shipping back to Sharon. We have, you understand, all the time in the world for this nonsense because we're waiting for my mother's ashes to come back from Pittsburgh.

My mother is being cremated in Pittsburgh because there are no facilities for it in Raysburg. My mother went to Pittsburgh two days ago, and no one can tell us when she'll be back. Until we know when she's coming back, we can't even put the funeral announcement in the paper.

My mother had two sibs, an older brother and sister, both dead, but they had kids, so I've got five cousins scattered around the country from Long Island to Portland, and I've called them all, and each of them asked, "When's the funeral?"—not that they thought they could manage to come to it, you understand, but if they wanted to send flowers or something—and I had to say, "I don't know yet. I'll have to call you back." The waiting is driving me crazy, and I'm not great company, so it's a good thing that Cynthia has her cataloguing to do.

I woke up in the middle of the night last night sick with fear. As irrational, ridiculous, absolutely wacky as it was, I couldn't stop thinking, Oh, my God, what if Maw isn't really dead, and now they're going to *burn her up?*

We don't get a lot of help with death these days. Despite all the yahoos blathering about Jesus on Sunday morning TV, I still find it hard to believe that anybody gets much comfort from Christianity (I don't know anybody who does, but maybe I move in the wrong circles). For most of us, the dominant myth system, the only one that carries any conviction, is a vague kind of pop science, and one of our basic doctrines is, "You are your brain." If your brain doesn't exist, then you don't exist, and nobody in their right mind wants to believe that, but what the hell are you going to do about it?

For the last forty-eight hours I have been having what I suppose you could call panic attacks, and I'm having one now. My mouth has gone dry, and my heart is racing, and I walk onto the sun porch and stare out at the river. Everything I see seems to be smeared over with a haze of pain.

"You okay, Larry?" Cynthia calls to me.

"No."

She arrives at my side and gives me a shake. "Come on, hon, let's get out of here. Let's go for a walk. Let's buy a case of beer and get drunk. Come on, let's do... *anything*."

What we've decided to do is walk to town. On the north end where my mother lived you won't see any houses older than '36 because they all got wrecked in the flood, but if you walk south toward the Suspension Bridge, you'll begin to see very old houses—"some of them must go back to the Civil War," Cynthia says, and she's much better at dating them than I am—and we've got to stop every few steps so she can look at another one. I'm feeling a perverse pride in all this—perverse because, after all, I had nothing to do with Raysburg being what it is today (all I did was grow up here), and in fact, most of the current citizens of Raysburg had very little to do with it either. The only reason most of those old houses are still standing is that their owners were always too broke to tear them down and slap up something really nice—like a dandy, up-to-date split-level rancher.

"Would you ever want to live here again?" Cynthia says. All I can do with that one is laugh.

Now that I'm out of the apartment, I'm beginning to feel better, and even the thought of my mother in Pittsburgh waiting to get herself burned up has become a distant abstraction without any juice to it (people don't die, we all know that). I've been looking forward to walking across the Suspension Bridge—it's one of the big landmarks in my childhood, and I still dream about it—but we're not more than ten feet over the river when I begin to get vertigo. "I'm a little dizzy, hon," I say to Cynthia. "Walk on ahead of me. I'll be right behind you—and don't stop until you're on the other side, okay?"

She gives me an odd look, but she does it. If I walk a few steps behind her and stare at her back—at her shoulder blades in her t-shirt to be exact—I'm all right. I can't remember when the bridge started giving me vertigo. When I was a kid, I walked across it a zillion times the same as everyone else did.

We arrive in town, and I move up to Cynthia's side. "Hey, what was that all about?"

"I don't like heights. You know that." I can see she wants to follow it up, and I see her decide not to.

We wander around downtown for a while. The mall in Ohio has drained away the business from Raysburg, and downtown has nothing much left in it but seedy discount stores. "We've got to bring Alison down here someday," Cynthia says.

"We do?"

"Of course we do. Don't you want her to see where you come from?"

I don't know how to answer that. It depends, I say, on the kind of person Alison turns out to be. That doesn't make any sense to Cynthia; of course Alison will want to see it. She can't imagine Alison being any kind of person who wouldn't want to see it.

Cynthia is charmed by downtown Raysburg. There are still signs that have been here forever—painted on the brick of old buildings—and she points them out to me as though she's the one who grew up here. And there are a few shops that have been here forever, and I point them out to her. As we walk by Rossiter's feed and hardware store—which looks exactly the way it did when I was four—there's a couple coming out. They're about our age, the kind of people you can tell at a glance are married with kids. The wife reads Cynthia's t-shirt and laughs out loud.

The husband has just bought himself the biggest, heaviest, bo-hunking weed-eater in the store; I own the same one, and I give him a look of man-to-man sympathy. He grins at me, looks away, then looks back and stops dead. "Oh, my God," he says, "Larry Armbruster."

I don't know him from—as my grandmother would have said—Adam's off ox. "Jesus, Larry," he says, "make me feel bad, why don't you?"

I'm smiling away like a maniac, but I haven't got a clue. "Give me a hint."

"Jeff Snyder," he says, sticking his hand out. Thirty-two years is an impossible jump, and I've got to stare straight into his eyes before I can connect him back to the kid I knew. The last time I saw him, he hadn't even started to shave yet. I also can't quite fig-ure out why he's so glad to see me; I never knew him that well.

Introductions are going around—his pretty wife's a Linda (with her honey-blond hair, Reeboks, and pink shorts and socks, she looks like a Linda), and once again he says "Larry Armbruster," and Cynthia gives me a puzzled, searching look, but I haven't got the energy to go through the name change business.

Jeff Snyder and I have obviously nothing to say to each other, yet we're stuck here on the street yattering away like a couple speedball insurance salesmen. He's just moved back to Raysburg this past year; Raysburg's having a renaissance, he says—"You wouldn't know the place." I tell them about waiting for my mother's ashes to come back from Pittsburgh. "That's rough," he says. "Why don't you come out to our place for dinner? Come on, Larry, I won't take no for an answer. Fire up the hibachi, burn a couple steaks, knock back a few brews—what do you say?"

I look at Cynthia, and I know she's thinking, oh, goody, just what Larry needs—distraction.

Back at my mother's apartment, Cynthia says, "So who's this Jeff guy?"

I went to a boys' military school. Whenever I tell people that, I get looks of profound sympathy—as though I must have suffered deep psychic scarring. I didn't suffer anything at the Academy that I didn't volunteer for, and if my psyche got scarred, it surely must have happened long before I got there. I liked the Academy. The only drawback was that it was hard to meet girls. I was the manager of the swimming team, and Jeff was on the swimming team. He was one of those spoiled country club boys with too much money, and he was a year younger than I was, and he swam the backstroke and the IM, and he was good but not terrific. "My yearbook's here somewhere," I say to Cynthia, "do you want to see us?"

I haven't looked at this picture in well over twenty years, and I try to imagine what I could have been thinking when they took it. Because I was the manager, I'm the only guy not wearing a swimsuit. Some of these guys I would have sworn I'd forgotten, but the minute I see their faces, I remember them. Jeff Snyder's sitting in the front row. He was one of those kids who look like they're twelve when they're seventeen, and I remember him as very much a little boy—a kid who liked to horse around and giggle. When I knew him, he was called Jeffy.

"My God," she says, looking at the picture of the swimming team, "it isn't just him, it's all of you—you're so *young*. You're just a bunch of little kids."

Standing in the center is the great Bobby Cotter, and it's hard even now for me to think of him as a little kid—although in the picture he doesn't look any older than I do. He was our team captain, undefeated in the IM two years in a row. Jeff, I'm remembering now, churned along in his wake and finished half a length behind him, but Bobby Cotter was so much better than anybody else in the valley that Jeff provided most of the excitement in the IM. Everybody knew that Bobby was going to win (the only question was whether or not he was going to break his own valley record); Jeff was the one who'd had to fight it out with the other team's best man.

The name attached to me in those days—it's right there under the picture—was Lawrence Armbruster, and I see that just about the same time Cynthia does. "I didn't realize you called yourself Armbruster in high school."

"Yeah."

"When did you go back to Cameron?"

"I don't know. In university, I guess."

"Hey, if you hadn't decided to change back, I'd be Mrs. Armbruster. I never thought of that. Wow, I don't think I'd like being Mrs. Armbruster—"

"Christ, what's the big deal? It's just a name. And you never would've been Armbruster anyway. I would've had to go back to Cameron sometime or other—I mean, I never was an Armbruster, not really. The name on my birth certificate's Cameron, for Christ's sake."

"What's the matter, hon? Why are you so upset?"

"I'm not upset."

Cynthia is the mistress of the significant sigh, and I get one now. She stands up, leaving me to my yearbook. "What should I wear?"

"I don't know. What you've got on seems fine to me."

"Oh, come on, Larry. Did you take a good look at his wife? I'm not going over there in tights and a t-shirt."

I sit and brood over the picture of the swimming team. I feel testy and ill done by, but I can't figure out who I think did anything to me. Cynthia's in the bath by now; I walk in, sit on the toilet. She's shaving her legs. "I'm sorry," I say.

"That's okay. I know this must be really hard for you."

"I tried to think that Bud was my father," I tell her. "I never quite made it, but I tried. He was going to adopt me, but he never got around to it. After I hit university, it seemed kind of silly to go on calling myself Armbruster."

"Did you feel bad... Oh, of course you felt bad. I mean, did it hit you really hard when your stepbrother died?"

"Oh, yeah," I say, and I hear how flat my voice sounds. "It hit me really hard."

Cynthia and I are standing on Front Street next to the Chrysler New Yorker, and, for no good reason I can think of, I suddenly want to go and have dinner with Jeff Snyder and his cute, blond wife about as much as I want to fling myself off the Suspension Bridge. "What's the matter?" Cynthia says.

"I don't know."

I'm leaning against the car, staring across the street between the houses at the river. It's seventy-some degrees and I'm chilled to the bone; my teeth are chattering. "Maybe I'm sick," I say. I catch myself making a motion I've made several times in the last couple days: I've reached into my shirt pocket for the cigarettes and lighter that aren't there.

"Christ," I say, "we hardly knew each other in high school, why the hell are we going to have dinner with him? What on earth are we going to say to each other? Maybe he really *is* an insurance salesman. God, they look straight as new drawn wire."

"Larry, *we're* straight as new drawn wire."

I've got to laugh at that. "Yeah, but if we are, we chose it from a number of options."

Cynthia says in her mom voice, "Look, Larry, if you don't want to go, we can just call them up and tell them you're not up to it."

I'm thinking hard, trying to figure out what's going on. I don't want to turn into a basket case so Cynthia has to talk to me the way she'd talk to Patrick. "No," I say, "let's go. I'll probably be all right once I get there... I'm a little shaky, can you drive, hon?"

Neither Cynthia nor I (thank God) are Valium types, but now I wish we were. I'd like nothing better than some instantaneous chemical I could dump into myself that would kill this horrible jangle. The world looks too bright—painfully bright—and I change into my sunglasses. "Jesus," I say, "how the hell long does it take to cremate somebody? Do you suppose there's a line-up—one little furnace and a big room stacked full of bodies? I'm beginning to feel like we're going to be stuck here forever. Jesus, I miss the kids."

Jeff's house is in Meadowland, out the pike, and I direct Cynthia up Raysburg Hill. We pass the statue of the Indian that's always been there, and it's all so damn familiar I might as well never have left. "I remember telling Jessie," I say, "that there's something about the Ohio Valley... I don't know, that I've always felt haunted by the valley. Like there was something here that was going to swallow me up."

"What did he say?"

"I'm not sure he said anything. I think it was one of those times where he just sat and listened. But I've been getting that feeling again. I'd almost forgotten the feeling. It's hard to describe, it's... This is a sad place, you know—at least it's always seemed sad to me. All the mills, and all the guys slogging away in the mills, and all the other guys out of work, and everybody drinking too much; and there's something here, something big and dangerous, really sad, and if I'm not careful, if I stay here too long, it'll—I don't know—suck me down."

"That sounds like your family," Cynthia says, and it's the perfect thing for her to say—because, of course, it *is* my family. There's a shift in my mind, and I'm back in my life again.

I put my hand on her thigh, and she gives me a smile. "Hey," I say, "you're being really great about this."

She replies with one of our standard jokes, and again it's the perfect thing for her to say, a line we've swapped back and forth for years: "When I said my marriage vows, did you think I was kidding?"

"No." And so we can laugh at it, I say what I usually say: "Thousands would, but I didn't."

By the time we get to Jeff's, I've convinced myself that everything's normal—absolutely non-threatening—and I'm looking forward to having a few beers and, maybe, forgetting about my dead mother for a while, and my sad, fucked-up family, and anything else the least bit depressing—for a while. Jeff and Linda meet us at the door, and Cynthia was right to change her clothes (she's usually right about these things); she's in one of her "classic" outfits, white linen blouse and shorts. Linda's changed into a jean skirt (it's tight enough but not too tight) and a brilliant blue sweater, one of those things that looks big enough to fit a linebacker and keeps sliding down to show off a shoulder (Linda has very good shoulders). I see the women check each other out. They're beaming away at each other with such fixed, focused grins that I can't tell what either of them is thinking.

We've got to do a tour of the house—a solid, middle-American wood frame from the twenties. Linda collects antiques, and Cynthia's eyes light up like beacons. The women get stuck in front of a Victorian wardrobe that Linda bought at a garage sale for twenty bucks. "One of the great things about the Valley," Linda says, "is that people down here think antiques are just old crappy furniture."

Jeff and I trail along behind our wives as they go from one ancient object to the next. Linda strips them down to the bare wood and then oils them, and they have the austere, venerable look of museum pieces. "*Won*derful!" Cynthia keeps saying, and I wonder if she's overdoing it. Jeff, I suspect, thinks these things are just old crappy furniture. He's filling me in on the missing thirty years. He is, of all wildly improbable things, a doctor. They've got a couple kids, and they're both out. "Shipped them off for the night," Jeff says with a laugh.

"Why the hell did you ever move back here?" I ask him.

They were living in Philadelphia, and he had to go to Pittsburgh for a conference, and then, on an impulse, he drove down to Raysburg to see what it was like. His dad had retired back in the seventies, and his parents had moved to Arizona, so he hadn't been down here since then, and he stayed with Bill Grubner— did I remember Bill? Yeah, he swam the two hundred free—so anyhow, he had a terrific time with Bill and his family, and he fell in love with the new Raysburg. He brought Linda down, and she fell in love with Raysburg too. "You know," he says, "somebody did a survey of the most livable American cities a few years ago, and Raysburg was right near the top."

"You're kidding me."

"No, it's true. "

He sounds like he works for the Raysburg Chamber of Commerce. "The crime rate's low," he says, "and the cost of living's super low. The schools are pretty good. Since Raysburg Steel's shut down, the air's clean. The city's undergoing a real renaissance. You wouldn't believe everything that's going on here now, Larry.

Shit, we've even got a little ballet company, can you believe that? There's a Victorian society, trying to preserve the old buildings, and Linda's very active in that. We've still got the symphony, and we've got poetry readings—yeah, really, I'm not kidding you. Poetry readings! Why, Raysburg's even got fruit-cakes now," he says, ignoring a dirty look from his wife. "They come through, look around, say, 'Wow, this is a damn nice little town, and there's other fruit-cakes here. Let's stay.'"

It's obvious that steel's dead here, but I've never known exactly why. I've lost track of the Valley over the years. "So what happened to Raysburg Steel?" I ask him.

"Oh, American steel just isn't competitive any more, Larry. Germany, Japan, I guess—that's where it's all gone."

"So where's the money come from?"

"What money?" he says, laughing. "Everybody's on welfare." It's the classic trade-off—jobs versus the environment. And it'd be nice to think that since the air's clean here, things are getting better. The truth of the matter, however, is that clean air here just means dirty air somewhere else, and there's nowhere, anywhere, far enough away that we don't have to worry about it.

"Tourism's bigger every year," Jeff's saying.

Tourism? I can't even begin to comprehend that one. People are going to pay money to see the sights in my old home town? What on earth would they want to see? The historic Ohio River, now the host to beer-swilling maniacs in speedboats? A bunch of non-functioning steel mills? The famous alleys of Center Raysburg where—back in the fifties—you could find the largest number of whorehouses per capita of any city in the United States?

As soon as we're settled on Jeff's new back deck (it still gleams with its first coat of paint), he's got to tell what pushed him over the edge. "I was doing damn well in Philadelphia, Larry. Believe me, *Damn* well." (Of course I believe you, Jeff.) He was walking out of an office building downtown in the middle of the afternoon and a very well dressed black man touched him on the elbow and said, "Excuse me, sir."

"He could have been any color, you know, Larry—white, yellow, pink, flaming magenta, who gives a shit? Just happened he was black. Dressed like a banker—gray suit, striped tie. Polite as could be. And the next thing I know, there's a knife pressed against my carotid artery, and my wallet's history. 'Have a good day, sir,' he says. Can you believe it? It wasn't like I was alone, or in a rough section of town or anything. People everywhere, on all sides of us, and nobody batted an eye. You know, the son of a bitch ran up five thousand bucks on my card before I could get the call in to Visa. Who needs it, Larry? I mean, *who needs it?*"

With less than a dozen polite feints, Jeff and I discover that if we're not exactly in the same political camp, we're at least close enough so we won't get into a roaring brawl, so now we can run through the standard blather about eight years of Reaganomics wrecking the country (God, somebody's got to do something about the deficit someday), and the asses getting taxed off the middle class (that's us) so the boys at the top can make their millions, as usual, and social programs will naturally get chopped, so the poor bastards at the bottom will be getting more and more desperate. "You could see the shit in L.A. coming from a mile off if you had half a brain in your head," he says—and what else can I do but agree? "If things weren't so screwed up, nobody could take a guy like Ross Perot seriously for longer than ten minutes," he says, "but the way it is, you know, he makes a hell of a lot of sense." Without asking me if I want one or not, he hands me another beer. "And you know the worst thing about George Bush?" he says. "The worst thing is, the sorry son of a bitch is the best we've got."

Somewhere in the midst of all this the terrible buzz is starting to come back, and I'm getting jumpy as a tomcat. I can't even sit still. I leap up and start striding back and forth across the deck like a visiting general, and, unlike myself, I feel a mad compulsion to talk talk talk. Cynthia, who usually does enough talking for both of us, can't get a word in sideways, and she sends me one of her significant looks, one that asks, "Are you all right?" I grin back and try not to look too much like an ax murderer out on a day pass.

Jeff, I've decided (and why am I surprised at this?), is exactly like the kid I knew in high school—except grown up. He's begun to call me "Lar" just the way he used to, and now that we've run through the Raysburg renaissance and the state of the nation, what the hell else can we do except talk about high school? So we've drifted into "Hey, do you remember so-and-so?" and "Do you remember when such-and-such happened, wasn't that a riot?"

"Hey, Lar," he says, "remember the rattlesnake?"

Ah, the rattlesnake story. Cynthia has never heard it, and apparently neither has Linda, and it should be good to get us through this interminable happy hour. The two-beer rule—as both Cynthia and I understand without having to say a word about it—is suspended for the night; in fact, I'm already on my third, and I can really feel the alcohol.

"Jeff was a real jerk-off in high school," I'm saying to the woman who married him (I've known her, of course, for all of about forty minutes). "Yeah, he was as cocky as they come."

"It's true," Jeff says, laughing, "I was."

One morning before classes we were in the biology lab—just "hacking around" Jeff throws in (I haven't heard "hacking around" in years)—and Jeff picked up a mounted rattlesnake head from one of the displays and started waving it in the air. One thing led to another, and, zap, he got me on the ear with a fang. It didn't hurt that much, but when I felt my ear, I found blood. So after morning formation...

And now we enter the world of infinite digression because our wives have just exchanged a look of womanly complicity (yeah, they may be assholes, but they're nice), and they've started asking questions, egging us on, so Jeff and I—aided by another round of suds—are engaged in the mutually fascinating project (and we have, you understand, the next million years to do this) of creating a vividly detailed account of life in the Raysburg Lancastrian Academy, circa 1960. We have to explain that we had military formation every morning, and that all our teachers were called "Captain" and that everybody had a nickname.

After morning formation, I went to see the biology teacher, Captain Penny—"The Farmer"—and asked him if I could get poisoned by a mounted rattlesnake head. He said he seriously doubted it. "Jeff Snyder, huh?" he said. "Why didn't you hit him?" (As I'm telling this, I'm astonished at how much I remember. It's as though I've just accessed a memory bank I didn't know I had.)

"Hit him?" I said. The question didn't make any sense to me. But I was a senior and a cadet captain, and Jeff was a junior and had no rank at all, and, from The Farmer's point of view, the fact that I should have allowed a junior to ding me in the ear with a dead rattlesnake made me a lousy officer. "What made him think he could get that familiar with you? If the boys don't respect you, it's your fault."

"Yes, sir," I said—that was what I was supposed to say—"but what about the rattlesnake? Do you suppose, sir, that I might be dead before the third period?"

"Of course not... Ah... maybe you'd better call your doctor. Go down and see the Colonel."

Colonel Sloan—known as "Old Liniment"—was our commandant. Two mornings a week he read to us from the Bible and the *Reader's Digest* and preached to us little sermons about the duties of being good cadets and Christian gentlemen. One of his stories, I recall, was about a paragon of a former cadet who, in the First

World War, crawled through a rain of machine-gun bullets into no-man's-land to retrieve his Academy class ring.

The Colonel, naturally, wanted to know how I'd managed to get bitten by a dead rattlesnake. "Well, sir, some boys were messing around—"

"What boys?"

"Well, sir... ah, Jeff Snyder."

Meanwhile, upstairs, Jeff was being run through the mill by Captain Penny. "He was really jagged off at me," Jeff says (Christ, I think, this guy's a walking gold mine of archaic slang). "You know what he said?" Jeff asks us rhetorically. "He said, 'If I was Captain Armbruster, I would have knocked you down, and if you tried to get up, I would have kicked you.'"

Meanwhile, downstairs in his office, the Colonel was saying to me, "What's the matter, Armbruster, are you afraid of him?"

"No, sir," I said.

"Then why didn't you hit him?"

"Larry," Cynthia says, "you always told me you *liked* going to the Academy."

"Let's get to the bottom of this," the Colonel said and stuck his head out the office door. "Guard! Go get me Jeffrey Snyder."

"Yeah, he really got to the *bottom* of it all right," Jeff says.

The Colonel started yelling at Jeff the minute he walked in the door. Then he picked him up bodily and threw him across the room. Jeff bounced off the couch, got up, pulled himself together. I walked over and stood next to him. The Colonel reached in his desk and took out a paddle. It was about two feet long and about eight inches wide. I remember it very clearly. It was highly varnished and had holes drilled in it. "You've never had a taste of this, have you, Snyder," he said in a voice I can only describe as "juicy."

"No, sir," Jeff said. His face was blank. Old Liniment was grinning ear to ear.

Jeff supplies the Colonel's next line (I've forgotten it, although it was entirely predictable): "If you're going to act like a baby, we're going to treat you like one," and he bent Jeff over the desk, got the paddle in a good, solid two-handed grip like a baseball bat, and hit him five or six times with a full swing. Each time sounded like a pistol shot.

Jeff stood up and swallowed once—I could see the rise and fall of his adam's apple—but, other than that, he showed no emotion whatsoever. The Colonel waved him out of the office. From where I was standing, I could see the open Bible on the Colonel's desk.

Cynthia gives me a wry smile. "How'd you ever survive?"

"What? You think there's something I had to survive?"

"Hit him," she says in a dumb-shit voice that's an imitation of me and Jeff imitating the Colonel. "When he's down, kick him. If he gets up, hit him again..."

Cynthia most emphatically does not like "boys' stuff," as she calls it. She will not watch "boys' movies" (anything about war, cops, or the Mafia). The quickest way to get her to walk out of the room is to turn on a ball game. She firmly believes that boxing should be banned. She thinks that any man who hunts or fishes is, by definition, a weirdly dangerous cretin. And the closest I ever saw her come to murdering Patrick was when he was going through his Ninja Turtle stage (he was five at the time) and enjoyed leaping out of hiding places to yell "Kawabunga!" and aim karate chops at her kneecaps.

One evening shortly after we were married, I was playing with Patrick outside. We were tossing a ball back and forth. Cynthia came out to watch us, and I saw a vast, loopy smile spread itself across her face until she looked like the Cheshire Cat. "Thank God," she said, "I don't have to do that any more." She meant, you understand, more than tossing a ball. So I seriously doubt I can convince Cynthia that there was anything good at all about the Raysburg Lancastrian Academy.

"There was a lot of tough talk," I say, "but it wasn't really all that tough."

"Oh, yes it was," Jeff says. "Tough as nails—marine boot camp, full metal jacket... No, Larry's right, it wasn't all that tough. It was kind of like the Boy Scouts."

"But you know," Linda says, "I kept thinking that what you guys were talking was child abuse."

A flicker of annoyance passes across Jeff's face. "Jesus, honey, don't make a federal case out of it."

To help him out, I say, "Oh, no, it wasn't child abuse. Far from it. I'd say it was more like vicious, perverted sadism."

"Hey," Jeff says, laughing, "that's it. Just the words I was looking for. Vicious, perverted sadism."

I didn't want to go to the Academy. I was scared shitless of going to the Academy. Good old Bud, my stepfather, had gone there, however, and he wanted "his boys" (as he called Johnny and me) to go there too. "It'll make men out of you," he said. I was twelve at the time, and I thought it would be pretty neat to be made into a man; I was even willing to undergo a certain amount of pain and suffering to be made into one. It never occurred to me that I might simply and naturally grow into manhood without having to undergo a certain amount of pain and suffering.

One of the patterns I identified when I was working with Jessie was what he called "doing things the hard way." I was so scared of the Academy I became the ideal cadet—at least for the first few years—and whatever they wanted me to do, I did it in spades, and I went out of my way to make things hard for myself. I hated drill, so I put so much effort into it that I won the competition at Final Drills two years in a row. I was afraid of guns, so I earned a string of riflery medals. I was never much good at sports, so I went out for one every season.

Football really was pain and suffering; I was so lousy at it that the only time our coach—"The Butcher"—ever put me in was when our opponents were such candies that he could have sent in the cheerleading squad and won. ("Well, Armbruster," he used to say, "if you can't be an athlete, at least you can be an athletic supporter—huh, huh, huh!") I ran the quarter mile, never scored a point in a meet, and threw up every time I competed—if you could call it competing. And swimming—well, you might think that in order to go out for the swimming team, the minimal requirement would be that you know how to swim. Any rational person would think that.

I was terrified of water, and I'd always been terrified of water. When I was little, a trip to a swimming pool meant a trip straight to hell. The other kids—with the accurate, nasty telepathy kids have about each other—knew that I was terrified and always dunked me the first chance they got, and I'd howl and cry, and my mother would say, "If you're going to act like a baby every time we come to the pool, I'm not going to bring you any more," which was, of course, exactly what I wanted.

Later on, my stepbrother Johnny and I were sent to day camp where we both succeeded in not learning how to swim. Johnny at least floundered around in the shallow end, but I wouldn't even do that. I would not jump into the pool. I would not put my face in the water. Why should I try? I was hopeless. I couldn't float, I couldn't do the dog paddle, I couldn't tread water. And when I clung desperately to a board and kicked like a demon—as I'd been forced to do countless times—I moved, very slowly, backward. The Academy had the best swimming team in the Ohio Valley.

My freshman year I decided to go out for the swimming team because I thought it would be good for me.

Our coach was an enormously fat man named Pete Saunders. In the real world outside the Academy, he was the Sheriff—and, if I were making this up, I would turn him into a thin man, because no one now would believe in an enormously fat sheriff, but it's even better than that. West Virginia sheriffs have always been elected, so every four years Pete traded the job with our other Sheriff, John Pettigrew, who was also enormously fat. You could have sent these guys to central casting they looked so perfectly like fat sheriffs—both of them must have weighed in at close to three hundred pounds—and I saw them once in an Elks Club variety show dressed up in pink tutus and doing the can-can together.

The only sheriff-like thing I could ever see about Pete was that when he was pissed off, his pale blue eyes could freeze your soul (the most pissed off I ever saw him was the time we came in for swimming practice and found a turd floating in the pool). My mother told me that back in his youth—before he'd become enormously fat—Pete had been so good in the water that she and her friends would go out to Raysburg Park just to watch him. He used to dive off the Suspension Bridge every Fourth of July, and even when I knew him, he'd still dive occasionally; at least once a year he'd get so mad at our divers he'd leap up, strip off his sweatshirt, and climb onto the board himself. "You can't be like a little kid taking a pee behind a barn," he'd yell. "Yup," he'd say, imitating the little kid going all slack and stupid with his dick in his hand, "well, I guess I'll just do her... No, you sure as hell can't dive that way." And then he'd dive.

Seeing Pete Saunders demonstrate a dive was—and I'm using the word exactly the way Patrick uses it—awesome: three hundred pounds of fat sheriff bouncing on the board, flying into the air, getting miraculously into a pike position, slicing—well, not exactly *slicing*, but at least entering the water in a perfect vertical. (The splash was also awesome.) He was beautiful in a weird way, and we'd all cheer when he did it.

Pete had a standard speech to open the swimming season: "This is the swimming team. The reason it's called the swimming team is because that's what we do here. We swim. If you're here for any other reason, please go home."

Then he told all the new kids to line up, dive into the pool, and swim a length. How I thought I was going to do that, I do not know (maybe I was expecting divine intervention), and when my turn came, I was so scared I must have been close to fainting—everything had gone blurry and I heard a great roaring from somewhere inside my head. I was so scared it never occurred to me to do anything other than what I was told, so I stood, walked forward until I was interrupted by the edge of the pool, and dived in. It wasn't much of a dive, but it was the first dive of my life.

I came up spitting water and thrashed about frantically. I could see the far wall bobbing up and down in the distance. It looked about as far away as London. I flung myself at it, doing the first dog paddle of my life. I thrashed about for a while until Saunders yelled, "Okay, son, that's enough."

I hadn't made it beyond the shallow end, so I let my feet touch bottom, walked over to the ladder, and climbed out. I doubt that I've ever felt more ashamed than I did at that moment. The other boys had been yelling and cat-calling, but Saunders told them to shut up, and I climbed out into a ghastly, humiliating silence. "Not a single one of you jokers has got any more guts than this guy," Saunders said. "Armbruster," he said, "you know what we really need around here? We really need a manager." I decided I was going to be the best manager the team ever had—and I was.

Right on through university, I continued doing things the hard way. I hated math, had no talent for it whatsoever, but it was

56

hard—and therefore good for me—so I kept taking more of it right up until I encountered the ultimate horror of the Calculus and had enough sense to drop before I got an F that would have kept me out of all the first-rate grad schools. I liked history, got easy A's in it, but decided to major in physics because it was the hardest discipline I could imagine—and lasted all of a term. I was a geology major for a while and then ended up in geography almost by default. It had enough math in it to be respectable, but it had its "soft" side too—not as soft as history, you understand, but soft enough so I could ace it.

The last time I saw my thesis advisor at Harvard was when he called me in to see what the hell I'd been doing all the previous year. (He hadn't got even a postcard out of me.) "Bring everything with you," he said ominously, "everything." His name was Bill Morrison, and he was a good geographer and a good man. When I'd still been behaving like a graduate student (rather than my high sixties incarnation as a hairy, incoherent, and hopelessly irresponsible mutant), he'd had me over to dinner to meet the wife and kids—and most professors don't do that. His field was perception studies, and he'd done some brilliant, ground-breaking work back in the fifties. He was a man I respected, and would have emulated if I could have figured out how to do it.

I brought everything with me. We went into an empty seminar room and spread it out on the table. As soon as he saw the masses of paper, he began to smile. No, the problem was not (as I'm sure he'd suspected) that I'd been doing diddly-shit; the problem was that I'd gone wandering off onto some lunatic excursion of my own and had done far too much of all the wrong stuff. "I'm thinking of changing my thesis topic," I said.

He did not want to hear that. "To what?"

"Well, I'm not really sure... Maybe a regional study, ah... Ohio River settlement, ah... changing cultural landscape, ah, you know, a morphology. I've been collecting a lot of material about the development of the iron and steel industry on the Ohio River—"

"Oh, God. What happened to your hazard study?"

"Well, the preliminary research is all right here. I mean, it could fit into the overall, like, you know, the overall picture. I've been reading Barrows—"

"Oh, you have, have you?"

Harlan Barrows was an American geographer who'd died only a few years before. He was one of the great cross-disciplinary geographers who kept widening the scope of the field. I'd just come upon his work, and I'd been devouring it like holy writ. "You know," I said, "his thing about, 'It's not the human fact that's geography, and it's not the environmental fact—it's the relationship between the two.'"

That formulation—simple as it is—had begun to resonate in my mind like a Zen koan; I kept having the feeling that everything in the universe was implied in that formulation. I was smoking a hell of a lot of dope in those days—not to mention a couple forays into the weird and wonderful world of acid—and I had begun to see, so I thought, how everything was connected to everything else, and I had experienced a mystical vision of the triumphant expansion of geography into every other discipline under the sun. Geography eats up psychology—chomp!—and anthropology—chomp!—and, wow, there goes sociology and ecology—chomp, chomp! Geography accounts for everything. Geography reunites the sciences and the humanities. Geography saves the world.

To do my small bit to contribute to the glorious and infinite expansion of geography, I planned to do a total study (by total, I meant *total*) of the Ohio River Valley. I would begin with the natural landscape, bring in the first settlers and the creation of the cultural landscape—or maybe I should start with the Indians—

but anyhow, I would describe the complex interactions between the evolving natural and cultural landscapes...

Dr. Morrison had extraordinarily black, bushy eyebrows. They almost had a life of their own. As I'd been talking, they'd begun to jump up and down on his forehead. Watching his eyebrows was so distracting that I had trouble hanging on to my train of thought. "Stop," he said.

"All right, Larry," he said, "maybe you will write a big book someday, but, in the meantime, why the hell don't you get your Ph.D.? Look, just go back and do the rest of your hazard study. Write it up. Compare it to previous hazard studies. Respond to the criticism, stand your orals, and you're finished, okay?"

I looked at him in wonder. It was so easy I knew I couldn't possibly do it.

Jeff has just slapped some steaks on the hibachi, and Linda's brought out tubs of deli salads, and I'm sure there's another case of beer in the fridge. With the approach of twilight the sky's gone a shifty pearlized color that looks extraordinarily lovely to me, and I haven't been this loaded in years, and—weirdly enough—there's nowhere I'd rather be than sitting on Jeff Snyder's back deck in Raysburg, West Virginia, with my wonderful wife (I suddenly feel a great, warm gush of love for her), talking about the good old glory days just like the jerk in the Bruce Springsteen song.

Jeff and I are playing the whatever-happened-to? game—mostly about guys on the swimming team. Whatever happened to Russ Anderson? Jesus, he was a hell of sprinter. Remember that start he had? Like a coiled spring. What happened to Ken Higgs, to Dougy Moore, to Tom McFee? The standard stuff—marriages, kids, divorces. Jerry Andrews? Cancer, huh? Christ, that's a bitch—he was just our age. Did you hear about Franky Gavin?

Killed in Vietnam. Jesus, you're kidding. A moment of silence for that one.

And of course we've got to talk about the great Bobby Cotter, undefeated two years in a row. I had a highly developed case of hero worship for Bobby Cotter. "You too, huh?" Jeff says. "I think we all did."

Bobby Cotter was the best swimmer anybody had seen in the Ohio Valley for years. His main event was the IM, and that meant he was a master of all four competitive strokes, and I thought that anybody who could do that was a cross between Houdini and Jesus Christ. In those days I could have told you every record for every event—school, pool, valley, A.A.U., age group, national, and world. I knew the personal bests of everybody on the team (even the freshmen), and I knew what they averaged in training because I wore a stopwatch around my neck and timed them. I kept meticulous records, and I sat up nights working out training schedules for our best guys (we had another hour of unofficial swimming practice after the regular practice ended), and I kept it all in what was referred to as "Larry's black book." Bobby Cotter said to me once, "You're more than a manager—you're a second coach." That made me happy for days.

Now something occurs to me that should have been obvious but hasn't been—when I was in high school, I didn't have the remotest notion of class distinctions. Oh, I knew that some of the guys had more money than we did—a whole hell of a lot more money—but I didn't think it made any real difference, and the stalwarts of the Academy swimming team were country club boys every one of them. They hadn't gone to the local, low-rent summer day camp at Waverly Park like Johnny and me; they'd gone to exclusive, expensive summer camps in New England. They'd had private swimming lessons. They'd gone through the A.A.U. age group program. Bobby Cotter had a swimming pool in his back yard.

A lot of the guys on the team—Jeff Snyder was one of them—used to go out to Bobby Cotter's in the summer; those who could swim (this was the swimming team, you understand, so that meant everybody but me) swam in the pool. I suppose I must have met Bobby's parents, but I don't remember them. His old man was the head honcho at Raysburg Steel, and he was hardly ever home. Bobby had a little brother who was something of a pest; we teased him mercilessly, and threw him in the pool, and made him cry a few times, and when he got to high school, he broke every freestyle record in the Ohio Valley.

The Cotters had a Polish lady who worked for them. She was a maid, I suppose, but nobody called her that. She knew all of our first names, and she'd make dozens of sandwiches and bring them out on a tray. It was a good time, a way for the swimming team to stay together over the summer, and it never occurred to me that I might not be welcome because I wasn't an out-the-pike country club boy, and I was right about that—I *was* always welcome. I think a lot of those guys didn't care any more about class than I did.

I find it depressing now to be thinking about Bobby Cotter. I tried to be just like him, and I always knew in my heart I couldn't be. I even admired his flaws—which, of course, I didn't see as flaws back then, but as virtues. That old clunker about the tough getting going could have been invented to describe him, and I thought his ironic, tight-lipped manner and dedication to murdering himself daily at swimming practice was the essence of real manliness. Looking back, I'd say he was a fiercely *driven* kid, closed in on himself, with something dark and unhappy to him. I hung around with him a lot, but I never knew whether he really liked me, and I still don't know. In the four years I knew him, he never revealed anything of himself to me. "I honest to God thought I'd see him in the Olympics," I say to Jeff.

"Yeah? Me too. There was one year, you know, when he was

ranked twelfth in the country. It was, let's see, my first year in university, so it must have been '62 or '63. I was absolutely certain I'd see him in the Olympics."

"So what happened to him?"

"I don't know. His family hasn't lived here for years."

Now, suddenly, for the first time, nobody has anything more to say. The twilight is settling over us, and we've ground to a halt. We could all use some food in our stomachs. High, high above us, a jet the size of a gnat is drawing a glowing silver thread across the sky. How I'm feeling is hard to describe—as though all the pieces of me are slowly drifting apart. I find myself playing, ever so gently, with a strange notion (thin and distant as the jet trail): seeing as I'm going to have to die someday, maybe there's something okay about it. (And I'm sure my mother doesn't mind that I haven't been thinking about her at all.)

"So," Cynthia says quietly to Linda, "how old are your kids?" I can feel the shift: the boys have had their fun, now let's get on to something *real*. Jeff can feel it too; he stands up, stretches elaborately, goes over to flip the steaks. I sit—happy to have arrived at this point of sodden immobility with my mouth finally shut—and watch Cynthia talking to Linda.

Cynthia's wonderful figure is a testimony to the efficacy of jumping up and down to music on her lunch hour (it's her PMS cure—when she misses a session at the wrong time of the month, she turns into the mom from hell). The way she wears makeup is a testimony to the year she spent behind the Lancôme counter at Park-Snow's. Most people can't believe she's forty. To be politically correct these days, we're not supposed to care about what women look like—but if you're a heterosexual male, do you believe that? I love the way Cynthia looks.

I love the way she's tipped herself forward toward Linda now, has turned her full attention to her. I love the way her left foot is arched (she's kicked her shoes off), the way her toes spread on the boards of the deck, as she pushes herself up to tilt forward. I love her Massachusetts accent, her dry sense of humor, the way she can giggle like a kid. I love the clean, straight way her mind works (I've never been able to find any duplicity in Cynthia). I love our life together. I love Alison and Patrick (and wish we'd called them tonight), and I love being married to Cynthia. My glory days weren't back in the fifties—they're right now.

"Have some carcinogens," Jeff says, and hands me a whole sirloin steak so big it's hanging over the edges of the plate.

"Thanks, doctor."

The food brings the boys down another notch: Jeff and I have turned into yawning zombies. We listen to our wives (the food's had the opposite effect on them; they're peppy as teenagers) as they find out everything there is to know about each other. They're both *second* wives. (Yeah, I thought Linda looked a lot younger than Jeff.) From his first wife, Jeff's got two grown kids, a married daughter and a son in university. (Good God, I think, two whole families. He sure married young and then did the straight trip the whole way down the pike.) Linda and Jeff's kids are at Raysburg High, pretty much on their own by now, and she's feeling at loose ends. She had a part-time job in Philadelphia, but in Raysburg? Forget it. Maybe she'll take some courses at Raysburg College. In what? She isn't really sure. She always wanted to write, but that's just kind of a dream, you know.

Much to my amazement, Cynthia is talking about Mrs. Epping. She has managed the segue into Mrs. Epping without bothering to mention that her unfinished degree was a doctorate; the self-deprecating way she's talking, it could even be a B.A.

"God, if I was close to a degree, I'd sure finish it," Linda says.

Cynthia wrinkles her nose. "Allie isn't even four yet."

"Oh, right," Linda says.

I never would have expected it, but our wives seem to have really hit it off, I can see that. They're leaning close to each other like a couple gossipy high school girlfriends. It's barely eleven, but I'm having a hard time staying awake, and Jeff's as silent as I am. Cynthia and Linda are making a date for tomorrow—we're going to walk around and look at Victorian buildings. And now it's time to go. I force myself to my feet, and so does Jeff. We yawn at each other. We both would have been delighted to be in bed an hour ago. He grins and punches me lightly on the biceps.

"Ah, Lar," he says, "the years go by like jackrabbits."

3

WE'RE BACK AT MY MOTHER'S apartment, and it's midnight. I'm stretched out on the bed like a catfish on the river bank, and all I want to do is sleep, but Cynthia's totally wired. She still can't get used to the heat, she says for the millionth time; she's stripped down to the buff and is padding in circles around the bedroom. "Wasn't it lucky we ran into Jeff and Linda?" she says. "I've met other doctors like that. Doctors can be kind of, well, simple. But he's simple in a nice way. And I didn't think I was going to like her. At first I thought she was... God, she seems like such a bimbo, but there's a lot more to her than that. Doesn't she have a cute figure?"

"Not as cute as yours, my dear."

"Oh, Larry, you don't have to say that."

"Yes, I do. Come on, hon, get in bed."

But she doesn't get in bed. "What do you suppose she was?" she says, "His nurse? His receptionist? I thought she was about thirty when I first saw her, but she's got to be older than that—"

"I didn't think she was thirty."

"I've always wondered what it would feel like to be *kept*. I probably wouldn't like it for longer than about six weeks. She's getting a bit of the mad housewife syndrome—the middle-aged antsiness."

Cynthia may not be *kept*, but I wonder if she isn't getting a bit of

the middle-aged antsiness herself. I haven't thought of this before—
at least not in a way that's as simple as this—but Cynthia will almost
certainly live into her eighties, and that means she's right smack in
the middle of her life, and I'm sure her current job beats the hell out
of what she did before—waitressing or selling cosmetics—but she's
spending a good chunk of her best years sitting behind a computer
in the Donaldson Insurance Agency, so I'd be surprised if she wasn't
starting to feel at least a little bit antsy. I know better than to ask her,
however; as high as she is, she'd tell me—for the next three hours.

"Did you bring any sleeping pills?" I say. Like most people our
age, we've got a bottle of them in the medicine cabinet for bad nights.

"Take a sleeping pill, Cynthia, and shut up," she says. "No, I
didn't bring any. I thought we'd be back home in two days."

She finally stops pacing and lies down on the bed with me.
Without even touching her, I can feel the energy crackling off her
like sheet lightning. In my best imitation of her father's plummy
voice, I give her one of his favorite lines: "Remember, Cynthia, balance and repose, balance and repose."

"Fuck right off," she says, laughing. "I thought you'd be asleep
by now."

"Not with you so cranked up. It's like trying to go to sleep in
the same room with a turbine."

"Just give me another minute or two. I am getting sleepy." But
she doesn't sound the least bit sleepy. Then she says—and it
sounds like a conversation opener—"I had a weird moment, one
of those times when you really *hear* what's coming out of your
mouth. 'Yeah, I'm Larry's second wife,' and it seemed so strange. I
don't think of myself like that."

"I don't either, hon. I've never really been married to anybody
but you."

"Hey, that's nice. You manage to say the perfect thing sometimes."

"Strictly by accident, you understand."

"Do you ever think about her?"

"Who?"

"Your first wife."

"Oh, God, honey, why don't you go watch TV or something?"

"I really want to know."

"You were a lot more connected to Danny than I ever was to Karen. We were just kids. We didn't know what we were doing." I want to add something more to put a firm end to the conversation. "We were the mismatch of the century."

But Cynthia doesn't want to let go. "Yeah, but do you ever think about her?"

"Hardly ever—and that's the honest-to-God truth, Cynthia Ann. Now will you please let me go to sleep?"

It has not exactly escaped my attention that there are certain parallels between my childhood and my current life. Having spent a couple years in therapy, I would have to be dumb as two boards not to see certain parallels—and even when I was trying my best to be dumb as two boards, Jessie wouldn't let me get away with it.

Because Bud Armbruster was the only model of a father I ever had, I bend over backwards to be *not* like Bud. For starters, I work—and that's a pretty big one, and so is not drinking much. Bud was never around, so I'm around all the time. Bud never gave a shit what Johnny and I did, so I made a huge behavior chart for Patrick, with merits and demerits, and posted it on the fridge. ("I appreciate all the thought you put into this, Larry," Cynthia said, "but I think you may have overdone it just a little.") Bud taught Johnny and me to tie a necktie and to drive a car and that was about all—except for giving us bits of enormously useful advice like "a gentleman knows how to hold his liquor," and "it's better to go to a cathouse than get a nice girl in trouble," and "if you can't go first class, don't go," and "clothes make the man," so I'm determined that I'm going to teach Patrick something. Luckily I have a pretty good idea of what will please him. I started him on his rock collection and his meteorological station, got him reading *Omni* and *National Geographic*. He's still young enough to think that a trip with Dad to the dusty old Peabody Museum, and a movie, and a burger at McDonald's afterwards is the next best thing to heaven. At the moment, he's saying that when he grows up he's going to be a geographer; I don't believe it for a minute, but I take it as a high compliment.

For a couple years I worried about Patrick's father. If my real father, the mysterious Matthew Cameron, had appeared at almost any time before I turned, oh, thirteen or fourteen, and he'd been a reasonably decent guy who showed any interest in me at all, I would have embraced him with open arms (at least I imagined I would have). Everything I knew about Patrick's father made me wary as a lynx.

Cynthia had supported Patrick's father while he was... I'm not sure what he was doing. For a while, I gather, he was building a sailboat. Cynthia thought that after Patrick was born, Danny would either get a job or take over at least some of the responsibility for the baby so she could go back to her job—"that's how naive I was," she says. (The days of her grants and TAships were long over by then, and—this is going to sound like a New Age soap opera, but it's true—she was waitressing in a vegetarian restaurant.) Danny did not get a job, and he did not take care of the baby, and, I gather, he expected his dinner to appear on the table every night the way it always had, so Cynthia called her dad who knew her well enough not to wire money, but, instead, sent her a one-way, non-refundable airline ticket back to Massachusetts. For months Cynthia felt guilty and worried about whether good old Danny could manage to support himself.

"It's impossible not to like Danny Seehagen," Cynthia used to say before I met him, and I'd think (but wouldn't say), Oh, yeah? I'll bet *I* can not like him. But she was right. It *is* impossible not to like Danny Seehagen.

Patrick's father is an astonishingly attractive man—tall, lean, tanned, with a big shock of sun-bleached hair, eyes as blue as the Mediterranean, and a smile like the sun coming up over a wheat field. He appears incapable of irony, or any kind of complexity for that matter, and everything that comes out of his mouth is so heartfelt, so sincere, so deeply *concerned*, that—I don't know—I wanted to wrap him up in a blanket to keep him safe from the mean old world. He seemed to feel most at home sitting on the floor with the children, and not only did he spend hours with his son, he spent hours with Alison who adored him.

Danny sat down with me one afternoon, bent forward so that our faces were only a few inches apart, fixed me with his gentle eyes, and told me that his name had been changed. He had met— he couldn't tell me exactly where, because he had been sworn to secrecy, but he could say that it was somewhere in New Mexico— a highly evolved soul who was channeling an ancient entity who had existed since before the creation of the universe. The ancient entity—we may know him as Ramaset—had told Danny that his name wasn't really Danny Seehagen. His real name was Kahari Seeker. So could I please call him Kahari.

It was extremely difficult for me to call a middle-aged, middle-class white American Kahari, but I made an effort. When Kahari decided he had been with us long enough (nearly ten days), he took me aside and asked me if we could have a private conversation. Sure, I said. The airline ticket that had brought him to Boston was half of a round trip that some lovely person had laid on him. In terms of getting back to California, he was, oh, a little short. I couldn't get my wallet out fast enough.

For me, the high point of Kahari's visit was a tiny incident that took place over the dinner table. We were all talking at once, and food was being passed, and forks were flying, and in the midst of the general chaos, Patrick said, in a clear, ringing voice, "Dad?" Everybody shut up, and Kahari and I both stared at Patrick. For a second or two, Patrick was thrown for a dead loss, but then—and he could have been a little boy in a cartoon it was that clear on his face—the light dawned, and he said, "No, not *you*, Kahari—I mean, *Dad*." I could have folded him into my arms and wept.

My watch tells me it's a quarter to two. "Are you still awake?" I whisper.

"Of course I'm still awake," Cynthia says immediately in a loud, angry voice. We turn over and look at each other.

"I'd kill for a sleeping pill," I say.

"Yeah, me too. We should have asked Jeff for something. Do you feel really bad, hon?"

"No. I feel okay. I'm just... exhausted, and I can't get my mind to turn off."

"Yeah, me too. You thinking about your mom?"

"No. You'd think I would be, wouldn't you? But I'm not. I seem to be doing one of these review-your-entire-life numbers."

"Terrific."

"What are you thinking about?"

"Oh, God, the kids, my job, everything that's piling up there—"

"Yeah. This is the shits, hon. You want to get up and watch TV?"

"You keep saying that! Jesus, I can't imagine anything more depressing. My goddamn period's two days late. Must be all the stress, or the heat or some damned thing. I feel like Maggie the cat."

To someone other than me, what she's just said might not have sounded like a very clear message, but I've been married to Cynthia for seven years. I'm not sure I can do anything about it, however, but I roll over and give her a little nibbling kiss to see if she's serious.

We've never been big on quickie sex. I think we both got our share of that in our twenties, and, with two kids, no matter how quick you are, sometimes you're just not quick *enough*. Alison usually sleeps like a log—except when she doesn't—and a suddenly opened door has occasionally disclosed Patrick standing silently on the other side. "Oh, nothing," he says when you ask him what the hell he's doing out there, "I just wanted a drink of water."

We usually plan it days in advance, arrange for the kids to spend the night at Cynthia's parents', get dressed up, go out for dinner, come back to the wonderfully empty house, light some candles, play around for an hour or so. There are certain advantages to middle age, and one of them is that it slows you down. By the time we've made it to bed, Cynthia's usual sexual style is one that I can only describe as *melted*.

She's not melted tonight. She seems to know exactly what she wants, and when she wants it is *right now*, and I've never known her so aggressive or in so much of a hurry. Just about the time I've decided I'm so tired I'll never catch up, she slides down, takes me into her mouth, and goes at me in a totally cold-blooded way, like: okay, let's see if I can get Larry in orbit in eight and a half seconds. There's something about how calculating she is about this—how goddamned knowledgeable—that's absolutely magnificent, and how could I ever have thought I was tired? She swings a leg over me—another surprise—and sinks down; she's so wet I've slipped into her without even a whisper of a glitch. For a few seconds we're at cross purposes, can't find a common rhythm; we're sweating and squirming and pawing each other in a kind of goofy, adolescent mortal combat, and I'm worried she's going to pop right off me, but then we're suddenly synched, and by God, there's no way we can lose.

With all the gentleness and consideration of ravening pit bulls we're working together—digging the same ditch, or plowing the same field, or any damn image you want—and the last coherent thought I have—my loud-mouthed mind has been rattling away up until now, you understand—is that it's amazing how I'd forgotten that sex is the only human activity that's genuinely worth doing.

Sweet Jesus, we're home. Cynthia is still straddling me. We have, I decide in retrospect, achieved that impossible Reichian Shangri-la, the simultaneous orgasm. At least I think we have. "Hey," I say, "did you come?"

"What the hell do you think?" she says. "*Now* we can sleep."

Cynthia's gone almost immediately; she's even snoring lightly. I roll over and feel myself start to drift away, and then—wham—I'm wide awake again. Something's not quite right; I can feel it like a big, dark hole in myself, and I can feel myself pulling back from it—something's wrong with me, something more than feeling bad about my mother being dead, but I don't have a clue what it is. Screw that, I tell myself, you can think about it tomorrow, and I squirm around in the bed, press my bum up against Cynthia's, arrange the sheet over myself just right, and, finally, I feel myself start to relax.

I don't know how much time's passed, but I'm dreaming. For a few seconds, I even know I'm dreaming. I've brought Cynthia and the kids to Raysburg because I wanted to show them where I came from, and now I seem to be in several places at once. I'm wandering around the big house halfway down Front Street where we lived right after my mother married Bud, but, at the same time, I'm driving around in Bud's Chevy looking for Cynthia and the kids because somehow I've misplaced them, and I'm driving too fast out the pike, skidding sideways over the s-bridge, and thinking, This can't be right. Cynthia can't be out here. What would she be doing out here? It doesn't make any sense.

Then I'm walking into the lobby of a building in downtown Raysburg, and I remember I'm dreaming, and I think how odd it is I've forgotten that. I'll have to make an effort to remember.

I'm walking into a place I haven't thought about in years and couldn't begin to locate now—and I'm getting more and more anxious and sad. It has a tile floor, and it's just been washed and smells of Lysol, and I know I've been there a million times. There's an old-fashioned elevator with a wrought-iron grillwork door, and there's a cigar stand with a blind man behind it, and I'm buying a peanut butter cup from him. "Is that a one or a five?" he asks me, and I see holes in his face where his eyes ought to be—and then I see Cynthia dressed in a Canden High majorette uniform come out of the elevator and walk across the far side of the lobby. She's got Alison by the hand. Patrick is dawdling along behind her, so, without getting my change from the blind man, I run after them, but then I'm back at our house on the Island, and the table's been set with all the best silver and china because the guys from the swimming team are already there.

Pete Saunders, our coach, is talking to my mother (they went to school together), and Jeff Snyder's there, and somehow he's both like what he was as a kid and what he is now, and I think, oh, God, I'm *dreaming*. That's what this is—it's a dream.

I keep looking around for Jeff's wife, but I can't see her, and I still can't see Cynthia or the kids. Our team captain, the great Bobby Cotter, looks exactly the way he did at eighteen, with his hair cut down to a half inch of burr, so thin his face is like a death's head. He's wearing his Academy uniform, and he's hunched forward in a way that seems threatening, and I know I'm supposed to be wearing my Academy uniform. He looks at me and scowls, and I think, He's right. Who am I trying to kid? I can't swim.

I don't want to be at a reunion of the swimming team. I don't belong there. I feel alone and scared. I've lost my wife and kids. But then my grandmother and I are upstairs. The dining-room table—still laid out with the best silver and china—has been moved upstairs, and we're looking out the window. It's late at night, and we're watching somebody approaching our house, walking up the sidewalk, and, for a moment, I'm sure it's Johnny. Then, as he gets closer, I see that it's not. I look at my grandmother, and we both laugh. "He really looked like Johnny for a minute, didn't he?" my grandmother says. "But of course it couldn't be Johnny. He's dead."

And then, just as quickly as if somebody shook me, I'm wide awake. I'm sweating out of every pore, and I'm scared shitless. My first thought is that "oh, it's only a dream" thing you do when you're coming up out of a nightmare, and I'm feeling a wonderful sense of relief because, as unpleasant as reality might be right now, it's nowhere near as unpleasant as that dream.

I listen to Cynthia breathing—she's really down deep—and I try to fall back to sleep, but I can't do it. I look at my watch, and it's nearly four—the hour of the wolf. Oh, terrific, I think, but I know there's nothing for me to do but get up.

I grab my clothes and slip out of the room, shut the door, get dressed in the dining room, and walk out onto the back porch. I look down over Front Street as I have so many times before. My hand's digging around in my shirt pocket, and when I realize what I'm doing, I'm bitterly disappointed—my eyes are stinging, that's how keen it is—and if there were a store open on the Island at four in the morning, I'd be smoking again. I consider jumping into the car and driving over to town but then think, Come on, Larry, get a life. Or at least remember the one you've already got.

I quit smoking by going to a group that met every Wednesday evening at the Sommerville Y, and now I'm remembering something the counsellor said: "The unfortunate thing is that you'll never again find a way to alter your brain chemistry in seven seconds." Okay, so I can't alter my brain chemistry, what am I going to do for the rest of the goddamn night? I lean against the porch railing, and I take about three deep breaths, and then I start to cry. There's lots of excellent reasons why I should be crying—I know that—but there's nothing in my mind at all beyond the cigarette I don't have, and I feel like a total idiot. I stand there and cry for a few minutes, and then it stops just as quickly as it started, and I'm thinking how weird that was, because now I don't want a cigarette at all.

Quitting was the hardest thing I've ever done in my life—and that includes football practice with The Butcher in August—and it took me six months before I could really say I'd done it and another year before I stopped bumming other people's at parties, and if my grandmother hadn't died, it never would have occurred to me to quit. My grandmother always felt eternal to me, more like a stone than a person, and her death made—I don't know how else to say this—a radical break in my life, like a fracturing along a fault line, and that took me totally by surprise, because if anybody had asked me, I would have said that I hadn't been all that close to her. I certainly never agreed with her about much of anything.

In my dream she was the way I remember her from when I was in high school—a woman in her seventies who looked easily ten years younger than that. She was only about five two, and she was solid but never fat, but she sticks in my mind as big and powerful—probably because a good part of my feelings about her go all the way back to my childhood when she took care of me while my mother worked. She and my mother lived together for so much of my mother's adult life that they developed a symbiosis—not altogether a healthy one—and, by the end, it took both of them to make a whole person. My mother was never quite right after my grandmother died.

My mother's job was to work and make money, and she did that; at home she spent a lot of her time falling apart—crying in her room with a cold cloth over her face (she had migraines, she said, and for all I know, she really did). My grandmother did the shopping, cooking, cleaning, and child care; even though he was no relative of hers, she took care of Johnny, as well as me, for years. She didn't talk about God, and she never went to church, but she was an old-fashioned Christian down to her toenails; if she was ever tired or if she ever felt anything less than wonderful, we never knew about it. Her favorite line was: "It's a great life if you don't weaken."

I lived with Karen for a few months before I married her, and my mother, for reasons known only to herself, decided to tell my grandmother about it. My grandmother called me up—and calling long distance to Boston was a big deal for her. "Larry," she said, "I just want you to think about something. Do you know how easy it is to ruin a young girl's life?" (Cynthia, when she heard that story, said, "If you'd still been living in 1910, she would have been perfectly right.")

Then, after Karen and I got married, I brought her down to Raysburg, and, much to my surprise, my grandmother liked her. "You did well for yourself, Larry," she said. "She's a sweet, sensible girl."

I can't imagine anybody who would have made a better daughter-in-law than Karen, but it was *my mother* who didn't like her. She never quite came out and said it, but it was plain enough: "She's a cute enough little thing, I suppose, *but* that giggle of hers would drive me crazy. She's got a good heart, *but* isn't she a bit of a scatterbrain? Oh, well, maybe she'll outgrow it, she *is* awfully young. I would've thought you would've picked somebody more serious." One night I found my mother hiding in the pantry crying. "Oh, honey," she said, "it's just so hard losing your son!"

I couldn't believe it. "Maw," I said, "I haven't lived at home since 1960."

"Don't pay any attention to your mother," my grandmother said. "She'll get used to it."

The last time I saw my grandmother alive, she was ninety-five and had shrunk up and become tiny and frail. She must have weighed less than a hundred pounds. Of course I didn't know it was the last time I'd ever see her; it never crossed my mind that she'd die before I got back to Raysburg (people live well into their hundreds all the time, we all know that). She'd never seemed the least bit senile, but when I sat down on the sun porch with her, she looked over at me with a bright smile and said, "Dad used to pour water down Shadyside Hill. As soon as it'd start to freeze, he'd go out every night after work and pour water down it, and the whole hill would turn into a big sheet of ice all the way to the bottom, and then we kids would go down it on our sleds. We'd just go sailing right down to the bottom—it evened out going down to the river at the bottom, so we could slow down. And then we'd pull our sleds back up to the top— Oh, but you wouldn't like that, would you, honey? You're scared of sleds."

I hadn't seen her in a year, and I thought, well, she's finally gone loopy on me. "You know, Grandmaw, I don't exactly do a lot of sledding these days."

"That's right," she said, looking right at me, "you're a big boy, aren't you now, Larry?" I was, you understand, damn near forty.

She looked out the window at the river for a while, and then she said, "I keep telling your mother to get out of the apartment, but she won't do it, and she blames it on me."

That was such a concise and accurate assessment of my mother I had to laugh. So did my grandmother. "She's just waiting for me to take a trip," she said, still laughing.

"Whatever happened to that nice little girl you were married to?" she asked me.

"We got divorced, Grandmaw, a few years ago."

"Divorced? Oh, that's right. I did know that. It's a shame. She was a sweet girl. I can't understand young people nowadays who don't want to get married, or when they do, they can't stick it out. What kind of life can you have without a family? And it's a shame how everybody moves away and goes so far away... Your father was a nice man, Larry, for all his faults. He never drank or ran around, and he always kept a job, and I told your mother, 'You stick it out, now, Dorothy. Don't think about yourself, you've got a little boy to raise,' but she wouldn't pay any attention to me."

That was the first time I'd ever heard my grandmother say a word about my father, and it was the perfect time for me to ask her about him, but somehow I couldn't do it.

"Well," she said, "and then she went and married that no-good Bud Armbruster. There's one thing that no woman should have to put up with, and that's a man who drinks. You don't drink, do you, Larry?"

"No," I lied, "not much."

"That's good. It's a crying shame what happened to Johnny. Poor little fellow. And if there's anybody to blame for it, it's Bud. You know, Larry, there's one thing for certain in this sorry world: you've got to take care of your kids, no matter what. Poor Johnny couldn't of been any more neglected if he'd been an orphan. Living alone down on the south end of the Island like that, and still in high school, imagine! Well, that's a long way back down the pike— I worry so much about your mother. I don't know what she's going to do after I go."

"Oh, Grandmaw, you're going to be around for a long time yet."

She looked right at me and laughed again. "Don't you try and kid me, Larry Cameron." I suddenly saw how old she was. Old, old, old—older than anybody.

"You should get married again, Larry, and have some kids," she said. "I don't think you'll be happy till you do."

That made me so mad I felt like wringing her scrawny old neck. "It isn't quite that easy," I said.

"Oh, yes, it is. Easier for a man your age than for a woman. The world's full of nice girls who want to get married."

I can't stop thinking about that dream. When I was in therapy with Jessie, I wrote my dreams down, and writing them down regularly makes them easier to remember. I was always trying to interpret them, but Jessie wouldn't let me do that. His standard question was: "Why is this coming up *now?*"—and that's what I'm asking myself: *why is this coming up now?*

It's strange how the closest thing I ever had to a guru in my life was Jessie. I never knew much of anything at all about him personally. He wore cardigans, and pants with pleats, and loafers. In his waiting room was a framed certificate that said he had his Ph.D. from Boston University, and I asked him once if he learned everything he knew in graduate school, and he laughed and said he hadn't learned a damn thing in graduate school. In his office was hardly anything at all—a desk turned sideways so that it wasn't between him and his clients, two chairs, a big file cabinet, white plastic venetian blinds on the window, an enormous color photograph of a landscape that could have been anywhere in the eastern United States (there were no buildings or people in it, just hills and trees). On the desk was a box of Kleenex—which told me that it was okay to cry in there, although I only cried once.

I used to wonder about him. Was he from a well-off background, or did he fight his way out of the ghetto? Was he married?

What was his opinion of Martin Luther King or Malcolm X? Did he have black—or, I suppose I should say these days if I want to be politically correct, *African-American*—clients who paid him something less than the sixty bucks an hour I was paying? But after a few months, I'd become so interested in what I was finding out about *myself* that I stopped wondering about his personal life.

So what worked? Cynthia's asked me that, and it's hard to explain. She's skeptical about therapists and therapy—to her, all that stuff comes out of the same granola bag full of nuts and flakes—and even though it worked for me, I'm skeptical too. I know there are a lot of dingbats calling themselves therapists— with and without degrees on their walls—but Jessie was very matter-of-fact, with no weird mysticism, and given the kind of person I am, I'm pretty sure if he hadn't been like that, I wouldn't have stuck with him.

We spent most of our time looking at the things I'd done in my life—and continued to do over and over again like a tape loop— to fuck myself up. "There's a space," he used to say, "between when we want something and when we do something about it. If we can pause in that space and *think*, then that's the only freedom we've got." In those two years I did a lot of pausing and thinking, and that's what changed my life—or, I should say, that's how *I* changed my life. It wasn't magic. It was hard work.

Shortly after Cynthia and I got married, I decided I didn't need to see a therapist any longer; for one thing, I was feeling pretty damned good about myself, and for another, the sixty bucks an hour seemed—well, as tight as our budget was (we were trying to save for a house), it seemed as self-indulgent as sushi once a week or silk underwear. I was afraid to tell Jessie I was quitting, but he surprised me by shaking my hand and congratulating me: "People shouldn't be in therapy a day longer than they need to be."

He suggested we go over what I'd accomplished in the past two years. It was one of those therapy assignments that a part of me always resists (what is this Mickey Mouse shit anyway?), but I did it. I'd accomplished a hell of a lot. I was no longer a drunk. I'd been promoted to senior editor, and, much to my surprise, I liked going to work. I'd taught myself to swim and had lost twenty pounds. I was married to a wonderful woman (much better than I deserved, I thought, although I didn't say that), and I liked her kid, and he seemed to like me, and we were planning to have a baby. For the first time in years I had the sense of going somewhere. "And do you feel alive?" he said.

That startled me. I'd almost forgotten what I'd said to him when I'd started. I'd run down a life checklist—drinking too much, shitty job, going nowhere, lousy luck with women—the sort of standard-issue miseries I suppose most people trot out in their first hour in a therapist's office. Then, having listened to myself—I'd never said all that stuff straight out like that to anyone, you understand—I felt a sludge-like gloom descend on me and said something I hadn't planned to say: "And somehow I don't feel like I'm *alive*. Do you know what I mean?"

For an eerie moment I imagined that he absolutely *had* to be thinking, "Jesus, what does this dumbass honky got to complain about?" But he said, "Yes, I do know what you mean," and he said it in a way that made me believe him.

So, the last time I saw him, I said, yes, I did feel alive. "Great," he said. "If you ever want to see me, I'm here," and I walked out and felt suddenly lighter—it was a feeling I remembered from finishing exams in university: hey, it's over and I'm free! I also felt sad because I knew I was going to miss talking to him. And I also had a tiny hint of an unpleasant, shifty, guilty feeling like I'd just weaseled out of something, although I couldn't figure out what I should have to feel guilty about—and now I've just decided that when I get back to Boston, I'd better call Jessie and make some appointments. Since I stopped seeing him, this is the first time I've ever felt like I really need help.

I'm sitting on the river bank as I did so many times when I was a teenager. There's a faint tickle of light over the hills above the river that tells me dawn's not far off, and maybe soon I'll be able to sleep. When I told Cynthia that I never thought much about my first wife, it was the truth, but I'm thinking about her now.

This is going to sound cruel, but it's not meant to be: Karen looked like a chipmunk. She had bright, happy, inquisitive eyes in a small, expressive face. She had chubby little cheeks. She was tiny and deft and did things quickly (she said that I "lumbered"). We met at a time when it was fashionable for women to look like children, and she did, but she didn't dress like a little girl on her way to a birthday party—she dressed like a little girl on her way to play school. She wore her dishwater blond hair either hanging straight, hippy-style, or in pigtails tied with bits of yarn (she knitted), and she favored yellow slickers, red rain boots, tie-dyed t-shirts, white athletic socks, and overalls in bright primary colors. When she was excited, she jumped up and down (really) and talked astonishingly fast in a voice that sounded like a tape speeded up. She was a naturally cheerful person who always tried to look on the bright side of things. With me, it was hard.

There's an exercise that's often done with geography students; the prof tells them to put away their books and draw a map of the United States from memory. The point of this exercise is not to make geography students feel like morons (although they always do) but to see the kinds of "mental maps" they have. When this was done to me, the map I drew was typical of what you get from most Americans. In my mental map, the Ohio Valley is an "area of brightness," so I drew it in enormous detail; the two coasts are fairly bright, but the middle of the country is an "area of darkness" so profound as to be practically stygian. What's west of Indiana? Who the hell knows? I didn't know then, and I still don't. Karen came from that huge, black nothing in the middle of the country—she was from Cottonwood Falls, Kansas—and maybe that's why I never understood her.

I thought it was exotic to come from Kansas, and I used to tease her about it. "Click your heels together," I'd say, "and you can go back to Kansas." When we first got together, she thought that was funny too, but I said it to her once too often, and she burst into tears.

When I met her, she was an undergraduate at B.U. I picked her up at one of those anti-war events we had in the Boston area about once a week in those days. I can't remember quite how we came to get married, although I'm pretty sure that if my draft board hadn't been sniffing at my ass, I wouldn't have done it. We planned to finish our degrees, and then I would get a job in a university somewhere, and she'd teach grade school. Well, she finished *her* degree.

I also can't remember quite how she finally decided to leave me—that is, I can't remember the exact details, although the fact that one night at a party I drank an inordinate amount of tequila and went home with a long-legged girl in a white leather miniskirt instead of with Karen might have had something to do with it. And the fact that the girl in the miniskirt was only the first of a series of girls (all of them wearing something other than overalls in bright primary colors) might also have had something to do with it. I got the divorce papers from Kansas and didn't contest it—how the hell could I? A couple years later Karen wrote me a long, chatty letter. She was living in some town in Kansas other than Cottonwood Falls. (Are there any towns in Kansas other than Cottonwood Falls? If so, name ten of them.) She was married with a kid, and happy as a clam—how was I doing? It was a friendly, forgiving letter, but I was not happy as a clam and didn't write back—and to this day feel like a total shit that I didn't.

I was the one who was fucking around, yet I was the one who wanted to stay married—does that make any sense? But right up to the moment we were holding hands and leaking tears at the airport, I also thought splitting up was no big deal. Then I walked into our Munchkin-sized apartment near Central Square and threw myself down onto our bed and cried in a devastated, heartbroken, uncontrollable way I'd thought only happened when somebody died, because the only other time I'd ever cried like that had been when Johnny died.

The next ten years was pretty much a write-off. Like many people I knew, I lived on next to nothing (that was somehow relatively easy back then), and I kept wondering if I shouldn't have stayed married to Karen. I felt totally blocked about finishing my thesis, but told myself that one magical day I'd wake up and feel like getting back to it. I'd already been doing odd bits of work for P. an' N. (Bill Plenart had called Dr. Morrison asking for a grad student to do an index for a book of readings, and that grad student was me, and I'd done them a dandy index), and I continued doing odd bits of work and continued to be known as "the kid from Harvard" long after I ceased being either a kid or from Harvard.

I wrote movie reviews for a number of little rags—sometimes for free and sometimes for twenty or thirty bucks a crack. I didn't know much about movies, but I thought I did because I'd read a few books translated from French. I got free passes and went to the movies ("the cinema" I would have said then) practically every night. I told people I was a critic (I never would have said I was a geographer), and the basis of my criticism was my *a priori*, and therefore irrefutable, conviction that any commercial feature made in the United States of America was, by definition, a piece of shit. One of the girls I slept with said I was "a good dumper," and that's accurate.

I was at my best (mildly amusing) when dumping all over a Hollywood movie, at my worst (impenetrable) when praising some pretentious exercise in tedium like *W.R.: Mysteries of the Organism.*

My main avocation was picking up girls. (Yes, I know they were "young women," but that's not how I thought of them then, and it'd be hypocritical to pretend that I did.) I'd never before had much luck with girls, and the discovery that it wasn't all that hard to get them to go to bed with me acted like a drug—I just couldn't get enough. This was the height of the sexual revolution (or whatever you want to call it), long before AIDS, a few years before anybody even gave a damn about herpes, and a startling number of girls were so aggressive I didn't have to do much beyond making eye contact with them. It also helped that I was *known*—at least in the small circle of bars and clubs where I was a regular—and had a certain *cachet* as a denizen of the artsy fringe. I wrote, you understand, *alternative* movie reviews. And everybody loves the cinema.

I thought the height of sexiness was the smooth, lean body of a girl who's just out of her teens, preferably dressed in something interesting—like jeans so tight she has to lie on the bed to put them on, or a miniskirt worn with sleek boots over the knee, or black plastic hot pants—and, given how refined my tastes were, it's not surprising that the girls who went to bed with me tended to be entry-level secretaries, file clerks, receptionists, waitresses, unemployed high school drop-outs, and students, lots and lots of students, from Boston's zillion colleges. My private code of ethics, such as it was, declared high school girls off limits, but a couple times I didn't know until afterward.

How many girls? I don't know. I was afraid to count. The sheer number might have looked like success to somebody else, but it felt like failure to me, because, weird as it might seem, all I really wanted was one of them. But even weirder—and this says something about the times—is that no one seemed to find anything terribly wrong with what I was doing; the worst I ever heard was, "Oh, Larry's going through his second adolescence." (The truth was, of course, that I'd never got out of my first.)

I did not enjoy the sex much. There are guys—I've met them—who claim to find it a turn-on to go to bed with somebody they've known for twenty-seven minutes, but I'm not one of them. I suffered from dreadful performance anxiety, and all I wanted to do was get the sex over with as quickly as possible (sometimes I'd find myself fantasizing about the one last week while I was screwing the one this week) so I could lie there peacefully afterward, have a smoke, and talk to them. I was a great listener, and anything they wanted to tell me was A-okay with me.

I heard about their parents, their jobs if they worked, their classes if they were students, and their boyfriends (a surprising number of them had boyfriends; some were even engaged). I enjoyed their company in bed—whoever the hell they were—and I enjoyed having breakfast with them the next morning, and I learned a lot about the hopes, dreams, ambitions, and philosophies of the kind of girl who answers the phone at a used-car lot, or is in second-year arts at B.U. and wears polka-dot platforms out to a jazz club. I liked almost all of them—some of them quite a lot—but I never saw any of them more than a few times. Looking back on it, the only good word I can find for all of this is *crazy*.

That period of my life ended pretty much the way it had begun—I drifted into it and I drifted out of it; at neither end was there much sense of volition. ("Who did it then?" Jessie would ask me years later.) Plenart and Northcott offered me a fulltime job; I didn't know whether I wanted it or not, but the world hadn't offered me much of anything lately, so I thought, why not? It'll only be for a year or two.

When anybody asked, I told them I hated my job, but I was doing real editing by then, and I found it curiously absorbing. I was living in a house in Cambridge with five other people, not your old-style hippy house but a quiet place where people worked at something and went to bed at a decent hour—a house full of oddballs like myself where everybody was friendly in a vague, distant way but nobody wanted to get too close to anybody else, because if you're over thirty and you're living in a house like that, you're obviously a loser, and the last thing you want to do is engage in a heart-to-heart conversation with some other vague, melancholy loser.

Working a standard-issue forty-hour week was a new thing for me, and it made me tired (Jessie thinks I was depressed in those days, and he's probably right). I always ate in restaurants, and then I'd go to a movie or home and watch TV. It got to be too much trouble to write my silly movie reviews. It got to be too much trouble to go out to the clubs, even on the weekends. I can remember sitting in the living room, enjoying the non-company of one of the polite, distant fellows I lived with, watching the late news on the tube, drinking the big glass of brandy I always had before bed, and thinking, Christ, it's been a long time since I've had sex with anybody.

For years I'd thought of my life as temporary. My real life, you understand, was being a graduate student at Harvard, and when I finished my Ph.D., I would continue with my real life, which would be teaching geography at a college or university somewhere. I always thought I'd get a job not in the black hole in the center of the country, but right at the edge of it—Ohio University, Indiana University, some place like that—and I imagined myself teaching geography (even physical geography, which was not my strong suit), and I knew I could do it. I imagined myself writing papers, giving lectures, getting tenured, and I knew I could do it. I imagined myself married with a couple kids—but I couldn't quite imagine my wife. She wasn't Karen. She wasn't any of the girls in polka-dot platforms. The best I could do was to think of her as one of the girls I'd admired in high school, one of the girls I'd been too shy—or too something—to ask out. For instance, Susie MacGregor, the majorette.

Bizarre as it was, I could remember the twenty-minute conversation I'd had with Susie MacGregor at the Friday night hop after the Canden–Academy game in 1959 more clearly than many of the events in my recent life. We'd both come straight from the game (I'd actually been in it for all of about forty-eight seconds), and she still had her uniform on. It was late in the season, and her legs were bright pink from the cold. And it wasn't just that she had the most beautiful legs in the Ohio Valley or that, to my mind, *nothing* (not even the steamiest of the pictures in Bud Armbruster's secret stash of men's magazines) could ever come close to being as sexy as a Canden High majorette, but she was also such a bright, bouncy, friendly, *intelligent* girl. So there I am, living my quiet but fulfilling life as a tenured professor at Ohio University, married to Susie MacGregor who's grown up into a splendid woman...

But one night, sitting in the living room with my glass of brandy, I realized that I was never going to teach anything anywhere or be married to anybody. Where the hell had my life gone? I was no longer, not by the wildest stretch of the imagination, a hotshot grad student. I was, God help me, getting dangerously close to forty. It had been a couple *years* since I'd been to bed with anybody. The girls had changed; they were wearing spike heels and disco jeans with rhinestones on their bums; when I admired them on the street, all I could think was, "Christ, they're too *young*." I was, you understand, about to enter my next incarnation as a drunken asshole.

The only time I cried in Jessie's office was also the only time that color—race, black and white, ethnicity, whatever you want to call it—ever came up after our first awkward meeting. I'd had a dream about him. It was one of those rare, totally convincing, three-dimensional, technicolor dreams I have every year or two, and I knew I had to talk about it, but I was embarrassed too. I'd been seeing Jessie for only a few months when I had it, and I wasn't sure how he was going to react.

In the dream, I was lost. I was driving an old car—to be exact, Bud Armbruster's Chevy that I learned to drive when I was sixteen. But I wasn't a kid in the dream; I was my present age. I pulled off the side of the road and started looking at my map, and I couldn't read it, couldn't make any sense out of it at all. It was like a map designed according to an entirely different set of conventions from ordinary maps.

"So the geographer can't read the map?" Jessie said.

I didn't think it was the right time to point out to him that there's a difference between a geographer and a cartographer. "Yeah," I said, "I guess that's right. What's it mean?"

"Don't worry about what it means. Go on, tell me the rest."

So I left the car and started walking and came to a big house. There was a party going on inside—hundreds of people—and I walked in, and nobody paid the least bit of attention to me. I found the phone and called Phyllis, and she started talking to me very fast—words coming out a mile a minute—and I kept saying, "Wait a minute, Phyllis, I'm lost. Don't you understand? I'm *lost*." But she just kept on talking faster and faster, and I realized that she wasn't talking to me at all, so I hung up.

I felt lonely and scared and desperate, and I yelled at the people at the party, "Please, somebody help me. I'm lost." And all the people looked at me for maybe half a second, and—zip—just went right back to their conversations as though nothing had happened, as though I didn't exist.

I sat down on a couch. I didn't know what to do. I felt totally alone. And then I saw Jessie walking over to me—except in the dream he was a Rastafarian. He was barefoot and had dreadlocks and talked with a Jamaican accent. "Hey, mon," he said, "cool out."

When I told Jessie this, I saw something hard and quick in his eyes—like a shutter snapping—and there was a pause long enough for me to take a breath, and then he laughed. "It's really funny," he said, "how you guys think of us," and that was his only reference to race in the two years I saw him.

"Okay," he said, "this Rastaman—did he say anything else?"

"Yeah, he said, 'Look around you, mon. There's a great party going on here. Good food. Good drinks. Lots of foxy ladies. Just cool out and relax.'" And I added, "You know, all that sixties bullshit."

"Right," Jessie said, "I know what you think about all that sixties bullshit. You've told me. But back in the sixties, did you cool out and relax?"

"No," I said. "I guess I never did. I tried to act like it. You know, I smoked a lot of dope and I drank too much, and I tried to 'go with the flow,' like we used to say. But it never worked for me. I never did enjoy it. I was always worried about something. Was I going to get drafted? Were Karen and I going to split up? Was I ever going to get my Ph.D. done? Then, after Karen and I split up, it was: Gee, sure is a pretty girl I picked up tonight, but am I going to be able to keep my erection up? It was like going through the motions of pleasure without any real pleasure. I always thought somebody else must be having a good time, because I sure as hell wasn't."

"Right," he said. "Is there more to the dream?"

There was more to the dream. The black man in the dream put his fingers on my chest and pushed, and I started to cry. When I told Jessie this, he got up and walked over to me and did one of the few touchy-feely things he ever did with me. "Show me how his hands were," he said, and I put my hands, his fingers, into the position they were in the dream. He pushed on my chest, and I felt a horrible cracking pain, and I started to cry.

He walked back and sat down in his chair. I kept on crying. He handed me the box of Kleenex, and I cried some more. "Why are you sad?" he said.

I said the first thing that popped into my head: "Because of all the years I wasted."

4

SINCE I'VE BEEN BACK IN RAYSBURG, I've been coming out of sleep weirdly disoriented, not sure of anything, but today I know immediately where I am—in the double bed in my mother's guest room. Without opening my eyes or moving a muscle, I can sense the furniture in the room around me, can feel that Cynthia's not in bed with me, and I also know (without knowing how I know it) that it's late in the day. I don't feel rested.

When I open my eyes, Cynthia, naked except for her wrist watch and her wedding ring, is standing by the side of the bed looking down at me, and I feel a tickle of irrational fear—it's like a long shudder. She's standing so silently, mysteriously, that I'm afraid to do anything to break the mood. The blinds are down; they're translucent and radiate an intense, hot, yellow light; the room is blazing with it. Cynthia's eyes meet mine. I can't read her expression. "What are you doing?" I ask her.

"Looking at you."

"What time is it?"

"Nearly noon. You should get up. We have to meet Jeff and Linda at one."

Whenever she climbs into bed with us, Alison always says, "I'm awake." She says it as though it not only explains why she's just arrived in our bedroom at a quarter of five in the morning, but also accounts for the entire order of the universe. "I'm awake," I say the way Alison says it, and Cynthia and I smile at each other. She's standing with her legs apart, her feet firmly planted on the carpet, one hand on the back of her neck, the other on her hip. It looks like a stance she could hold forever. "What on earth are you thinking about?"

She doesn't answer for a moment. "Looking at somebody asleep is, I don't know, poignant."

Cynthia has never got back down to what she weighed before Alison was born. No matter what she eats, she always stays a few pounds heavier—and complains about it—and I suppose it'd be nice for her if she lost those few pounds, but I don't give a damn about them. She looks great to me. "Hello, naked wife," I say.

"Hello, husband," she says. "There's fresh coffee on. I've been up since... I guess a little after seven."

"Why'd you get up so early? What have you been doing?"

She shrugs. "That's when I woke up. Just been trying to finish things off." I can tell she's not a happy camper.

"Did the funeral home call?"

She shakes her head, so I call them for the hundred millionth time, but my mother is still not back from Pittsburgh. "Could be today," they tell me, "let's keep our fingers crossed." Keep our fingers crossed, huh? Oh, yeah, we'll certainly keep our fucking fingers crossed. This is beyond being nightmarish; it's like waiting for Godot.

"I should've called in to work a couple days ago," Cynthia says. "They didn't expect me to be gone this long. But I wanted to be able to say, 'I'll be back on the such-and-such—'" She shrugs.

"Are you sorry you came?"

"Of course I'm not sorry I came. I actually like Raysburg. From everything you've said about it, I didn't expect it to be such a pretty little town."

"Yeah? That's not exactly how I'd describe it." She gives me a long look.

"I didn't get to sleep until, I don't know, it was around dawn," I say.

"Yeah, I was sort of vaguely aware of you being up. I'm kind of worried about you."

I'm kind of worried about me too, but I don't want to say so. "I'm okay. Thanks for last night."

"Thank you too. Yeah, that was nice, wasn't it?"

We take our coffee into the living room, and I suddenly see us as my mother would if she were alive. She'd be shocked down to her toenails—her son and daughter-in-law sitting on her living-room couch naked as two newts.

"Thank God for Jeff and Linda," Cynthia says.

"Yeah, right."

I feel about as speedy as a loris. We're both—it's obvious—a bit depressed. I tell her my dream, and what she says about it is perfect: "Should I buy a majorette uniform while we're down here?"

Her note cards and manila envelopes and stacks of paper are arranged in a neat pattern on the floor. She picks up a couple pages of letter paper and hands them to me. "Look," she says, "somebody copied out all of 'The Chambered Nautilus.'"

"That's my grandmother's handwriting."

"Yeah, it didn't seem like something your mother would like. 'Build thee more stately mansions, O my soul, as the swift seasons roll—'"

"That's my grandmother. She used to quote that."

I hand her back the poem, and she packs it away inside a folder. "I got as far as making a year by year outline of your mom's life," she says, "but there's too many holes in it, things I just don't know about—and then I wondered what the hell I was doing it for."

She shrugs. I shrug. "What holes?"

"Oh, just little ones—like from when she was born till when you were born."

I laugh at that. "Yeah, that's kind of a hole for me too."

My mother wasn't exactly forthcoming about her life. It's odd: my grandmother talked readily about herself, told me endless stories of growing up in a little farming town on the Ohio River, but remained to the end a mysterious figure to me; my mother didn't like to dwell on the past, as she put it, and told me so few stories of growing up that I could retell them all to Cynthia in ten minutes, but my mother always seemed to me as transparent as a water glass.

"In high school, she liked going to dances," I say. "If you asked her, that's always what she'd talk about. The dances out at Raysburg Park. A lot of the big bands came through.

"Oh, there's one story she told me a million times. There was a famous trumpet player who was playing here, and she was riding in some guy's car, and they could hear the band. I don't know where the hell the band could've been playing that they could hear it driving on the National Road, but they could—and the trumpet player held the last note of a song as they went all the way up and over Raysburg Hill. It was like an epiphany for her."

"That's a nice story."

"Yeah, it is. It's... Oh, I just had one of those dumb, obvious thoughts. The stories I've got in my head right now are all the stories I'm ever going to get."

"Yeah, I know, hon. It's really sad, isn't it? We should have taped her or something."

"Remember what she said at Christmas? 'I never had much luck with men. I married two losers in a row.'"

"Yeah," Cynthia says, smiling.

"If she hadn't been pissed on vodka, she never would have said that. And remember what she said when I asked her about my father? 'I'd tell you if I could, honey, but I spent so many years trying to forget him, I guess now I can't remember a damn thing.'"

Cynthia laughs, and then we both fall silent. "We'd better get dressed," she says.

I don't know what Cynthia's thinking about, but I'm thinking about my father. He's like a black hole in my childhood—just a large, central absence. His name was Matthew Cameron. I am named for my grandfather, Lawrence Cameron. All I know about either of these men is his name.

I suspect that I look like the Camerons, although I don't know for sure, never having met any of them. (I certainly don't look like my mother or anybody else in her family.) The Camerons were from Pittsburgh. My father—I'm guessing here—must have come down to Raysburg to get a job. He worked for Raysburg Steel in some sort of office capacity; after he and my mother split up, he moved back to Pittsburgh. I don't know why the marriage failed; my mother has said both that she left him and that he left her, and whenever I'd point out the contradiction, she'd deny it.

I couldn't have been much more than a year old when my parents split up, and I have no memory of my father whatsoever. For all I know, he may have married again, and I may have half-sibs. Cameron is a Scots name. If you don't already know that, you can find it out in a library fairly quickly—as I did when I was twelve.

Of course all of this, as they say, "came up" in therapy. It came up fairly early on in the game. "How far is Pittsburgh from Raysburg?" Jessie asked me. He had been taking what appeared to be excessively thorough notes about my "family of origin," but now he stopped and gave me one of his long, inquisitive looks.

"About sixty miles."

"And you never looked him up?"

"No."

"Why is that?"

"Do you think I should have?"

"I don't know whether you should have or shouldn't have. I just want to know why you didn't."

I still don't know why I didn't. The first thing I said to Jessie was that my mother had obviously hated my father, and I must have picked up something of that from her. Then, after spending a long time staring at the wall in Jessie's office, I said that I'd always had a feeling of—I don't know—being pissed off at him, or something like that, because he'd never looked *me* up. Both those statements are true, but I can't help feeling that they explain nothing. I have been in Pittsburgh many times in my life, and I've never bothered even to look for my father's name in the phone book. It's almost as though I don't want to know anything about him.

Now, thank God, we're out of the apartment. We're walking through downtown Raysburg with Jeff and Linda, looking at old buildings. "Built around 1861," Linda says, consulting her guidebook. "It had the first electricity in Raysburg."

We've crossed to the other side of Main Street to get a better look, and we've all assumed the same stance—tilted backward in gawking wonderment—so we can read the carved words at the top of the building—W. T. STAUB. "We look like four hoops from South Mud," Jeff says.

As Victorian buildings go, I suppose it's a dandy example. The uppermost section has a huge arch cut out of it with a window stuffed in the middle. The next section, which appears absolutely unrelated to the one above, has a fat bay window flanked by ornate carvings that look like abstractions of some strangling weed. The ground level has a modern facade and houses a little shop that sells moonshiner dolls, corncob pipes, porcelain pigs, and a multitude of objects—ashtrays, pennants, place mats, mugs, bumper stickers, fridge magnets, and pillows—that say, "Almost Heaven, West Virginia."

"They started generating electricity here in 1882," Linda informs us.

"It's wonderful," Cynthia says with no irony whatsoever—she really does think it's wonderful. I'm feeling like I'm going to start screaming at any minute, but I'm doing my best not to show it.

"I keep trying to tell the Raysburg Victorian Society," Jeff says, "that their next project should be a walking tour of Raysburg's historic whorehouses: On this location in 1802, Madam So-and-so established the first French-style bawdy house west of the Alleghenies. Notable figures to get laid here include Henry Clay, Andy Jackson—"

"Oh, fuck off," Linda says.

"Why not a tour of locations where Joe Patone had somebody shot?" I say, doing my best to fall in with Jeff's goofiness. "Note the distinctive display of bullet holes splattered across the—"

"Why don't you guys go drink a beer or something," Cynthia says.

"Oh, no. We're really enjoying this, aren't we, Lar?"

"You bet. Wouldn't miss it for anything. What's next?"

Next is a younger building—turn of the century—with two angels carved onto it. We dutifully stop and look at the angels. Then there are a couple more buildings from the 1860s; they just look like buildings. (It's hard for me to stop seeing downtown Raysburg as anything other than the dumb, familiar place where I grew up.) Then there's another really gaudy one, and we've got to stop to admire it. The word "Apotheke" is carved over a window; "Apothecary?" Cynthia says.

"Right," Linda says, "a German drug store. There were lots of Germans here."

"Jawohl," Jeff says, "undt ve isst shtill here."

"Your family's been here a long time?" Cynthia asks him.

"Five generations. My great-grandpa had a brewery—we're in the book."

Linda flips to the right page and hands the guidebook to Cynthia. "Oh, yeah," Cynthia says, "the Schneider Building—built by Thomas Schneider, president of Schneider's Brewing Company—has a motif of hops carved into the facade."

"Yep, we've always been big on hops."

Even for a jerk-off like Jeff, it's impossible not to respond to Cynthia's delight in local history, and he launches into a quick rundown on the Germans of Raysburg. "It got to be pretty hard to be German after the First World War," he's saying. "My grandfather told everybody we were Swiss."

We're down to the lower market by now, and Cynthia spots a used book store. "Here goes the rest of the day," I say to Jeff.

"I have to look, don't I?" Cynthia says. "I'll only be a minute. I promise."

We follow her in. She heads straight for the dusty shelves in the back beneath a hand-lettered sign that says VICTORIANA. "Hey, Lar, here's the ticket," Jeff says. He's found the table with the old *Playboy*s and *Penthouse*s.

"Oh, great," Linda says, and to Cynthia: "What's the difference between a man and a U.S. Savings Bond?" Cynthia shakes her head. "Savings Bonds mature," Linda says.

"Do I deserve that, Lar?" Jeff says. "Tell me, do I deserve that? Okay, then, how many blonds does it take to change a light bulb?"

Linda presses her fingers against his lips. "Truce?" she says.

Cynthia kneels on the floor so she can peer into the farthest corners of the bottom shelf. "Why don't you guys go on ahead? I'll catch up."

"No, no, no," we all say. "Take your time." But the last thing I want to be doing is wandering around a book store; the strange haze of pain has come back like a fine curtain between me and the world, and it's hard for me even to read the titles.

Then I hear a little gasp from Cynthia. It's a sound she might make if she'd just pricked her finger with a needle. As I hurry over to see what's happened, she's standing up slowly. With her bare hands, she wipes the dust from a book and passes it to me. The title is *Alice McDonnell—A Story for Today;* the author is Mrs. Clarissa Coltsworth Epping.

"It's a late one," Cynthia says. She's whispering. "Nineties. It's one of her last really good ones." She opens the cover and we both read the inscription written with a nib pen in an old-fashioned hand with lots of loops and swirls: "To dearest Delia on her sixteenth birthday, from your loving Aunt Myrtle, Raysburg, West Virginia, January 14, 1897."

I look up at Cynthia. Her lower lip's quivering and her eyes are flooding. I wrap my arms around her, and she presses her face into my chest for a few seconds. Then she steps back. "Oh, God, I'm sorry, Larry. I don't know what happened to me. This is really silly."

Cynthia likes to think of herself as a rational person; strong emotions take her by surprise, and she's always embarrassed by them. "Don't be sorry," I say. "It's okay."

I hand her my handkerchief. She's left a wet spot on my shirt. "It was a shock, or something—I don't know what. Of course she'd be here. She was immensely popular all the way through the nineties. It was just—oh, I don't know."

She pats her eyes, blows her nose, hands me back the handkerchief, pastes on a smile, and sings out in a cheery voice, "Hey, Linda, guess what I found."

We're walking back up Chapline Street toward the car, checking out a few buildings we missed on the way down. Cynthia and Linda are a few steps ahead of us, deep in conversation. "Bright lady you've got there," Jeff says.

"Tell me about it."

"You ought to encourage her to go back to school." Neither he nor Linda have figured out that what Cynthia abandoned was a Ph.D., and I'm not about to tell them.

"I've been doing my best," I say, "but that's not her idea of a good time."

My attention's been caught by a building across the street. I know I've been in it, but I can't remember when or why or what's inside. It looks like it used to be an office building—like it might still be one. "Hey, Linda," I call to her, "what's that building?"

She stops walking and looks at it. "I don't know," she says. "It's not in the book."

"It's late," Cynthia says, "twenties. See the art deco carving?"

I don't give a rat's ass about the art deco carving, but I'm suddenly very curious about what's inside. "Wait a minute."

I've crossed the street, climbed the steps, and walked in before it occurs to me to wonder what I'm doing. Inside is a lobby. There's nobody in it. The floor is made of small black-and-white tiles. I walk across the lobby to the corner where the cigar stand should be—the cigar stand with the blind man—but it's gone. I turn, and right where I know it's going to be is the elevator with the wrought-iron grillwork door. I know I've been in here with Johnny.

There's a ringing in my ears—or a buzzing or some damn thing—and I'm suddenly so hot I feel like I've stepped into a blast furnace. I've always thought "break out in a sweat" was just an expression, but that's what I've just done; sweat's pouring down my face in buckets, and I'm having trouble seeing anything. I've never fainted in my life, but I have the horrible suspicion that's exactly what I'm going to do, and I imagine myself keeling over and my head going smack like a melon on those goddamned hard tiles. I know I've got to get my head down. I spread my legs, bend at the knees, and tip forward.

Jeff arrives at my side and slips an arm around my waist. "Hey, Lar, what's the problem?"

Cynthia and Linda have followed Jeff in. I hear Cynthia make a little anguished gulp—"Oh!"

I straighten up slowly. My head's clearing, but I feel sick at my stomach. "No problem," I say. "I just felt a little faint, that's all."

I know now what waiting for my mother's ashes to come back from Pittsburgh feels like. It feels like waiting to find Johnny's body.

Jeff takes my left wrist and finds my pulse. He gives me a long, dark look. "Lar," he says, "you know what I'd like you to do? I'd like you to lie down on the floor here. Come on, I'll give you a hand."

"Jesus, why the hell should I lie down on the floor?"

"Just do it, honey, please," Cynthia says.

He wraps his arm around my waist and guides me down until I'm stretched out on the hard tiles. I feel like a total fool. "Any chest pains?" he says.

"No."

"Any pains anywhere?"

"I felt kind of sick at my stomach—like I was going to throw up."

"Oh," he says, "how is it now?"

"It's going away."

He stands up and says to Cynthia, "I wouldn't mind putting him under observation for a day or two, do an EKG—"

"Hey," I say, "talk to *me*. I'm right here." He sinks down into a squat next to me. "What the hell are you talking about?" I say.

"You feel faint—sweating, tachycardia, fifty years old. What do you expect me to think?"

"You don't have to convince me you're a doctor. I believe you."

He laughs at that, but it doesn't stop him. "When's the last time you had your heart checked?"

"I don't know—six, eight months ago."

"EKG?"

"Hell, no. Look, Jeff, I've been going to the same doctor for years. He's at Harvard, for Christ's sake. If there was anything wrong with my heart, I'd know about it, wouldn't I?"

"Not necessarily. You get any exercise?"

"I swim."

"Jesus, Lar," he says, softly, almost under his breath, "when the hell'd *you* learn to swim?"

Then, with me stretched out on my back and him hunkered down next to me like a garage mechanic, we go through my entire medical history. He wants to know who in my family had heart trouble, what diseases I've had, when I quit smoking, how many years I've been swimming, how many times a week I swim, how far I swim, how I've been sleeping lately, what I generally eat, what I ate that day.

"Look," I say, "I'm under a lot of stress. That's all it is."

"What? You think stress doesn't affect the cardiovascular system?"

I turn so I can look right at him. The view is like something from a pretentious movie—just behind Jeff are Linda's pink socks and Reeboks and Cynthia's white socks and Nike cross trainers; I look up and see both women staring down at me with sickly, frozen faces. Cynthia's so upset she's wringing her hands. I fix Jeff with what I hope is my most commanding gaze. "This is absolutely ridiculous," I say. "My mother died, and I feel shitty, okay? That's all there is to it, okay?"

I know with absolute certainty that there's nothing wrong with my heart; I'm also enough of a geographer not to trust the things we know with absolute certainty, and Jeff's planted a nasty doubt in my mind. I feel horribly, disgustingly mortal, and the only thing I can do about it is stand up. Jeff doesn't try to stop me. "For the record," he says, "I'm strongly recommending an EKG."

"For the record," I say, "fuck off."

"Larry," Cynthia says in a sad, small voice.

"That was meant in good humor," I say to Jeff.

"You cut me to the quick," he says with a wink.

Cynthia wraps her arms around me, and we stand there hugging like lovers who haven't seen each other in a couple years. "I'm all right," I tell her.

We walk back out into the sunshine, and again I reach for the cigarettes I haven't smoked in ten years. Everybody's looking at me like I'm the latest exhibition from Patagonia. "I feel fine," I say. "No dizziness, no nausea—no symptoms. There's not a fucking thing wrong with me."

"Except you're a little fried around the edges," Jeff says. "How about some Valium?"

"Fuck, no. I just want my mother's ashes back."

"So let's go see if she's back," Cynthia says.

We troop silently around the corner and half a block up and into the funeral home. Young Jim Kleister—the latest incarnation of undertaker Kleisters (they've always taken care of the dead people in our family)—greets me with, "Oh, Mr. Cameron. We've been trying to call you. We received your mother's remains about an hour ago."

Jeff and Linda discreetly step back outside. Cynthia and I follow Young Jim (that's to distinguish him from his father, plain Jim) down a hall and into a side room. Young Jim can't be much older than twenty-five, yet he's already mastered the difficult art required in his profession of radiating a mixture of manic cheerfulness and profound gloom. With an odd gesture—it resembles a bow—he presents us to a box resting on a table. It's a little square box of highly polished dark wood (I suppose I must have ordered it, but I can't remember doing it). It's not much bigger than a box for storing silver. There's a metal plate screwed onto it; engraved on the plate are my mother's name and her dates.

My entire mother is in that little box. I touch the smooth, dark wood and start to cry. Young Jim offers some Kleenex—not to me but to Cynthia (that's how good he is)—and, with another motion that's almost a bow, backs through the door and closes it behind him. I stand there bawling my head off. I wish I believed in the immortal soul, but I'm not sure I do.

After I've finished crying, I don't feel much of anything—just numb and blank. Cynthia and I hug. I see that now she feels worse than I do; her eyes are spilling over with tears, but she isn't crying, and she can't seem to say anything. "Let's get out of here," I say.

Jeff and Linda have looks of such sympathetic, sappy miserableness pasted onto themselves that I have to laugh at them. Then we're stuck there on the sidewalk, looking at each other like four penguins on an ice floe.

"You want to be alone, Lar?" Jeff says.

"No. That's the last thing in the world I want."

"Want to go back to our place?" he says. "Want to look at more old buildings? I don't suppose I can talk you into an EKG, huh? Want to—I don't care what, you name it. We're at your disposal."

"Is there any place," I say, "where we can go for a swim?"

For someone who never was much of a jock, I have an oddly intense love of athletic facilities. I love gyms, weight rooms, running tracks, locker rooms—and pools, of course. I love walking in and smelling the chlorine. I can be in the lousiest mood in the world, and the smell of chlorine will pick me up. It's a hot, sunny afternoon, and Jeff had been willing to bet that anybody with any sense would be in an outdoor pool, and he was right. We're at the indoor pool at the Canden Y, and we've got the men's locker room to ourselves.

"You doing okay, Lar?" he says.

"Oh, yeah. You still worrying about my heart?"

"What do you think, asshole? It's my job to worry about your heart."

With the feigned nonchalance of a couple slightly-older-than-middle-aged men acutely aware of the sands of time cascading down the old hour-glass (at least I am), we're stripping off our clothes and flinging them boyishly into lockers, while—covertly, you understand—we're checking each other out. Neither of us is exactly what anybody would call lean, mean, and superbly conditioned, but for forty-nine and fifty, we're not doing half bad.

Once I was out of the funeral home, the last thing in the world I wanted to do was walk back into it, so we went to Jeff's, and I called Young Jim Kleister, and we decided on the date for the funeral. Then I called the *Raysburg Times;* the obituary was all set to go, and the funeral's the day after tomorrow, and there's not all that much left for us to do. Cynthia's even made us a plane reservation. It's just now beginning to sink in, and I feel spacey with relief.

"I can just see it," Jeff's saying, "you drop dead in the pool, and your wife's got a six-million-dollar malpractice suit going against me, and I'm standing there explaining it all. Well, yes, I did think he might have had a mild heart attack, so, naturally, I figured the best thing to do was take him swimming—"

"Oh, for Christ's sake. You don't honestly believe I had a mild heart attack, do you?"

"Larry," he says—and it's the first time I've seen him be totally serious about anything—"there's absolutely no way for me to know, unless I do some blood tests and an EKG on you, and even then I might not know. All I've got to go on is your medical history, and your medical history tells me you probably didn't..." He hesitates.

"Yeah?"

"I'm going against the grain here. When we're talking hearts, we should be practicing a very conservative, very defensive, brand of medicine. Having said all that, if I honest to God thought you'd had a heart attack, I wouldn't have brought you to a swimming pool, now would I?"

That takes the wind right out of me. "Jeff," I say. "I don't think it was my heart. I think it was something else."

"So do I," he says. "Stress. And a swim's probably the best thing for you, but you know, I could be wrong."

I don't know what to say to that. We walk through the showers and into the pool. Our wives haven't appeared yet, and the only other person there is the lifeguard. She's perched on a chair high above the water, her toes curled around the rungs, and she's so engrossed in the book she's reading she doesn't even look up. She's wearing an old sweatshirt that says "LIFE'S A BEACH" (there are no beaches within three hundred miles of Raysburg). She looks about twelve, and I can't help wondering if she's capable of hauling a full-sized adult out of the deep end.

We sit down on a bench. Jeff yawns and stretches. "Got all the gear, I see." He means my cap and goggles and nose clip and plastic thongs. All he's got is an old pair of trunks.

"You betcha. When I decided to take up swimming, my first rule was to make it as easy and pleasant as possible—I never liked getting my face wet."

Just as I meant him to, he's laughing. "You're a card, Lar."

"Jesus, Jeff, what are you—a tape recorder? Don't you ever forget any slang? Don't you ever *retire* it? A *card!* Good Christ, Jeff, that's not even our generation. That's our parents' generation."

This is exactly how we used to tease him back in high school when he seemed so much younger than the rest of us—when he was such a perfect straight man that we couldn't resist—and I wonder why I've fallen back into it. Maybe I'm getting even with him for playing doctor. How on earth did he get to be a doctor anyway? It seems so unlikely.

"I didn't have a whole hell of a lot of choice," he tells me. "My old man was a doctor, and he was paying the bills, and that was that."

"What kind of doctor are you?"

"Brilliant, first-rate, what do you think? No, just a GP. I used to be a cardiologist, but I got out of that. Too many assholes like you who wouldn't do what I told them."

"You like being a doctor?"

"Well, you know, Lar, after twenty-some years you get kind of tired of sick people."

He's grinning. He shakes his head. "The only kind of medicine that makes any sense is preventive medicine, but nobody wants to hear that. Nobody ever stops smoking if I tell them to—or lowers their fat intake, or takes up jogging, or whatever the hell you tell them. There's just an endless line of these poor fuckers with something wrong with them, and sometimes they get better, and sometimes they get worse. If they get worse, I send them to a specialist, and if they get a lot worse, he sends them to a surgeon, and he cuts them up, and then they die." Now he's got me laughing.

We both peer toward the entrance to the women's locker room, but there's still no sign of our wives. "You swim much?" I ask him.

"Not as much as I should. Four years at the Academy and then four more at Ohio State. All my associations with swimming are competitive, and doing it for fun just seems, I don't know, weird."

"Were you any good at Ohio State?"

"Oh, hell no."

And here come Linda and Cynthia finally. I'd had enough presence of mind to throw my swimming stuff into my overnight bag when we were leaving Boston (that seems like a million years ago), but Cynthia didn't bring a suit with her, and Linda has lent her one of hers. Cynthia's wearing a beach towel over it, wrapped around and tucked in at her waist like a sarong.

"Thank God nobody's here to see this," she says under her breath, and I don't know what she's talking about. She takes me by the hand and leads me off on a little stroll around the pool, and then, when we're on the far side, she whips off the beach towel and turns around to show me. Linda's old suit is a black-and-white one-piece, and in the front it's as modest as can be, but on the bottom in the back there's nothing but an inch-wide strap that runs all the way up to the waist. "Wow," I say.

"Like that, huh?"

"Oh, sure."

"Yeah, I thought you would. It even embarrassed Linda. She kept saying, 'Oh, God, I'm sorry. I forgot how it was cut. Oh, I haven't had it on in ten years.' She must have said that a million times. 'Oh, I haven't had it on *in ten years.*'"

Looking at my wife's bare ass (the suit frames it rather neatly, I've got to admit) is giving me a distinct tingle, and I have a quick, vivid flash of making love last night. "If that's Linda's taste in swimsuits," I say, "I'd love to look in her lingerie drawer."

"Oh, I'll bet you would."

We've made it over to the lifeguard by now, and I can't resist looking to see what she's reading. It's a Stephen King novel.

"Larry?" Cynthia says, and I can hear that there's something bothering her that's more serious than wearing Linda's slutty swimming suit.

"What's the matter, hon?"

She shakes her head. "I'm all teary." She touches her breastbone to show me where she feels the tears.

"What's wrong?"

"I don't know. Just the... you know, life, death, and the human condition. Christ, will I ever be glad to get home." Then she turns and looks me right in the eyes. "You scared the shit out of me, hon. Will you have a check-up when we get back?"

"Yes, sure. There's nothing wrong with me."

"I know that. But will you have one anyway?"

"Sure. Yes, yes, I really will."

Jeff walks lazily to the edge of the pool, dives in, and goes blazing by us. I'm delighted to see something left of the beautiful, light, whippy stroke he had as a boy. "Look," I say to Cynthia. "Pretty stroke, huh?"

Dutifully she looks and says, "Oh, yeah," but she could care less about swimming strokes.

Linda has settled onto the edge at the shallow end; she's paddling her feet up and down in the water. "You've got the right idea," Cynthia says to her.

Jeff slams into the wall like he's finishing a race, bobs up, shakes the water off himself. "Well, there's my exercise for the year."

I climb down the ladder because I don't like jumping in; I walk around past the women's feet. "How about it, girls?" Jeff says, and to me, "Think we'll get them in the water?" He gives his wife's ankle a light tug.

"Not a chance," I say, "Cynthia thinks swimming laps is nuts."

"Right," she says, "you might as well be a hamster on a wheel."

"But jumping up and down to teeny-bopper top-forty rock," I say, "while wearing baby pink Spandex tights—in a class with a cute name like 'Super High-Tech Body Burner'—that, you understand, is a perfectly sane activity for a grown woman with two kids."

"Don't give me that, Larry," she says, laughing, "you love it."

"You're right, I do." I put on my cap and goggles and nose clip. "I'm going to do forty meters," I say, "so I'll see you guys sometime tomorrow."

"Easy," Jeff says.

"With me, it's always easy."

I push off. The water feels like velvet against my skin. Until I get warmed up (ten or twelve laps), I alternate a lap of backstroke with a lap of freestyle; after that, I swim all freestyle. I use the nose clip for the backstroke to keep the water out of my sinus cavities. If you're breathing right, you don't get water up your nose, but who gives a shit about breathing right? The only thing in the water any slower than me swimming freestyle is me swimming backstroke, and it will average out to nearly a minute a meter, but I don't care. I'm not racing anybody.

Cynthia is probably telling Jeff and Linda the story of how I learned to swim. She loves to tell that story because she thinks it's weird, eccentric, and delightful that her husband taught himself to swim when he was in his forties—and he did it by reading books. I didn't start that way; I started with private lessons.

The friendly, helpful, and impossibly optimistic young woman I was paying fifteen bucks a half-hour to teach me to swim was about the age my daughter would have been if, like Jeff, I'd had a daughter in my twenties. Like most swimming instructors, she swam beautifully and had never experienced any difficulty whatsoever in learning to swim. She did with me what everybody else had always done—gave me a kick board and told me to kick—and when I kicked like a frenzied demon, I moved slowly backward in the water the same as I always have and always will forever. I stopped after two lessons and went to the library.

I read—I won't say all—but certainly most of the books written about swimming in the last twenty years. We're used to taking things on authority; we like to believe that people who write books know something; if I hadn't been trained in human geography—hadn't read dozens of perceptual studies and hazard studies in which it has been demonstrated time and time again just how profoundly the perceived environment can differ from the real environment—I might not have believed what I discovered: that most of the people who write about swimming don't know a goddamn thing about it. If you don't believe me, compare photographs of championship swimmers with the ridiculous things that are written about them. The people who write these books can't even see what's right in front of their eyes.

I'm exaggerating, of course, but not by much. I gave up on the texts and stared at the photographs until I got bug-eyed. My freestyle stroke is modeled upon that of a wonderful channel swimmer; in her prime she held half a dozen records for swimming across huge bodies of water; someone had photographed her throughout the entire cycle of her stroke, and I finally learned from those photographs what nobody had ever said to me—that you can swim perfectly well with no kick. Oh, her legs do a slow, gentle flip-flop to give her stability in the water, but she's not getting any forward propulsion from her legs; the main thing she's doing is keeping them straight out behind her so they won't create drag. Of course I'm not even remotely as good at it as she is, but I can swim a mile that way. As I said, I'm not racing anybody. I just want to get my heart rate up, and keep it up for a while, and I do that.

Like me, Patrick is a total klutz in the water, but I'm teaching him to swim with my method, and it's working just fine. I keep thinking that there's something enormously significant about all of this—something that could be generalized and made to apply to a hell of a lot more than swimming or learning to swim. If I could ever figure out what it is, maybe I could write a paper about it.

Some of the most odd and interesting thoughts I ever have come sailing in out of nowhere when I'm swimming, and now—on lap eighteen—I remember walking out of the old elevator and across the tiled lobby to the cigar stand. Johnny was with me. We always bought peanut butter cups from the blind man. The memory is absolutely clear. It was a specific day. It was raining out, and I could hear the rain—and smell it. I try to find more memories, but that's it—no more pictures in my mind—but I've been left with Johnny to think about.

When I was eight, my mother married Bud Armbruster. He had a son named Johnny who was seven. No, I didn't think it would be fun to have a nice, new father and a brother (as my mother put it); I wanted to go on living with my mother and grandmother the way I always had. I remember crying about it a lot, but nothing I said or did had any effect.

When I first met Johnny Armbruster, I didn't like other little boys much, and didn't trust them, so I was wary of him, but I could see right away that he wasn't the kind of little boy who was going to haul off and punch me for no good reason. If you have kids of your own, it helps you remember being one, and watching Patrick grow up has refreshed my memory. Eight-year-olds know more than what most adults think they do—although a kid's knowledge is selective and unreliable. At eight, I knew that any boy whose mom has died is bound to be sad, and I knew that Johnny was sad, and I was afraid of his sadness as though it was something I could catch like the measles.

I was a quiet kid. Johnny was even quieter. But I was a good kid (now I think that I was far too good for my own good), and Johnny's quietness was deceptive; he was capable of doing really rotten things—so rotten that they instantly became family legends. What I didn't know at eight—or at eighteen, or, for that matter, at twenty-eight—was that doing really rotten things can also be a way of being sad.

Once—this was shortly after his mother died—he quietly took a carton of eggs from the fridge, tiptoed through the kitchen, opened the door to the basement, sat down on the top step, and methodically threw the eggs—all twelve of them, one at a time—into the basement. The hot-water heater was directly at the foot of the steps; the eggs made an omelet in it (at least that's how the adults told the story), and the omelet cost Bud a hundred bucks. Johnny also wet the bed, wet his pants, and sleepwalked (or at least they said he did; I had a hard time believing it). When he sleep-walked, he peed between the banisters down into the front hall.

Johnny loved playing with matches. Most adults smoked in those days, and he watched them carefully; he was extraordinarily adept at whipping a pack of matches off a table and into his pocket before anyone noticed, and things around Johnny frequently burst into flames. (He always appeared to be totally surprised when they did.) He burned his hands several times, but that didn't stop him; the worst he did—at least the worst he did when he was little—was set fire to the living-room drapes. His standard defense: "I just wanted to see what would happen."

When I first met him, he took me into his room to show me his scrapbook. He collected pictures of whiskey bottles clipped from ads in magazines. Some brands, I gathered, were harder to find than others; his ambition was to collect at least one picture of every brand there was. Later on, he showed me the real thing. We stood—secretly, of course, and quiet as ghosts—on two chairs and looked into the kitchen cupboard to see where Bud kept his bottles. Bud had a lot of bottles. I didn't know enough at eight to think that there was anything odd about Johnny's scrapbook or Bud's bottles. I had very little experience with grown men, and it was easy enough for me to believe—I'm not sure how I would have put this at eight—that one of the primary distinguishing characteristics of grown men was that they loved and collected whiskey bottles.

However different Johnny and I were in many ways, we were both sad, inward kids, and after the initial strangeness wore off, we banded together against the rest of the world, and he was, I suppose, my best friend until I was well established at the Academy—well, no, not that exactly. We fought too much to be friends. He was more like my brother.

I'm on lap thirty-two—that's eight more to go—when I

remember what was in the building with the old elevator and the cigar stand. There was a barbershop on the third floor. It always seemed a mysterious, secret place to me, hidden away inside that building, and it was where Bud went to get a shave and a haircut, and he used to take Johnny and me there. The barber was a black man—a Negro we would have said then—and there was a manicurist, a very pretty girl who looked just a shade darker than white, and I can remember wondering if someone was that close to white, how you could know for sure she wasn't white.

Johnny and I went in there once looking for Bud, and we caught him kissing the manicurist, and that's a memory I didn't know I had. Now I can see it in my mind: she had on one of those tight, straight fifties skirts, and Bud's hand was cupped around her ass, and he was giving her, not a passionate kiss, but a big, silly smooch. I didn't care what kind of kiss it was; I was so shocked it was like a physical sensation—an electric buzzing over my skin.

In my memory, Johnny and I are walking across the tile floor toward the cigar stand. I can hear the rain, and I can smell it, but I can't remember anything more—that is, I can't remember any more vivid details like the smell of the rain. We went to see a movie at the Court on that day when it was raining—I can remember that—and when we came out of the theater, it was still raining, and—picking up the pace of my last few laps—I see Cynthia and Linda's feet under water at the side of the pool every time I turn at the shallow end, and I see the rain when Johnny and I came out of the theater and the whole world looked wet. I remember the stoplights gleaming on the wet street, the brilliant colors of them against the slate-blue light from the sky, and walking across the Suspension Bridge with Johnny, and I remember the rain on the river, the way it drifted, and unfolded, in gray layers down the river. The Suspension Bridge had wooden flooring then, and I remember how it rattled when a car went by, but I can't remember what Johnny and I were talking about. I know we talked a lot when we were kids, and I wish I could remember exactly what we talked about, but I can't. And then I remember getting to the end of the bridge and turning up Front Street; it was a route I'd been walking my entire life—it was more than familiar, it was eternal—and I must have been right around Patrick's age, and remembering this makes me think of Patrick in a different way, because I was a complete person by then, somebody with a full set of thoughts and feelings, and I know I was talking to Johnny about something important, but I can't remember what it was, and that makes me sad. I wish I could remember what we talked about. I can't ask him, because he's dead. Why can't I remember?

5

IT HAS BEEN OVER A WEEK since I've been in the water, and I can feel it in my muscles. I'm so tired I could fall asleep instantly—or at least I think I could—and my brain has turned to mush, and I can't imagine anything I'd rather be doing less than fighting with my wife. I'm pretty sure she doesn't want to be fighting with me either, but it's one of those fights that once you're in, it seems impossible to find a way out.

"It isn't as though we haven't talked about this," Cynthia says. We're back at my mother's apartment, and Cynthia's supposed to be changing for dinner, but she's pacing up and down.

"Right, right. Yeah, we've talked about it." I'm lying on the living-room couch—not totally horizontal but getting there. "But look, hon. Isn't it a wonderful owl?"

The owl is perched on the coffee table. It's a carved wooden owl, fully owl-sized, so realistically painted that from a few feet away it looks real. Cynthia doesn't care what a wonderful owl it is; she thinks—or at least for the sake of the argument has decided to think—that I'm cultivating some bizarre, warped, fantastic streak in our daughter.

"Alison is not an owl," Cynthia says. It's one of those statements that leaves me absolutely nothing to say.

"She's already got a dozen owls anyway," she says.

"Yes. Right. Why the hell did you let me buy it?"

"What was I supposed to do—get in a big fight with you in front of Jeff and Linda?"

"No, but you could have said, 'Hey, Larry, maybe we should talk about this.'"

"What's to talk about? You don't care what I think. You're just going to go ahead and do what you goddamn well—"

"Hey, this is ridiculous. Alison doesn't—"

"Yes, she does. We've got a daughter damn near four years old who thinks she's an owl. You encourage her."

"For Christ's sake, Cynthia. I can't believe we're doing this."

She takes a breath to yell at me, and then she doesn't. "I can't either," she says and sinks into a chair. Her mouth turns down like a Greek tragedy mask. She shakes her head and tries to laugh. "Oh, fuck, it is a beautiful owl—if you like owls." She wraps her arms around herself, bends forward, and starts to cry.

I take her by the hand and lead her into the guest room. We lie down on the bed. Cynthia hates crying and has a hard time giving in to it; I think she sees it as a kind of weakness—for herself, at any rate (she never minds it when I cry, although I don't very often). Now she's crying so hard she's thrashing from side to side. Her fists are clenched; she keeps arching her back like a landed fish, and a steady, wordless wailing is pouring out of her. I've shed all my tears in the funeral home, and I feel sympathetic but detached—and exhausted. She cries with her eyes shut, the tears streaming out from under her closed lids. When she begins to quiet down, I take her into my arms. "Oh, God, Larry," she says. "I'm sorry."

"You don't have to apologize every time you feel something."

"Oh, fuck right off."

"Okay."

"I hate it when she talks in her goddamn squeaky little owl voice—and then you hoo at her, you asshole."

118

"Sorry. I won't hoo at her any more."

"Oh, I don't care. Hoo at her all you want. Christ, I want to go home."

I start to drift off to sleep, and Cynthia says, "Larry? Take care of yourself please. I know you're going to leave me alone someday, but I just want you around as long as possible, okay?"

"I will," I say. "I promise."

I'm not even aware of falling asleep, but the next thing I know, Cynthia is kissing me on the cheek. "Hon. Come on."

I push myself up. I was so far down I was totally unconscious—no sense of time passing at all, and a part of my mind says, yeah, that's the way death must be—nothing at all. I feel about as useful as an old, leathery lizard, and sometimes I just wish the hell I could shut my mind up. I look at my watch and see that I've been asleep for over an hour. Cynthia's changed into her sailor dress, redone her makeup, and she looks sparkling fresh. She's great at pulling herself together when she has to. "You okay?" I ask her.

"Oh, yeah, I'm okay," she says with a wan smile. "My period just started. I'm going to call the kids, okay?"

I drag myself into the bathroom, splash water on my face, take two Tylenols. I can hear Cynthia on the phone talking to her mom—I can tell it's her mom by the tone of her voice—and I'm remembering the dream I had last night. There were too many dead people in it—my grandmother who's been dead since 1980 saying, "It can't be Johnny. He's dead." And my dead mother, talking to Pete Saunders, our old swimming coach, who's dead. And the person who looked like Johnny—maybe it was Johnny, dead or not.

When Johnny was laid out in Kleister's funeral home, lots of his friends from Raysburg High showed up, and some of them cried buckets, and I was a bit surprised—and glad—that he'd made so many friends at Raysburg High. But the only one of *my* friends who came to see him—and pay his condolences to me—was Bobby Cotter. I have never understood the significance of this.

I had many closer friends than Bobby Cotter, and I didn't think they were any less my friends for not showing up at the funeral home. Johnny had only been at the Academy a couple years, and he'd been a quiet boy, and I don't blame anybody there for not remembering him. Many of my friends, when I saw them, did manage to mumble something like, "Heard about Johnny. Sorry." Beyond that, they didn't want to talk about it, and neither did I. They did exactly what I expected of them, exactly what I would have done, and that was enough.

Johnny was the first dead person I'd ever seen, and it's a testimony to the skills of the folks at Kleister's that he looked as presentable as he did. Part of his mouth had been reconstructed—a kind of Halloween plastic mouth had been inserted in one side— but other than that, he wasn't too bad. He'd fallen off his bike the week before and got cinders in his hand, and they were still there. That really got to me—the cinders in his hand—and I don't know what else to say. The effect of seeing somebody dead, somebody you knew really well, isn't something you can say much about that will be any different from what anybody else says. No, I don't think it's barbaric to have an open casket. People who tell you they're glad they saw the body because otherwise they wouldn't have believed it—not deep in their hearts—are right. I saw his body, and I believed it deep in my heart. I've never cried so hard or so long in my life.

I was one of his pallbearers. My mother kept trying to talk me out of it. "It's pretty rough if it's one of your own," she said. "Are you sure you want to do it?" It wasn't that I wanted to do it—I *had* to do it. None of my friends were at the funeral, and I was glad they weren't.

I was really surprised when Bobby Cotter walked into the funeral home. He could have got a parent to come with him, I suppose, or some of the guys from the swimming team, but he didn't; he came by himself. He had a suit and tie on. I thanked him for coming; he shook my hand in a grave, formal way, but he didn't say "I'm sorry." I took him over to look at Johnny, and we stood there looking down at Johnny, and then Bobby said, "He looks dead."

"Yeah," I said, "he is dead."

We stood there looking down at Johnny a while longer, and then Bobby slapped me on the shoulder and left. I've never told this story because I'm pretty sure that anybody who heard it would miss the point and think that Bobby behaved like a total boor, but I think what Bobby did, and said, was one of the most truly gracious gestures I've ever experienced. It fit perfectly into the world we shared—the Academy, the swimming team—and it acknowledged the exact truth of what was going on. Yeah, Bobby, you were right. He was dead. He was dead as a post.

On the phone, Cynthia's saying, "Daddy got you a beautiful new owl, honey. Just wait till you see it."

But when I talk to her, Alison doesn't mention the owl. She says, "Daddy, I miss you."

For a few seconds I can't say anything. "I miss you too, honey."

"You come back right now, please."

"We'll be home the day after tomorrow. That's really soon, you know."

"You come *right now*." She's not kidding.

I look at Cynthia. My mind's a blank. One of the standard things I say to Alison is, "Hey, kid, I'm not God," and once she astonished me by looking me right in the eyes and saying, "Yes, you are, Daddy."

121

Right now, I wish the hell I *was* God. "What's the matter, Larry?" Cynthia says.

Then I locate the voice I use when I want at least to *sound* like God. "We'll be home before you know it, Allie. Now you go tell Grandmaw to give you some ice cream. You tell her Daddy said so."

When I get Patrick, he says, "Hey, it's getting pretty boring here."

I know him, and I know the tone to take with him: "Well, I'll tell you, Patrick, my boy, it's getting pretty damn boring here too."

We've heard the steam calliope playing ever since we parked up on Market Street, and we're walking fast, just short of running. We turn the corner and see Jeff and Linda standing on the wharf look-ing anxiously up the hill for us. Jeff grins, waves, points at his watch, and makes a come-on gesture. Linda starts up the gang-plank. I grab Cynthia's hand and we take off, lickety-split. About halfway down the hill I start worrying about my heart.

"Talk about cutting it close," Jeff yells over the calliope and hus-tles us onto this cute—a bit too cute—reproduction of an old-time pleasure boat. She's a rear-wheeler all tarted up in red and gold; she's called *The Belle of Raysburg*, and this, once again, is Jeff and Linda being textbook hosts, doing everything they can to show us a good time and give Cynthia her beloved nineteenth cen-tury—or at least what passes for it in 1992.

We pause, out of breath, looking down at the river as the gang-plank goes up. The calliope falls silent, and it's too silent—the sound's been chopped off and my ears are still ringing with it. "Sorry we're late," Cynthia says, "we fell asleep."

Simultaneously, Linda is saying, "Oh, Cynthia, you're wonder-ful." She claps her hands to show how wonderful. "You look like a Victorian schoolgirl."

It's an accurate description, and you would have thought Cynthia planned it. She didn't plan it. She's wearing the only dressy outfit she brought with her—one of her favorites—and she would have worn it even if we'd been going to a dog fight. It's a white dress with navy trim; it has a skirt just above the ankle, and it has that—whatever it's called—that little square cape thing hanging down the back like on a sailor suit. She wears white lace-up boots with it, and she does look like she stepped out of an old photograph.

Linda, however, did not step out of an old photograph. She's got on skyscraper heels and a tight little knit number in electric blue. Cynthia would have worn something like that only if she and I were alone and had planned to go to bed right after dinner, and I can see her searching her mind for a return compliment when the calliope kicks in again and saves her the effort. Jeff and I are just two middle-aged goofs in sweaters.

A fellow wearing a straw boater and garters on the sleeves of his striped shirt says, "This way, Dr. Snyder."

We have what appears to be the table of honor; there's no one else near us, and we're perched at the edge of the railing looking out over the river. Cynthia's mind must have been working the entire time, because, at the next pause between calliope tunes, she says to Linda, "Wow, you sure look terrific in that dress. You've sure got a great figure."

Linda blushes—it's odd, and kind of nice, to see someone blush these days—and she makes a dismissive gesture. "Oh," she says in a strangled little voice, "thanks. So do you," although the only part of Cynthia's figure that shows is her small waist.

We're under way, the big wheel going THWACK-thump, THWACK-thump. A pitcher of beer's arrived already, but Linda wants white wine. Cynthia thinks white wine's pretentious, but she says, "Oh, that sounds nice."

Jeff and I pour the suds, and I've just decided that, by God, I deserve to have a good time. Cynthia must be thinking something similar—she's singing along with the calliope. "My God," Linda yells, "she knows the words." Then it's the chorus, and it turns out to be "Ta-ra-ra Boom-de-ay" and we can all sing that much.

The calliope, thank God, wheezes to a halt. "You feel okay, Lar?" Jeff says.

"Sure. Stop worrying about my heart, will you?"

"Oh, I gave that up. Anybody who can swim a kilometer with a stroke as rotten as you've got hasn't got a damn thing wrong with his heart."

The cold draft tastes good. Jeff and I are facing the West Virginia side, and we watch the lumpy, green hills unrolling behind the buildings of downtown Raysburg. We've already done the good old high school days; what on earth have we got left to talk about? Our wives are moving right along, however; Linda's asked Cynthia how she got interested in the nineteenth century, and Cynthia's giving her usual answer about falling in love with Edith Wharton in high school, and I've heard it all before, so I'm listening with only half an ear. What's more interesting is watching Cynthia check out Linda's nails. Linda must have just done them. Most of the time Cynthia's nails are chewed, ratty stubs, and she thinks having perfect, polished nails is... I'm not sure what, something like disgustingly effete ("Who has time for that shit," she says), but when she's feeling really down, she gets a manicure.

"Where'd you say you live?" Jeff asks me.

"Sharon. It's near Boston."

"Nice town?"

"Oh, yeah." I give him my geographer's summary of Sharon. Lake Massapoag is the reason there is a Sharon, and the town followed a pattern of development that's typical in the northeastern

United States. They used to pull a lot of iron ore out of the lake. (Some of that iron ore almost certainly made its way into the blast furnaces of Raysburg.) Then, when there was no more iron ore, what was left was a recreation facility—the perfect site, first, for summer cottages, later for a bedroom community for people like me who work in Boston.

"There are no pools in Sharon," I tell him, "because everyone swims in the lake—except me. I don't like lakes. They're silent and stupid and don't go anywhere. If God had meant me to swim in Lake Massapoag, he wouldn't have given me a perfectly lovely twenty-five-meter pool six blocks from where I work."

"You're a funny guy, Lar," he says. "You ever think about moving back here?"

I laugh, and then I see that he means it. "It'd be a long commute," I say. "Your work's portable, doctor."

"It'd be a good place to retire to."

"Retiring? Who's thinking about retiring?"

"Me," he says with a grin.

"Yeah? Christ, you're not even fifty. What would you do?"

"Sit on the bank, watch the crawdads die."

They've got the waitresses dressed up like Kitty in "Gunsmoke," and ours doesn't seem to mind it. She's a breezy kid with a sense of humor, and Cynthia finds out right away that she goes to Raysburg College. Jeff orders half a dozen appetizers. Our wives are moving so easily from one topic to the next you would have thought they'd known each other for twenty years; now they're doing the kids. Jeff and Linda's daughter's thirteen and is giving Linda the fits. "I read somewhere that the age of first sexual contact keeps getting younger and younger—like for a lot of girls it's twelve. *Twelve.* Jesus. I keep talking to her about AIDS, but I just think it goes in one ear and out the other."

"How old's your oldest?" Jeff asks me.

"Twelve," I say with a laugh, "but I can't imagine Patrick making it with anybody."

"Oh, yeah?" Cynthia says. "Have you had a good look at some of the little sluts in his class?"

Gawky little Patrick with his smudgy glasses and his hair hanging in his face? Well, I guess stranger things have happened, and some of his classmates are, well, to put it kindly, not exactly the way I would have thought twelve-year-old girls ought to be. "There's too damn much money in Sharon," I say.

"And it's your little owl we're going to be worried about in another few years," Cynthia says to me.

"Convent school," I say.

"Right," Linda says, "on the North Pole."

"Not a whole hell of a lot you can do about it," Jeff says. "Get them interested in sports maybe."

"I don't know why we should expect them to be any different from the way we were," Linda says. "I mean, *really*—when you think about it."

"Yeah, I do expect them to be different from how I was," Cynthia says. "I wouldn't want any kid to be the way I was."

"Oh, you couldn't have been that bad," Linda says.

"Are you kidding? If AIDS had been around, I'd be dead."

"You?" Linda says. She's actually shocked, and I see Cynthia react to that. She gives me a quick look: Hey, Larry, help. Get me out of this.

"I bet we were all fairly wild," I say. "It was the times."

Linda's still having trouble believing it. "But you seem so *conservative*," she says to Cynthia.

Whatever Cynthia's feeling always shows right on her face for all the world to see, and she's been thrown for a loop. "Conservative? I'm a registered Democrat." As lame as that was, it was probably the best she could do. I don't quite understand what's happening.

And Linda won't let up. "No, I don't mean politics. I mean... you know."

Cynthia looks out at the river. After a moment, Linda touches the back of Cynthia's hand and says, "Did I say something wrong?"

Cynthia turns back to Linda and smiles. "Oh, no. It's just that conservative's a bad word for me—sort of on a par with serial killer. I never thought anybody would ever call me conservative."

That opens another near-fatal hole in the conviviality, and I can't think of a thing to say. Linda doesn't know Cynthia, but I do, and I know what Cynthia's doing—she's thinking. Finally Cynthia says, "The way things are these days, you just try to live a decent life, and you find out you've turned into a reactionary." She smiles. "I don't know what the hell I am, not really. The radical middle."

That's done it finally—everybody's relaxed again, and she's off the hook. "Yeah," Jeff says, "it's what used to be called liberal."

There's a pause, and then Linda goes right back at it: "Yeah, I'd be dead of AIDS too."

"Hey, Lar," Jeff says, "how'd we end up with these two wild ladies?"

"Beats the hell out of me."

Despite the pressure she's getting from all directions telling her to lighten up, Linda is not about to lighten up. I can see that she's really upset. "You're right," she says to Cynthia. "I've just been kidding myself. I don't want Kristin to grow up the way I did, but it looks like she's going to. She won't even talk to me any more."

"Come on, Linny," Jeff says, "it's a stage. She'll turn out all right—just like her mom."

"I hope so," Linda says. "Her mom just got through by the skin of her teeth."

With some people you can make it through dinner—you can make it through an entire series of dinners, years of them—and no matter what, everything will always stay polite and on the surface;

Linda, I can see, is not one of those people. Up until now I haven't really registered Linda—certainly haven't taken her seriously—and I'll bet that happens to her a lot because she's a pretty blond and dresses to show off and appears to be—and probably is—totally without guile. "A lot of us just got through by the skin of our teeth," I say to her, "excepting, of course, this one here." I pat Jeff on the shoulder.

He laughs at that. "Oh, Lar, you don't know the half of it."

"What pisses me off," Cynthia says, "is how nobody gives a damn about us... you know, just ordinary people with kids. There's either the lunatic right or the lunatic left. If you talk about family values, you immediately get yourself lumped with Dan Quayle."

"Oh, right," Linda says, laughing, "I know exactly what you're talking about. I was in the dentist's office with Krissy the other day, and I picked up a magazine, and there was this article called 'Does Anybody Care About the Family?' And I sure get the feeling that nobody cares, so I started reading it, and I kept agreeing with everything she said. You know, like people from dysfunctional families are going to be dysfunctional adults, so the family's the most important institution we've got, so why isn't anybody doing anything about it? And it started out making a lot of sense, talking about taxes and daycare, and I'm going, right, yeah, that's telling them—and then, all of sudden, right out of nowhere, I find out who *really* cares about the family. You know who that is? Jesus."

Cynthia cracks up. "Sucked you right in, did it?"

"Oh, yeah. I threw the damn thing down, and I thought, hey, I've just been tricked."

"That's right," Cynthia says, "and you know what the trick is? They've cut the middle ground right out from under us."

"Naw," Jeff says, "it's still there. It's about the only thing that is there. None of that noise on television means a goddamn thing anyway."

"Oh, you never take anything seriously," Linda says.

"Do I deserve that, Lar? Tell me, do I deserve that? I'm a very serious guy."

He takes a big drink of beer and grins at everybody. "You don't believe me, huh?" he says. "Well, there was a time when I honest to God thought that if Barry Goldwater wasn't elected president, that would mean the end of the American Republic—and he wasn't elected, and that was the end of the American Republic. Then later on, I did a little turn-around, and I honest to God believed that if George McGovern wasn't elected president, that would mean the end of civilization as we know it. Well, shit, he didn't get elected either, and that was the end of civilization as we knew it. But then a few years after that, America was once again faced with a terrible moment of crisis because—and I honest to God believed this—if Ronald Reagan was not elected president, then there would be no hope for anything whatsoever. Well, Ronald Reagan was elected president, and guess what? After eight years of him, there was no hope for anything whatsoever. And you don't think I'm a serious guy? Well, I'll tell you, friends and neighbors, of course I'm serious. This time I'm voting for Ross Perot."

We're all laughing. "See what I mean," Linda says.

We're going with the current; we're floating by Millwood now, and there's an abandoned coal tipple, and the abandoned Staub glassworks, and one of the Raysburg Steel plants all boarded up. The sun's still high—it's making quarter-sized spots of fire on the water as we go churning along—and it strikes me that this is the perfect place to be, going with the current down the big Ohio.

I loved maps when I was a kid because I'd figured out early that the world was a shifty place and wouldn't stay put, and maps give you the illusion of making it stay put, and I used to stare at them for hours and memorize the names like a catechism. Now, back in some dark corner of my memory, I find the names of old river landings on the West Virginia side: Millwood, Kate's Rock, Moundsville, Cresep's Landing...

Everybody comes from somewhere, and Linda's from Norristown—so close to Philadelphia that's where she always knew she'd go as soon as she got the chance. "What's Norristown like?" Cynthia asks her.

"Oh, it's a great place," Linda says. "We've got the state insane asylum."

Our waitress arrives with our appetizers—an absolute avalanche of them—cheese sticks, jumbo shrimp, meatballs, artichoke hearts, vegetables and dip. It's perfect—floating down the river and drinking cold draft and eating jumbo shrimp with hot sauce. On down the river—Proctor, New Martinsville, Sistersville... That's the river in my mind; here on the real river, the sun's still high, and the *Belle of Raysburg* hasn't even made it to Moundsville.

Linda was one of three kids, she says, "the one in the middle— the one who was always trying to make everybody happy." Her old man worked in the wire factory; her mom drank—it's a sad, familiar story—and Linda was ashamed to bring her friends home. She'd never know whether or not her mom would be passed out on the floor.

That's my cue to tell Bud Armbruster stories. Bud's mom was living on his dad's pension—which was next to nothing—and she'd been saving for years, a nickel here and a dime there, so there'd be enough money left to bury her. "I don't want to be a burden to anybody when I'm gone," she used to say, and when she died, Bud bet the money on the World Series and lost it. My mother paid for old Mrs. Armbruster's funeral.

"Oh, great," Linda says, laughing—it takes another grown-up kid of an alcoholic to laugh at a story like that. "You ever have a problem with it yourself?" she asks me, "I mean, like you know—drinking?"

"Oh, sure."

"Yeah, me too." She's drinking wine, and I'm drinking beer, and we give each other bittersweet smiles across the table while Jeff grins at us. "Yup," he says, "but we all quit years ago—except, of course, for tonight."

But again Linda—and I'm getting to like her for this—won't let go. "Did you get any help for it?"

"Yeah, I was in therapy for a couple years."

"I did the AA thing for a while," she says with her sad smile, "you know, children of alcoholics. It really helped. God, it's a hell of a way to have to grow up."

"You bet," I say.

These days we would say that Bud Armbruster was an alcoholic, but back when I was a kid, people didn't talk like that. They just said he was a drunk. He'd had an excuse for a while; his wife had died of cancer. But after a few years—after he married my mother—he'd run that excuse out, and he was known to our neighbors as "that no-good Bud Armbruster." He had all the bases covered: he was a social drinker and a solitary drinker, a daily drinker and a binge drinker. For years he had the biggest office supply business in town—typewriters, adding machines, file cabinets, office furniture, and all the stuff that goes with them—and his main client was Raysburg Steel, so of course he made good money. He never had any trouble supporting himself until he met Maw, but after that, it seemed to get very hard for him.

I got used to Bud not working and being drunk all the time, but I guess my mother didn't; when I was seventeen, she left him. I could see why she did it, but still I didn't like her splitting us up. Bud and Johnny moved into a little place down on the south end, and I ended up right where I'd started—with my mother and grandmother in an apartment in Belle Isle. Bud had got himself a job as a night clerk over at the McClain, and they gave him a room, so when his shift was over, all he had to do was walk a few feet and he could pass out. Johnny, to all intents and purposes, was living alone. Sometimes I'd manage to get a case of beer, and I'd take it over to Johnny's, and we'd sit and get pissed and watch his old, snowy, black-and-white TV. He was the only sixteen-year-old I knew who lived alone.

Johnny died the summer after my senior year in high school, and Bud never recovered from that. It doesn't take a whole hell of a lot to hold down a job as a night clerk; all you have to do is sit there and remain vaguely coherent, but he kept getting canned. Each hotel he worked in was farther south—sleazier, cheaper, grubbier than the last one. He ended up in the ultimate crap-hole down by the old Staub glassworks in Millwood; it was more of a whorehouse than a hotel. He died of drink in his fifties. I was at Harvard and didn't bother to come back for the funeral.

Even though he was the author of, well, if not all, then at least the better part of his own tragedy, there's no way I can see Bud's life as anything other than tragic, but I don't want to talk about it that way, not tonight, and I certainly don't want to talk about Johnny, so I search my mind looking for Bud Armbruster stories that are funny—or at least can be told so they're funny.

Bud, I tell them, had two employees—an elderly single lady named Ethel Harmen who kept the books and a first-rate repair-man named Charlie Schwab who serviced everything Bud sold. For a few years Miss Harmen (or "Stupid," as Bud always called her) and Charlie ran the business while Bud drank. He supplied all the office equipment for Raysburg Steel—not just for the main office but all their plants up and down the river—and as long as that contract was in place, the business could float. One winter when we had a lot of snow, he took off to Florida for a month. My mother was mad as a hornet. He came back tanned practically black, walked in the door, and said, "I feel great. I haven't had a single drink of whiskey the entire time I was gone."

My mother should have known better, but she lit up like a Christmas tree. "Oh, honey, that's wonderful."

Bud laughed and said, "I've been drinking gin."

Raysburg Steel changed management—it was when Bobby Cotter's dad came in, I think—and they put the office equipment contract out to tender. Bud was furious. I can remember him pacing up and down, saying, "Who the hell do they think they are?"

"I imagine they think they're Raysburg Steel," my mother said.

"On principle," he said, Bud refused to bid, and six months later he was bankrupt. His creditors knew him; in a matter of hours, they stripped his office and warehouse right down to the paint on the walls. While he was sitting in the Silver Stein getting loaded, they took his Buick off the street. (I drove the old Chevy down to the south end of the Island so they wouldn't find it.) Luckily, we were renting our house, so they couldn't get that. They would have taken the furniture—and they tried to make my mother responsible for his debts (which included several thousand dollars worth of bar bills)—but she got a lawyer and stopped them. (It took her two years to pay off the lawyer's fees.) For months afterward tough guys in trench coats kept coming around, and Bud hid out in the upstairs bedroom where he wept and drank bourbon. My mother brought him his dinner on a tray.

Linda's laughing again, but Cynthia doesn't think it's the least bit funny. "She should have shot him," she says.

"For a while there," I say, "after Bud went bankrupt, she was supporting herself and me—and Bud and Johnny and my grandmother. She owed her soul to Household Finance. She went in to see her boss at Raysburg Steel. She'd been there, oh, I don't know, fifteen years. And she asked him for a raise. He said, 'Mrs.

Armbruster, you're already one of the highest paid women in the Ohio Valley.'"

Linda's laughing like she saw the punch line coming, but Cynthia's too angry to laugh.

"How much do you suppose women made in those days?" I say. "Dick-shit is what they made—"

"It's what they still make," Cynthia says.

"So she went across the river to Carleton Garment, applied for the office manager's job there and got it. It still wasn't a whole hell of a lot, but it was more than she was making at Raysburg Steel. She came back the same day and told Bud she was leaving him."

"Why'd she put up with him as long as she did?" Cynthia says.

"I don't know. I think she felt sorry for him."

"There's a funny dynamic with alcoholism," Linda says, "like a lot of times the partner thinks they deserve it."

"Any drunks in your family?" Jeff asks Cynthia.

"For a few years my father did fairly well at it."

I've never heard this. "Golden-Mean Warren?" I say. "Really?"

"Oh, yeah. He had... I guess you could call it a mid-life crisis. I was just in high school, and I didn't care what he was having. He was drunk a lot, and then he ran off with a woman—"

I really can't believe this. "Warren?"

"Oh, yeah. He was only gone about a week, but I thought the whole world was going to fall apart. Mom damn near left him."

So much for balance and repose.

We're floating on down the river, and I'm thinking about Bud. He was a likeable man in spite of everything, usually a jolly, ridiculous drunk, or a sad, quiet one, and when he was nasty—and he sure could be nasty to my mother—it was always verbal. He never hit anyone in his life, and he was pathetically transparent, and there's something almost touching about being as monumental an asshole as he was.

"I couldn't love you more if you were my own," he used to say to me with the slushy sentimentality of a man with most of a fifth of Four Roses in him—and it was true that he did ignore me just as much as he ignored Johnny. Occasionally he'd decide that he was going to do something with "his boys." I remember once he took Johnny and me to Pittsburgh to see a ball game; it had never registered on him that neither Johnny nor I gave a shit about baseball.

For a few years I tried my best to think of him as my father, and I still dream about him even after all this time. In the last dream I had of him, he was immaculately groomed just as he always was in real life. He had brilliantine in his hair and was wearing a tuxedo and was standing in the shallow end of the pool where I swim on my lunch hour; he was drunk as a lord—which was nothing unusual—and he was playing a trumpet. Bud never played anything, let alone a trumpet, but in the dream, he played so sweetly it made me cry.

And on down the river. Atkinson's Landing was too small to make it onto the map, so I'm not sure where it is. That's where my grandmother's from. The packet boats carried coal and tobacco, livestock, the U.S. Mail; they'd toot their horns and everybody would come running down to the landing. My grandmother grew up cooking for farm hands; those were the days when you had pie with every meal, and they had a whole pantry for pies. No sidewalks, no streetlights, no electricity, no indoor plumbing. "People scrubbed their outhouses white as clouds," my grandmother told me when I was a kid. And on down the river. Friendly, Long Reach, Raven's Rock, Wade, St. Mary's...

"I always wanted to have a family," Linda says, "but I was scared to death of it because my own family was so fucked up. I wasn't sure I could do it. Then, well, your kids come along, and you're *doing* it, you know, any old which way, and all you can do is the best you can. I'm really glad I had kids."

"How about you, ace?" I ask Jeff. "You glad you had them?"

"Oh, sure. I'm glad I had them, but I always felt like they just sort of jumped out at me."

"Oh, yeah, they really just jumped out at you," Linda says. "Right."

"Well, maybe not our two, hon, but my first two sure did. You think any sane man would have two kids while he was still in med school? Jesus. 'Guess what?' Candace says, 'I'm pregnant.' 'Wow,' I say, 'that's weird. We've been so *careful.*' 'Oh,' she says, 'I must've forgot to put the diaphragm in.'"

"She really did that to you?" Linda says, and I'm surprised that she's never heard this before.

"Oh, you bet," Jeff says, "and that wasn't even the half of it."

There's a bit of a hole in the conversation, and Cynthia comes in to fill it up: "How'd you guys meet?" she asks Linda.

"Oh, it's ridiculous," Linda says, "he picked me up in a bar. You know, he didn't even tell me he was a doctor. He didn't tell me for the longest damn time. When I met him, he hadn't worked for months."

"You're kidding."

"Nope," Jeff says. "I was, well, when I left Candace, I didn't have a clue where to go. All I knew was I had to get *out,* so I called up a buddy of mine from med school. He had a practice in Philadelphia. I'd never been to Philadelphia in my life, and I said, 'Hey, you want a house guest for a while?' and he said, 'Sure,' so there I am in Philadelphia, and Candace and I are screaming at each other long distance. She's going to court, and by God, I'm going to *pay*, she says, and I'll never see the girls again, ever, ever, ever—and then her dad's calling me up, and *my* dad's calling me up, and ole Doc So-and-so, the head of the clinic where I worked, is calling me up, so I just thought, fuck all of you, I'm going out on strike. I'd decided I was, you know, going to *find myself,* all that horseshit. I didn't know what I wanted to do, but I sure as hell didn't want to go on being a doctor."

That's just totally destroyed everything I thought I knew about Jeff Snyder, and I'm so astonished I don't know what to say.

"I was all set to marry him thinking he was just another jerk-off," Linda says, laughing. "I used to circle the jobs in the paper and leave them on the table—you know, like little subtle hints. It took damn near six weeks before he confessed."

Cynthia is absolutely delighted by this. "What on earth did you think?" she asks Linda.

"I thought he was putting me on. I go, 'Come on, Jeff. Get real. You're not a doctor.'"

"Oh, this is wonderful," Cynthia says, "just like a fairy tale. And you were going to marry him anyway?"

"Oh, yeah, there was never any doubt in my mind I was going to marry him."

The sun's setting on the Ohio side, throwing long shadows onto the West Virginia side. I am—why am I surprised at this?—drunk. Not stupid drunk, but drunk with that wonderful singing lift that makes you think that there's something to be said for alcohol after all. But I know enough to slow down. I lean back and watch the hills roll by.

"All I ever wanted to be," Linda is saying, "was a Bryn Mawr girl. Fat chance of that." As soon as she graduated from high school, she went to Philadelphia, got a job as a file clerk—and this is a familiar story too—took night classes at a secretarial college, went to clubs, drank too much, screwed around. "You ever wear polka-dot platforms?" I ask her.

"No," she says, "but I had a pair of bright red ones. Oh, God, I can't believe the things I did. What's the weirdest thing you ever did?" she asks Cynthia.

"Hey," Jeff says, "what's this? We in a Madonna movie, or what?"

"I'm not going to tell you the weirdest thing I ever did," Cynthia says, laughing, "I haven't even told Larry."

"I went to bed with a guy I hadn't known more than a few hours," Linda says, "and he had handcuffs fastened to the head of the bed, hidden under the pillows, you know, all set to go. Click, click, and there I am—wow, like, Mommy! Help! I've never been so scared in my life. I screamed and cried, but he wouldn't unfasten me. He goes, 'Come on, relax, and you'll like it.'

"There was no way in hell I was going to relax and like it, but there was nothing I could do about it. Oh, God, it was like—I don't know, it was like, you know, being at the dentist's with no anesthetic, and you're totally helpless. Ughh. It still makes me shudder. I actually prayed—dear God, if you get me out of this, I will never, never, never go to bed with a man I don't know, ever again in my life. Of course I didn't keep the promise longer than a month—but, oh God... You know that scene in *Cape Fear*, where he handcuffs her? I couldn't watch it. I had to get up and go to the can."

"I blew four guys in a row at a party once," Cynthia says in a dry, flat voice. I am, in spite of myself, shocked—more by the fact that I'm hearing this for the first time in company than by anything she might have done years before I met her.

"Those were my good old grad school days," she says, "and that was, you know, liberated behavior. We were all reading Foucault. He was a heavy duty French writer who was really big back then," she supplies for Linda, "and he was big on madness. We kept talking about Nietzsche and Artaud and de Sade—we never read much of them, of course, but they all went mad, so we thought they were really where it was at."

"You were working on, what, your master's in English?" Jeff says.

There's a pause a fraction of a second long, and I'm sure I'm the only one who notices it, and then Cynthia says, "Yeah, Christ, I had a wonderful time. The second meeting I had with my thesis advisor, he screwed me on the floor of his office."

"Oh, no," Linda says with a squeal.

"Oh, yes. I didn't like it all that much, but I took it as a high compliment, a... I don't know, a kind of authentication. And he gave me a pair of black panties with no crotch in them—which I dutifully wore whenever I saw him—and a long reading list. All the most trendy, up-to-date, with-it bullshit you could possibly imagine."

This is also the first time I've heard about the panties. "I thought he was a Hart Crane specialist," I say.

"He hadn't thought much about Hart Crane since his first hit of acid. God, you should have seen what was on his reading list— Carlos Castaneda, *The Crack in the Cosmic Egg*. Foucault, of course, and Saussure, Barthes, and those guys. *The Story of O*—

"Oh, no!" Linda says. I can see she's enjoying the hell out of this insider's view of academia.

"Oh, yes, yes, yes. A major work, you know, a serious critique of the poverty of everyday life. And I, being a good girl, read every piece of junk he wanted me to. I even plowed through all those French guys, but I didn't understand a word of it. I might as well have been reading Sanskrit. And you can imagine just how extremely useful all of this was for someone who was supposed to be writing a critical study of a nineteenth-century American woman novelist. Oh, Jesus. And that was education?"

Cynthia's been interrupted while we order dinner. We decide to go "heart smart," as Jeff says, and we order fish—four different kinds so we can share them—and a California Chablis to go with it, and I know that as tired as I am, I'd better go easy on the Chablis or I'll end up falling asleep before the boat gets back to Raysburg. I'm right at the perfectly balanced edge, and I want to stay there. "Huh-uh," I say to the offer of more beer.

"You're a wise man," he says.

"Not wise, doctor, just fifty."

Now Cynthia's telling Jeff and Linda about going to Massillon. "I was scared to death. We all thought that America was the most corrupt and evil nation in the history of the world—except for maybe Nazi Germany—and Ohio was in the very belly of the beast. I was sure if I wasn't careful, everybody would take one look at me and realize I was a weird, dangerous radical and, I don't know, stone me in the town square or something."

Cynthia settled into her work in the Epping Museum in the basement of the town library, and Mrs. Epping's granddaughter—she'd put the museum together in the first place—kept dropping in to see if she could be any help; when she saw how serious Cynthia was, she insisted that Cynthia stay with her. Mrs. Epping's granddaughter was married and had four kids ranging in age from six to nineteen. The kids idealized Cynthia and treated her like one of the family. "They thought I was a real California girl." She helped out around the house, cooked a few meals, picked up and dropped off the kids at softball practice and piano lessons, "generally made myself useful." She even went to church with them.

"For the first time since I was about fourteen," Cynthia says, "I wasn't screwing anybody. I never thought I'd be a proponent of chastity, but my God, was it ever a relief! And there was nobody around who wanted to talk about radical feminist post-constructionist deconstructionist semiotic anything—and that was *really* a relief. And the Thompsons weren't red-necked Nazis; they were kind, decent people who thought the Vietnam war had been a tragic mistake and that Nixon was a crook. And the kids were bright and funny and were dying to get out of Massillon as fast as they could, and I was amazed to hear myself saying, 'You know, there's a lot to be said for staying right here.' I got back to California, and it was like the emperor's new clothes. All I could think was, you guys don't know *anything*."

She stopped sleeping with her thesis advisor; she had a hard time working up much interest in the latest critical debate or revolutionary article; she still kept plowing along on her thesis, but she'd brought so much material back from Massillon her heart sank every time she looked at it. She knew by then that if she were ever going to teach, it would have to be at some quiet little backwater—maybe at a tiny college in some place like Ohio.

"So then I solved all my problems in one fell swoop," she says, "I got pregnant with Patrick."

"Oh, yeah," Linda says, "I know *that one* all right."

It's almost night by now, and we're still headed south. The green, lumpy hills keep unwinding, and around the bend there's always more river. No one has bothered to tell me how far this silly little boat goes, but I don't care if it keeps on going all the way to the Mississippi. I drift away inside myself for a few minutes, and when I come back, dinner's here, and we've got Cajun cod and planked catfish (so of course I've got to do the old joke about throw away the catfish and eat the plank); we've got the fisherman's platter (it's all French fried—so much for heart smart), and some baked thing full of shrimps and scallops. The portions are enormous. Jeff starts dividing them up so we all get some of each.

The Chablis arrives in a wine cooler, Jeff pops it, takes the first sip. "Beats turpentine," he says.

We're all of us a bit pissed by now, and we've hit that wonderful point you always hope for in a social evening but you don't often get—when everybody's feeling great at the same time, and everybody likes everybody else a whole hell of a lot, and there's no effort to the conversation. Cynthia's Massillon stories have set Jeff off, and he's telling us about living with his first wife.

"You should have seen the house we had," he says. "It cost half a million bucks, and everything was glass. Glass ceilings, glass walls, windows in the glass walls, mirrors on the real walls so you'll think they're glass walls. That was so you could see the wonderful view—and the view was absolutely nothing. That's what they've got out there in Arizona—absolutely nothing. And we had, count them, two cleaning ladies working day and night. The whole goddamn place smelled like Windex. And I used to get lost in there, like I couldn't remember which was the way in and which was the way out—and we got written up in a local magazine so everybody could say, 'Gee, look at those silly assholes living in a glass house.'"

We're all of us finding Jeff's story riotously funny. He's a natural-born storyteller, and his timing's perfect.

"I was making so much money—I didn't even think they *printed* as much money as I was making, and as fast as I was making it, we spent it twice as fast, and I was working, oh, maybe sixty, seventy hours a week, and I don't know who the hell Candace was screwing—no, you must never never never call her Candy—because she sure as hell wasn't screwing me. And me? Oh, I was dicking nurses by the dozen. I couldn't even keep track of their names, so I just called them all 'Debbie'—and then my old man retired and bought another glass house a few miles down the road so he and Mom could watch their grandchildren grow up. And I hate my goddamn old man. He was the one, you know, who got me into that whole fucking mess in the first place.

"So there I am living in a glass house in the middle of the desert with a woman I don't like, and two kids who never see me, and my dear old parents right up the road, and four horses out back—and there's nothing I hate worse than horses—and I lose another patient. Hey," he says, holding up the bottle of Chablis, "we seem to have cleaned this one out," and he waves at the waitress.

"Oh, come on, Jeff," Linda says, "we don't need any more."

"Come on, yourself, Linny. If we don't drink it, we can always dump it in the river."

"So you lost a patient?" Cynthia prompts him.

"Oh, right, yeah. I lost a patient. So, big deal, right? You're talking cardiology, you're talking losing patients—you've got damaged goods to start with. You're supposed to get used to it—except I've never quite got used to it, and I keep thinking there must be something wrong with me because I let it bother me. Like good old Doc What's-his-name, been in the business for years, and he's making pots of money, and doesn't give a shit how many patients he loses, so why should I? I must be a total wimp or something. And I went into cardiology in the first place because there's money in it, and I'm making pots of money, aren't I? So what's the problem?

"Well, one of the problems was angiograms, and there's a percentage of patients you're supposed to lose—like, I don't know, say, one out of a hundred—but I was losing a lot more than that, and I was beginning to wonder if it wasn't me. You know, like maybe I was screwing it up. I spent a lot of time reading up on it, and if I was screwing it up, I sure as hell couldn't figure out how.

"So I lose two in a week. And I think, hey, this is ridiculous. You can't lose two of them back to back like that. And then I do the third one the next week, and zap, he checks out on me. I just couldn't believe it. I felt like I'd been run over by a dump truck. I was too depressed to even get drunk. I kept thinking, it's really got to be something I'm doing. You don't do a routine procedure like an angiogram and lose three in a row. You maybe lose one every month or so, but you don't lose three fuckers in a goddamn row, and, of course, after you lose them, they're dead. You know, like *dead*. And dead, my friends, is one of those medical conditions that's irreversible.

"So I go home and try to talk to Candace about it, and she says, 'That's really too bad, Jeff, but I'm sure you'll figure it out. Oh, by the way, sweetheart, I'm going to redo the living room.' And I threw a few things into a bag, and took a cab to the airport, and that was the end of that."

There's a pause while we all look out at the river, and then Linda picks up the ball. "And then a few months later I meet him in a bar," she says, "and it was one of those things when you get together and it's bingo—perfect fit. You just know it."

"We picked each other up on a Friday night," Jeff says, laughing, "and we couldn't get out of bed till Sunday afternoon—"

"And I got the worst yeast infection of my life," Linda says.

"But it was worth it, wasn't it, sweets?"

"You know what really got to me?" Linda says. "I thought he was cute, but in those days I thought *a lot of guys* were cute. Well, I'm allergic to cigarette smoke, and whenever I'd be in a bar too long, my nose would start to run—and he handed me his hand-kerchief. Like I didn't say anything, and he didn't say anything. He *saw* my nose running and handed me his handkerchief—a nice linen one, all fresh and pressed—and I looked at him, and I thought, wow—"

"That make any sense to you, Lar?" Jeff says, laughing. "Would you think that was a really big deal? You see a girl's nose running, you hand her your handkerchief. Isn't that what you do?"

"Maybe you do," Linda says, "but most guys don't. So naturally

I took him home with me, and the next morning I woke up, and the first thought I had was: *I want a baby*. He's still sound asleep, right? And I'm lying there, and my mind's going a mile a minute, and I counted back to my last period, and I thought, bingo, right on. And I thought, that's ridiculous, what if you never see him again? And then I thought, that's okay, then you'd have the baby.

"Well, that one's really scary. I had to think that one through. So I thought, okay, what would you do if you were all by yourself with a baby? Well, I'd just got, really, my first halfway decent job, and they had benefits, like, you know, *benefits*—like maternity leave. And then what? If you want to keep working, you've got to... But Lorraine—that's my sister—was just separated, got a couple kids, needs some extra money, and she goes absolutely apeshit over babies, and I thought, well, maybe, and so I had to work through everything, you know, to see if I could really do it—alone, you know—and I thought, hey, it's going to be really hard, but I can do it. And then I thought, well, I'll have to take care of myself, get out of the bar scene, maybe join AA or something, like, you know, clean up my act. And I really wanted to do that. I'd been wanting to do that for a long time.

"So Jeff wakes up, and I go, 'Hey, I want to have a baby,' and he doesn't even hesitate. He goes, 'Sure.'"

"Oh, Christ," Jeff says, laughing, "and you know what I thought? I thought she'd just said, 'Marry me,' and I'd already decided I was going to marry her. It took us a couple weeks to get all that sorted out. You talk about your risk taking, Jesus. It was like holding hands and jumping off a cliff—like we didn't know each other *at all*, and by Sunday afternoon, we were just, well, we just couldn't do it any more. I couldn't even walk straight. I mean, I'd even rubbed the skin off my prick. And we got up and drank margaritas and listened to Neil Diamond—"

"No, *you* drank margaritas. I drank soda water—because I just *knew* I was pregnant—and yeah, that was Krissy. I know it sounds corny, but I've never been happier in my life."

"I just drank those goddamn margaritas," Jeff says, "and we listened to Neil Diamond over and over again for hours." He winks at me. "And if life has any meaning, I'll tell you, Lar, I sure as hell knew the meaning of life that day."

I don't know where we are, but we're turning around, making a loop around a tiny island with nothing on it but trees. There's not much light left in the sky, and what there is has gone gray as smoke. Our waitress brings the second bottle of Chablis. Jeff pops the cork and fills each of our glasses. Then, smiling, he raises his glass. With a slow, deliberate gesture, he offers each of us a toast. "Here's to us," he says, "the adult survivors of damn near everything."

6

JUST AS SHE SAID SHE WOULD, my mother's landlady arrives at three. While we've been here, May has slipped into June, and when we got up this morning, we found that the temperature had shot up into the eighties. Cynthia is wearing nothing but bra and underpants; she's fastened her hair up in a high pony tail; there's a haze of sweat on her forehead like a faint oil slick. We're neither of us feeling exactly what you could call wonderful. The doorbell rings, and I look at my watch, and yep, it's exactly three. "Shit," Cynthia says and vanishes into the bedroom.

I take one look at my mother's landlady, and I hope to God she doesn't die before she gets out of here. She looks older than my mother did. She walks with a cane, and she has hell of a time making it up the stairs. She's wearing a violet pants suit with bell-bottoms that must have been the height of fashion for the golden-age set, circa 1970; she's lost weight since then, and she's a wizened-up little monkey inside it. She sinks into a chair. "Oh, Lord. Could I have a glass of water?"

There's nothing to put water in. The useful junk left for Sharon this morning; the useless junk was hauled off to the dump about an hour ago. Then I remember that we'd put our toothbrushes in a cup in the bathroom, so that will have to do. The old woman reaches for the water, and I see that she's got one of those diseases that makes you shake constantly. The lenses of her glasses are so thick that her eyes are astonishingly magnified and seem to take up half her face. She's peering up at me with those goggle eyes, and I'm finding this too depressing for words, and I'm suddenly, irrationally, mad as hell at Cynthia for leaving me alone with her.

"It's the living-room furniture, you said. And the TV?" She has a hard, thin, querulous voice. "There's two beds, you said. Is that what you said?"

"That's right."

"Well, I don't know. What else did you say? Did you say the stove and the ice box?"

"Aren't they yours?"

"Good heavens, no. They're not mine. And those drapes? Did we talk about those drapes?"

"Mrs. Campbell, you said you wanted me to leave the drapes up."

Cynthia appears, barefoot in her sailor dress, and sits down on the arm of the couch. "Well, I don't know," Mrs. Campbell says. "I just don't know."

"We didn't leave anything that Larry didn't talk to you about," Cynthia says in the voice of sweet reason.

"You can't get much for old furniture these days," Mrs. Campbell says. "What do we say a hundred dollars?"

I feel like breaking the old bag's neck. "Forget it. You can just have it all, okay?"

Mrs. Campbell looks at me with her bulging, fishy eyes and starts to cry. There's something horribly sad about old people crying, and, for a moment I'm afraid I'm going to start bawling right along with her. "My mother thought very highly of you, Mrs. Campbell." I don't know whether that's true or not, but the words came out of some automatic phrase bank and are certainly something that my mother could have said. "I'm sure she would have wanted you to have it."

That makes her cry even harder. "Oh, dear. Oh, dear." She fishes a little handkerchief out of her violet purse and dabs at her face with it. "Oh, and you've cleaned it all up too. That was really nice of you kids to do that. Thank you for doing that. I was going to have Tiffy—that's my granddaughter, you know, Jerry's daughter—I was going to have her in, but now I don't I have to. But now I've got to advertise it. Do you suppose I can advertise it as furnished? Well, anyhow, semi-furnished. I just can't believe your mother's gone. I felt so sorry for her after your grandmother died. The people downstairs, you know, they come and go every six months. It's a shame the way life is sometimes. Just last month we sat right here and had a real nice talk. Oh, I just can't believe she's gone. I'm so sorry for your loss."

I can't say a word, not even "Thank you." She paws around in her pants and pulls out a roll of bills held together with a rubber band. "Here. You take this."

"No, I can't possibly take it, Mrs. Campbell."

"Yes, you can. I won't hear another word about it."

I help her back down the stairs. I keep shoving the roll of bills at her, and she keeps shoving it back. There's a battered, piss-yellow Datsun waiting for her with a girl behind the wheel. The girl has mirror sunglasses, a black tank top, three earrings in each ear, and a rose tattooed on her tanned left shoulder. She's smoking, and she says, "Hi," and I imagine it's got to be Tiffy. I get Mrs. Campbell settled in the passenger seat, and she reaches through the open window and pushes the roll of bills into the pocket of my shirt. "You're in my prayers, Larry," she says.

Back in the apartment, I peel the rubber band off the bills and count them out. "You didn't take it, did you?" Cynthia says.

"Christ, it just seemed easier."

The bills are ones, fives, and tens, and they add up to exactly one hundred dollars. "You shouldn't have taken it," Cynthia says.

"Lay off, will you."

Cynthia gives me a sharp, bird-like look, and I see her decide not to say anything. "I've got to be alone for a little while," I say. "I won't be gone long."

Before now I couldn't have imagined ever feeling so bad that I'd say to Cynthia, "I've got to be alone." I don't like being alone and never have, but I feel so miserable I don't want anybody to see me like this, not even my wife. Last night, floating up and down the river on the *Belle of Raysburg*, I'd been so happy I'd been damn near ecstatic. Cynthia had been the most wonderful wife in the world, Jeff and Linda my very best friends, and I'd felt like the luckiest man in western civilization. I woke up this morning feeling like dog shit. I haven't had wild mood swings like this since my twenties, and I'm scared.

I walk straight down to the river bank. It's private property, but I don't care. It gets hot in Massachusetts in the summer, but there's a quality to the heat here that Massachusetts can't touch. I feel like a scrap of fatty bacon sizzling in a pan, and it's not even July yet. Jesus, I think, how did I ever manage to live here?

I woke up this morning remembering things I haven't thought about in years and wished the hell I wasn't thinking about now. During that long period of my life—mid twenties to damn near forty—when I couldn't have been wasting my time any more efficiently if it had been shit I'd been flushing down the toilet once a day, I used to think—in fact it was the main thing I thought— *Who gives a fuck?* I didn't trust strong feelings in myself—whether they were good or bad—and I didn't trust them in anybody else, and I was ready at the drop of a hat to make fun of anybody who took anything seriously, because, as we all know perfectly well, nothing means anything. Phyllis, the best I could tell, had no sense of humor whatsoever (with her, a clever academic wordplay passed for a sense of humor), and she used to say to me, quoting somebody or other, "He who laughs has not heard the terrible news." And I'd say back to her, "If you can't laugh, you might as well be dead," but it wasn't until I was working with Jessie that I saw how easy it's always been for me to go for the laugh. I'd tell him some ghastly, pathetic story from my life, and he'd say, "That's really sad. Why are you laughing?" And sometimes—not every time but sometimes—I'd stop laughing, and then I'd let myself feel, for maybe a second or two, just how horribly sad it really was. When I thought I was a movie critic, *of course* the only American director I liked was Woody Allen.

Right now I don't find much of anything funny. The sense of pain smeared over everything is so strong I'm not sure I can see anything at all of the world outside me but an ugly blur, and I'd be delighted to trade this in for that ordinary, old, familiar, stupefying, enervating, bone-grinding depression that goes with "Who gives a fuck?"—but I can't seem to be able to do that. I haven't felt this bad since—well, since the last time I felt this bad.

It's funny what set me off the last time. I was going into my second year of doing whatever it was I was doing with Phyllis, and she was putting together a book of readings on gender, and I was flipping through the galleys and saw the name "Cotter" and that stopped me. It's not a common name. Then I was astonished to discover that the Cotter in the book was Bobby's big sister. I'd only seen her a few times in my life, and I'd certainly never talked to her. I'd never been interested in people's big sisters, only their *little* sisters, and I couldn't even remember what she looked like beyond a vague impression of somebody in one of those full-skirted cocktail dresses girls wore in those days. I sure as hell didn't know she wrote anything.

There were biographical notes on the contributors. Bobby

Cotter's big sister was, of all weird things, a poet. She had grown up, I read, in a "bleak, gray steel-manufacturing center on the Ohio River where, in the fifties, the air pollution was so severe that one rainfall was recorded that was more acidic than battery acid." It's distinctly unpleasant to see your home town summed up in a sentence like that—even if you know it's true. (Phyllis wrote the sentence, and she's never been to Raysburg.)

I read the poems. The headnote Phyllis had written for them said they were "a powerful deconstruction of gender identities in the 1950s" and, for all I know, they might be. The one I remember best is about a young girl riding down the river past the steel mills while wearing her first nail polish. The poems were better than anything Phyllis had to say about them.

Finding those poems depressed me for days, and I couldn't understand exactly why, although it wasn't too hard to find specific things I found depressing. I found it depressing that Raysburg had produced a major poet (at least Phyllis said she was a major poet), and nobody in Raysburg had ever heard of her—or was likely ever to hear of her. I found it depressing that Bobby Cotter had never made the Olympics. I found it depressing when I remembered how much money the Cotters had, and how I'd been so goddamned dumb I'd thought it didn't make any difference— when, of course, it makes more difference than almost anything else. I found it depressing that I'd spent so much energy trying to be exactly like Bobby Cotter, but I'd imitated his worst qualities instead of the only thing that saved him from being a miserable little prick—his strange, dark graciousness—so that when I was imitating him, all I did was make myself into a miserable little prick.

I found it depressing that my grandmother had died and left my mother alone in a little apartment overlooking the Ohio River with nothing to do but watch television and call me up once a week to complain about it. I found it depressing that my own life was so pointless. So I'd got out of the Ohio Valley, so what? I'd done very little to help myself (it was as though I'd never understood what the stakes were), and for all the good it was doing me, I might as well have stayed there. I found it depressing when I remembered all the times I'd been stupid or downright self-destructive, pretentious or unkind. And eventually I realized that I found, well, not just Johnny's death, but his whole goddamned life depressing.

He never did very well in school; he never failed a grade, but for years he teetered just at the edge of it, and I imagine somebody these days would say he had a learning disability. I don't think he had any learning disability. He had no trouble learning anything he really wanted to learn, and he had an uncanny talent for putting his knowledge to practical use.

The first of his demonic little devices I remember we called "The Patent Fuse-blower." It was an electrical plug with its wires wrapped around each other and then covered with a massive amount of electrical tape so Johnny wouldn't electrocute himself, and he must have been nine or ten when he made it. When my mother would take us to visit one of her friends, he'd wait until he was out of sight of the adults—all he needed was a few seconds—and then he'd shove the damned thing into a wall socket, whip it back out and into his pocket. "Oh, my God," my mother would say, "another fuse blew. I just can't believe it!" She never figured out what was happening.

When we started at the Academy, Johnny went into the library there and looked up gunpowder in the encyclopedia. We had the ingredients in our chemistry set. He quickly used up our little bottles, but it's not hard, even if you're twelve, to buy saltpeter, charcoal, and sulphur. Right from the beginning, his concoctions burned, but he wanted them to explode.

He kept looking for exact instructions. We were both avid

shoppers from the Johnson Smith catalogue; we sent away for whoopee cushions, dribble glasses, cigarette loads, Chinese linking rings, and booklets on ventriloquism, card tricks, and the secrets of Houdini's escapes. Johnny kept looking through the catalogue hoping to find a booklet entitled *How to Make Gunpowder*, but Johnson Smith didn't sell anything like that. He went to the public library and found detailed descriptions of gunpowder, but nothing he read gave him the exact proportions of the ingredients or a set of clear, simple, step by step instructions for putting them together. "They don't want me to know how to do it," he said.

He worked on it for a year or more. I got used to hearing—from the basement or the back yard—an intense, sinister hiss as his latest mixture burned but didn't explode. A burning mixture of sulphur, saltpeter, and charcoal has a powerful, distinctive smell. There were three adults living in our house, and why not one of them said anything—even something as innocuous as "Hey, do you smell something funny?"—I'll never know.

By the summer he turned fourteen, he was certain he'd got it right, and I was just as curious as he was to see if he had. We waited for an afternoon when all the adults were out. He'd soaked a toilet paper roll with paraffin, crammed it tight with his gunpowder, and fitted it with a fuse. (He'd learned by then to make perfectly good fuses.) It looked like a stick of dynamite from a Bugs Bunny cartoon. He set it on the railing of the back porch and lit it. We ran to the far side of the back yard and waited—and waited. "I made the damn fuse too long," he said, but we were too scared to go check on it.

We sat down in the grass. "Maybe it's gone out," he said. I didn't think that was very likely because he'd tested fuses for months up in our bedroom, and none of the ones in his latest batch had gone out. Then we heard—not the standard hissing noise—but something that sounded like an explosion in slow motion:

FWAAAAAAA-THUMP. A small, oily cloud of dense, black smoke rose from the porch. We ran back to see what had happened. A hole about six inches long and an inch deep had been blown out of the porch railing; the wood was still smoldering. Fragments of burning wood and paper were scattered around the yard.

We sanded down the hole and repainted it. No one ever asked us why there had suddenly appeared in the back porch railing a deep indentation covered with fresh, shiny paint, and Johnny stopped working on gunpowder. Looking back, I think he may have scared himself—but, more to the point, he'd also found by then somebody catering to the kid underground to sell him atom pearls, M-80s, and cherry bombs, and they worked a hell of a lot better than homemade gunpowder. My mother eventually told Johnny that one more explosion and she'd send him to reform school. She never would have sent him to reform school (I'm not even sure it was legally possible), but I think it was the worst threat she could imagine, and it worked. If he blew anything up after that, it wasn't around our place.

If he hadn't died, what kind of an adult would he have been? I didn't have the remotest idea, but I couldn't imagine a long, happy, productive life for Johnny. What the hell chance had he ever had?

It was the dead of winter—which, in Boston, is the perfect time for being depressed out of your skull. I was drinking a lot in those days (that's putting it mildly), but this time I really did it right. I bought, not a bottle, but a *case* of Scotch. I'd outgrown my living-with-losers phase by then, so I was in a little apartment in Sommerville, and I sat in it and drank Scotch. I was supposed to have a date with Phyllis that weekend, but I didn't show up, and I didn't call to cancel it, and when the phone rang, I didn't answer it. I sat in front of the TV, let it play whatever it wanted to, and drank the way I imagined Bud used to drink—not for fun, not for anything, just drinking. (Could we call this the Zen approach to alcohol?) Somewhere in the midst of all this I kept having a nasty thought over and over again; it wasn't a particularly complex thought (if it had been, I couldn't have had it), but it was a thought I couldn't shake—*There is something seriously wrong with me.*

I didn't go to work on Monday, and I didn't bother to call in. I crawled out of bed, and I drank. I did this until—and God knows why it finally got to me—the smell of Scotch made me throw up. To this day, I can't stand the smell of Scotch. When I did manage to make it back to work—I'd been gone a week and a half, and why they didn't fire me, I'll never know—I went straight into Steve Segal's office. "Hey," I said, "what's the name of that therapist you've been telling me about?"

Now I feel like the whole center of my life has been sliced away, and it could have been only a few minutes ago I walked out of the big house halfway up Front Street and down to the river as I did a million times when I was a kid—because I just had to get the hell out of there. When I was working with Jessie, I spent a lot of time trying to remember—no, more than remember, trying to *re-live*—events from my childhood. I wasn't very good at it. I kept finding areas of darkness where there should have been a memory but there wasn't, and when I did remember things, they usually seemed as distant and insubstantial as if they'd happened to somebody else. But now I'm remembering so intensely that the past is more real than anything in the bleak, squashed present.

It's Sunday afternoon, and it's hot as blazes, and Bud Armbruster is standing in the middle of the kitchen floor. In the last year he's gained a lot of weight, and it's all gone straight to the front of him—made a big, swollen belly—and he's started wearing his shirts hanging out to try to disguise it, but it only makes it look worse. He's shaved and cut himself; a scrap of bloody toilet paper is clinging to his cheek. His hair is slicked back, and he's wearing a sports shirt, one of the gaudy ones he brought back from Florida, but he's still got his pajama bottoms on, and he's barefoot. He's standing with his legs spread wide apart as though the kitchen is a boat going down the river, but, by God, he'll be damned if it's going to throw a man like him. He's smoking, holds the cigarette pointed in toward himself, cupped in his left hand, and he's forgotten it. The ash is about an inch long, and I know that pretty soon it's going to hit the kitchen floor, and then my mother will get even madder than she is already, and I know she's really mad because she isn't saying anything at all. Johnny and I are standing silently on the porch looking in through the screen door. To see us, all you'd have to do is look in our direction, but nobody seems to know we're there—and there's nothing unusual about that.

Bud is plastered like a wall, but there's no sign of what he's been drinking, and there's nothing unusual about that either. There are bottles hidden all over the house, as Johnny and I know because one rainy afternoon we found eleven of them—eight pints and three fifths. After Johnny entered our findings into a notebook (Basement shelf behind the paint cans, 1 pint Four Roses, 3/4 full; Living room book case, behind Mark Twain, 1 fifth Canadian Club, 1/4 full...) we put each bottle back exactly how we had found it. "You're drunk, Bud," my mother says, "go back to bed."

"I am not drunk," he says, speaking so slowly and carefully he sounds like a radio announcer. "How can you say that? How can you say that to me? I haven't had a drop to drink in a week. But you don't trust me. That's what it comes down to, doesn't it? That's what it always comes down to in the end. How do you think that makes me feel, huh? When your own wife doesn't trust you, how do you think that makes you feel? And even if I was drunk, I'd have plenty of reason, wouldn't I?"

"I give up," my mother says.

Neither Bud nor my mother can see her, but Johnny and I can—my grandmother has just come down the hall and stopped outside the kitchen door. She stands there with her arms folded, listening.

"Go on back to bed," my mother says to Bud. "I don't even want to talk to you when you're like this."

"Oh, no. We've some serious talking to do, some very serious talking and planning to do, but you don't want to talk. Oh, no. When I was doing okay, I was good enough for you then, huh? When there was lots of money coming in? But when my luck's running the other way, when I'm having a setback, you don't want to talk. 'For better or worse,' it says in the marriage vows, but you don't want to talk. Well, I'm going to talk to you, Dorothy, and you're going to listen. There's going to be some big changes made around here, believe me. And they can either be for better or for worse, and that's entirely up to you. Right now, when I'm right on the edge of getting on my feet again, you can either be for me or against me. You can either act like a wife, or throw me away like an old piss-pot. It's entirely up to you, Dorothy, believe me." This is pretty much Bud's standard speech.

The ash finally hits the linoleum. Johnny and I look at each other and exchange a wordless grin. My mother takes her glasses off and rests her face in her hands.

Bud notices the cigarette, puffs on it, butts it out on a saucer, presses both hands down on the kitchen table and leans forward toward my mother. "Do you know what I'm going to do, Dorothy?" he says. "But only if you force me into it. I'm going to move out of this goddamn hoity-toity house I got for you. And you can live with your goddamn interfering mother the whole rest of your goddamn life for all I care. And I'm going to put Johnny in the children's home. If you want to see that happen, well, you just go right ahead. The choice is yours, Dorothy. The choice is entirely yours." Some of this is new—the part about putting Johnny in the children's home is new—and Bud must have spent the morning dreaming it up.

"I've heard just about enough of this," my grandmother says and steps into the kitchen. "You sober up, Bud Armbruster, and you go get yourself a job, and then you can talk about 'for better or for worse.'"

"You see, Dorothy?" Bud says, leaning farther over so his face is only a few inches from my mother's. "You see how it is?"

My mother isn't about to see anything; she's bent forward with her face pressed firmly into her hands. She doesn't say a word, and she doesn't move a muscle.

"Whose side are you on, Dorothy?" Bud says. "You've got some hard thinking to do, Dorothy, and some hard choices to make, believe me. How things go from here on out is entirely up to you."

"That's enough of that," my grandmother says. "You just get out of my kitchen."

"Dorothy? Are you going to let her talk to me that way? The choice is yours, Dorothy."

"I said that's enough of that. And I meant what I said."

Bud pushes himself back from the table. He is—it's plain on his face—afraid of my grandmother. Wobbling, he sidles around her; she's staring right at him, but he won't meet her eye. He stops just inside the kitchen door and lights a cigarette. He still won't look at my grandmother or anywhere near her. "Dorothy?" he says. "Dorothy, are you listening to me? If you force me—if you force me to do it—I'll put Johnny in the children's home. I swear to God I will."

"You'll do nothing of the kind," my grandmother says. "That's the most ridiculous thing I ever heard of."

My mother's face is still pressed into her hands, but she says, "Mother, don't pay any attention to him. He's just drunk. He doesn't mean it."

"The hell I don't. I am not drunk. I have not had a drop to drink in over a week. I'm doing my best, and I mean every word I say. But if you go on the way you're going, you're going to force me to drink again. Dorothy? You know that, don't you, Dorothy?"

"Get out of this house."

"Did you hear that, Dorothy? Did you hear what she said to me? What's wrong around here is plain as the nose on your face, and you talk to me about drinking? Good God. Take the beam out of your own eye, why don't you? Well, Dorothy, I'm sorry to have to say this, but the choice is yours. It always has been. You've run the show from the moment I met you. Well, I'm sorry, but if that's the way it's going to be, then I guess that's the way it's going to be. Just remember—it was entirely up to you, and you failed me again."

Then, using the wall as a support, Bud makes his way though the door and down the hall. There's a crash of books from the living room as he retrieves a bottle (later, without comment, my mother will go in and put the books back on the shelf). Within the hour he will be—and Johnny and I both know this from previous experience—passed out cold. He and my mother haven't slept in the same bed for several years now; Bud has the little room that used to be the sewing room, and when we walk by the door, we'll hear him coughing and snoring. Because he's passed out early today, he'll be awake again around dawn. We'll hear him wandering around the kitchen, running the tap, taking aspirin. He'll groan and talk to himself while he's doing this—and sometimes he'll sit at the kitchen table and weep loudly. Sometimes he'll yell, "Dorothy. Please, honey, help me. I can't stand it any more." But my mother will never come down. Some mornings he'll go back to bed and sleep till noon. Other mornings he'll start drinking right away.

"Dorothy," my grandmother says, "why do you persist in giving him money so he can buy it?"

My mother is still hiding behind her hands. She will get up later and go upstairs and spend the rest of the day and evening in bed with a cold cloth on her face, and tomorrow morning she'll be back at work in the downtown office of the Raysburg Steel Corporation. "Mother," she says, "I really wish you wouldn't interfere."

"Interfere? Well, honey, you may not know it—and Bud may not know it—but *I* still know what's right and what's wrong."

Johnny and I have the two twin beds in the attic. That night I wake up and hear him crying. A chill goes through me. I hate to cry, and I hate to hear other people cry. "What's the matter?" I say.

"Dad's going to put me in the children's home."

When I come back, the apartment's so silent I'm afraid for a moment that Cynthia's left. But then I find her lying on the bed in the guest room reading the Mrs. Epping novel she got for seventy-five cents. She's stripped back down to her bra and underpants, and when she looks up at me, she's smiling. "Feel any better?" she says.

"Not much."

She gives me a look that seems about equally split between sympathy and annoyance. "We'll be home tomorrow night," she says in a voice exactly like she'd use to say to Patrick, "Cool it. Dinner will be ready in five minutes."

I sit down on the edge of the bed. The last thing I want to do is act like Bud and start yelling, "Help, help, help," but that's exactly what I feel like. "So how's Mrs. Epping?"

"Oh, great. I read them all too fast the first time through, and I missed a lot. I think this might be one of her very best."

"Oh, yeah?"

"I'd always thought that James didn't have any influence on her at all, but now I can see it plain as day," and she starts telling me about Mrs. Epping's narrative technique. I follow her for a while, and then I dial out. She's positively bubbling over, and I can't help thinking it's not fair that she can be so cheery when I'm not—although I don't know why the hell it shouldn't be fair, or even if it isn't fair, what difference it could possibly make.

She stops in mid flight. "You don't really want to hear this, do you? I'm sorry, Larry. God, you look awful."

"It's all right. I'm okay. I just want this to be over." I get up and walk into the living room. There's nothing more depressing than a stripped apartment waiting for a new tenant.

Cynthia follows me. She's still holding the Mrs. Epping novel with her finger in it to mark the place. "Hey," she says, "I'm really sorry I managed to enjoy myself for a few minutes there."

It's an invitation to laugh, and ordinarily I'd laugh, but today I can't. I have no reason to be, but I'm so mad at Cynthia I could strangle her, and I hear myself saying—it's like somebody else's voice coming out of me—"Jesus, your dad sure spoiled *you* rotten. All you had to do was reach out and take what you wanted, and you just couldn't do it."

There's a pause exactly like the long inhalation between the moment when Alison hurts herself and the moment when she starts to cry—I can see Cynthia's lower lip quivering—and then she starts to cry. She turns and runs back into the bedroom and slams the door.

For a moment I hate myself so much I'm paralyzed, and then I follow her. She's thrown herself down onto the bed, and she's sobbing. Great, I think, now I've made her feel just as bad as I do. "Hey, I'm sorry."

"Fuck you," she says.

"I didn't mean that. I really didn't."

"Yes, you did. That was really ugly. That was the worst thing you've ever said to me."

"I'm sorry. I'm really sorry."

I can't imagine anything sadder than this, and I can't think of anything that's going to make it any better. Then, suddenly, without planning to, I start to cry too. It feels like a dam breaking, and I'm afraid I'm not going to be able to stop. I sink down onto the floor and lean back against the wall.

The minute Cynthia hears me crying, she stops. She's kneeling down on the floor in front of me. "Shhh, it's okay," she says. "We'll get through this, and then we're going home."

Today nature isn't doing it. We've driven out to Waverly Park, and we're walking around the lake, and it should be making us feel better, but it's not. It's that deadly West Virginia combination—hot, high humidity, and not even the faintest suggestion of a breeze. It's late in the day, but the sun is still burning furiously away, and I can't help thinking about the ozone layer and the radiation that's beating down on our bare heads. I feel stupid and slow and filled with pain, and all I want to do is go back to what used to be my mother's apartment and stand in a cold shower. On top of all this, Cynthia has fallen silent, and I know—in spite of how sympathetic she was trying to be just a few minutes ago—that she's mad as hell at me and she can't pretend any more that she's not.

It's hard for me to talk, and I have to plan what I say before I say it and then work up what seems like an enormous amount of energy to get it to come out of my mouth. "What are you thinking about?" I've planned to say for about a dozen steps, and now I manage to get it out.

"You don't want to hear it."

"Yes, I do."

She gives me another of her quick, sharp looks from the side. "I was just trying to reconstruct your thought process—you know, to how you got to what you said."

"Oh, God, honey, I haven't felt this bad in years. It just popped out of me. It didn't mean anything."

"Yes, it did."

The nasty silence resumes, and we trudge on. Even through my sunglasses, the glare off the water is making my eyes burn. "Let's go back to the car," I say. She doesn't answer. Walking around the lake appears to have become some grim assignment we've got to complete no matter what.

"You were probably thinking about your mother and the horrible, shitty life she had and how hard it was for her," Cynthia says, and she's not bothering to disguise how angry she is. "And you've got this myth in your head about what a wonderful, warm supportive family I've got, and I've *told* you it isn't true, but you— It's like you don't process the information. And you think I just walked away from my Ph.D. like, I don't know what, in a fit of pique or something."

I hadn't been thinking anything at all like that. Before I said what I did, I hadn't been thinking *anything*. But I've got to admit it's a pretty good guess.

"You think I've got this perfect father–daughter relationship, and it just isn't true. Oh, I get along fine with my dad now. He's mellowed out a hell of a lot in the last few years, and I think he feels guilty about neglecting me when I was growing up. So, yeah, we do get along just fine now, and yeah, I do admire him, I always have, but there were times when I was growing up, he was a real son-of-a-bitch. And, yeah, we had money and he did give me lots of *things*, but I was never spoiled. Not in the way you think I was anyway."

"Look, hon, this is kind of—I don't know. You don't have to convince me."

"Yes, I obviously do have to convince you. This probably isn't the right time or the right place, but I really want to tell you this. I want you to get it clear in your head. It was not a barrel of laughs being the daughter of the great Dr. Warren Lewis. He wanted one of his kids to be a scholar, and he was sure it was going to be Tony, and any idiot could see that Tony didn't have a hope of being a scholar, and I kept going, 'Me, me, me, I'm the one,' but he never took me seriously—because I was a girl. Talk about classic—that's a bad pun, isn't it? But, yeah, it was classic. Straight A's, National Merit Scholar, astronomical board scores, straight A's at Radcliffe—and none of it counted because I wasn't a boy."

Now that she's started talking, it's coming out fast in a hard, mechanical voice, and, in spite of the heat, she's walking faster, and there's nothing for me to do but keep up with her. She may think she's told me all this stuff before and I hadn't really been listening—or, as she said, processing it—but a lot of it she never has told me before, or at least not in this clear, coherent way so it makes, as Jessie would say, a pattern.

She started reading her dad's books when she was twelve or thirteen, and she couldn't believe that any one human being could know as much as he did. She read Plato and Aristotle so she could talk to him about them, but she knew it didn't count because she didn't read them in Greek, and she never worked up her courage to talk to him about them. She wouldn't take Latin in high school because she was afraid even to try. Then he had his mid-life crisis and ran off with his woman—"I never knew anything at all about her, not even her name"—and for the next year or two the main question was whether or not her parents were going to get divorced, and Cynthia entered her wild phase. "I was mad as hell at him, and I really wanted to get him, and I didn't even know it.

Oh, I knew I was mad all right, but I thought it was the war and the general rottenness of America."

She read R.D. Laing and decided that the family was the root of all evil; she read Marcuse and Germaine Greer and bleak European fiction and incomprehensible, depressing poets who wrote without any capital letters, and she smoked dope, and screwed guys twenty years older than she was—and went on to the Cliff where she still managed to stay interested in the nineteenth century, and she still got straight A's. Her senior year she wrote a paper on Kate Chopin that her prof said was the best undergraduate work he'd ever seen. He told her to submit it to journals and gave her a list of them. She gave it to her father.

"I waited and waited and waited, and weeks went by, and finally, I said, 'Hey, dad, did you read my paper yet?' And he looks up at me with his big, goofy smile, and says—and he sounds surprised—'Yes, I did read it. You know, Cynthia, it's not half bad.' And that was high praise. The highest praise I ever got. But I never submitted it anywhere, because I'd be damned if I was going to submit a paper that was *not half bad.*

"Even before I went to Massillon," she says, "I was beginning to have this awful sick feeling that there was something wrong somewhere. I can remember waking up in the middle of the night once with a horrible feeling of dread. I'd just written another paper—I remember I'd quoted Adorno and talked about the death of art— and I'd got an A on it, and I realized I didn't believe a single word I'd said. And I kept reading more and more stuff to try to figure out what I did believe, and the more I read, the more I felt totally lost. And my father was one of the greatest scholars in America, and it never crossed my mind that I could talk to him about it— and I was right. I *couldn't* talk to him about it."

We've made it almost around the lake, and I can see the New Yorker waiting for us not more than a hundred yards away, and all

I can think about is getting in it and going to some place air-conditioned and drinking about a gallon of cold beer.

"And then when I was in Massillon," she says, "and was staying with the Thompsons, I realized that the problem wasn't *the* family, it was *my* family. I mean, nobody in my family was getting beaten up or abused, but it was a family that didn't work. And the Thompsons were a family that—well, you know, it wasn't all Beaver Cleaver, but it was a family that worked, and the longer I stayed with them, the more it made me look at my own family.

"For instance, why had there never been any rules for me? Why, when I was fourteen, was I allowed to wear leather mini-dresses and go wandering around Harvard Square picking up men? Why was I allowed to stay out all night? Why was I allowed to bring men home and screw them in my bedroom? It wasn't just permissive, and it wasn't just the sixties, it was *nuts*. It was like nobody gave a shit. And meanwhile Tony was getting so much pressure he ended up in Mass General with a nervous breakdown or whatever it was. And why did my father never talk to me? And why did my father never talk to my mother? And why—lots of things."

She stops walking, and I stop walking. "They fed me," she says, "and they paid for my clothes, and that was about it. They never gave me any help whatsoever growing up, and anything I ever got that counted for anything, I had to get on my own, so don't you ever ever *ever* say to me again that I was spoiled rotten."

The Kappa on Edgemont—it's one of Raysburg's eternal places; I used to come in here with my mother when I was a kid, and she told me she used to come in here when she was dating in high school, and now I've come in here with my wife and I've got kids of my own (although I haven't seen them for so long they're beginning to seem like little ghosts in my mind), and—I find myself adding stupidly—and my mother is dead. We're sitting at a table in the corner farthest from the door. Without realizing I was doing it, I've picked a safe place with my back to the wall so I can see everything that's going on. It's almost as though I don't want anybody to sneak up on me.

I'd been dying for a cold beer but I didn't order one. "Bring me about a gallon of iced tea," I said. The warning bells had been going off in my mind, and in that pause Jessie used to talk about—the space between when you want something and when you do something about it—I'd thought, no. As shitty as you feel, the last thing you want to do is dump alcohol in on top of it.

Cynthia, however, has downed a Miller Lite in thirty seconds flat. I know she's still mad. She's only a few feet away, but I feel miles distant from her. She's run out of words, and I wonder if she's hit an internal block like mine so it's impossible for her to talk. "Why don't we have dinner?" I say.

It takes her a long time to respond. Then she says, "Why don't we go over to Jeff and Linda's?" They'd told us to drop by if we felt like it. They'd even told us we could spend our last night there if we felt like it.

"No," I say. I can't find the energy to add anything.

"Oh, fuck."

"What's that mean?" I say.

"I can't take much more of this."

"More of what?"

"You don't want to do anything to help yourself, do you?"

"Oh, for Christ's sake."

Cynthia sighs. "Come on, make an effort, will you, Larry? You're pulling me down like a stone."

I'm still trying to think of something to say when she says, "Besides, I've got to borrow something from Linda for the funeral."

"Why?"

"The only dressy thing I've got is my sailor dress, and I can't very well wear that to a funeral."

"Why the hell didn't you bring something else?"

"I didn't know your mother was going to die, did I? Jesus, Larry, you've been sniping at me ever since you got out of bed this morning. None of this is my fault, you know."

"I know it's not."

Cynthia orders another beer. I order some cheese sticks. Her beer comes, and she drinks half of it. She closes her eyes and sits there without moving. A couple tears come sliding out from under her closed eyelids. "Oh, honey," I say and take her hand.

She opens her eyes. "You're not having your beer," she says as though she's just noticed.

"I feel too bad to drink. If I've been sniping at you, I'm sorry."

"You said you were dying for a beer. It seems really sad you're not having one. God, we're both so depressed. I just think we need other people to help us get out of it."

I consider that. "Yeah, maybe you're right. It's just, I don't know, I'm not exactly a barrel of laughs. Yeah, we can go over to Jeff and Linda's if you want."

That seems to make her feel better. She finishes her second beer. "I'd better stop," she says, looking at the empty glass.

"Go ahead and get drunk. I'll drive."

She looks straight at me. "I feel really terrible about Mrs. Epping. I feel like I let her down. I don't give a shit about the god-damned Ph.D., but—" She takes a deep breath and looks away as though she's just become totally fascinated by the people at a far table. Her eyes are flooding.

After running through at least a dozen things in my mind, I decide to say: "What are you thinking about, honey?"

"Nothing," she says and signals our waitress, holds up her empty beer bottle. "Maybe we should eat dinner," she says.

So we've had dinner, and we still haven't found much to say. We're going back to get our things, and then we're going to Jeff and Linda's. I hate the new bridge that carries Route 70 across the Island, and I refuse to drive on it. "It's cut the Island right in half," somebody wrote on the questionnaire for my hazard study so many years ago, and that's right; it's destroyed the character of the Island, and after everybody my age dies, nobody will remember the way it used to be—a quiet place where people knew each other and there were real neighborhoods. Nobody will remember the victory gardens down on the river bank and how much fun it was to go down there on a summer evening with all the neighbors.

I drive across the Suspension Bridge and turn up Front Street. It will be the last time I'll ever see the apartment that used to be my mother's. I don't know what I'm feeling, but whatever it is, it's not great.

A couple blocks up Front Street I pull over and park. "What are you doing?" Cynthia says.

"I don't know."

I want to walk on the new bridge, but I don't quite know how to say that to her. I don't want to have to explain anything. "Come on. I want to show you something."

It takes Cynthia a moment to catch up. I'm glad she doesn't ask me what's going on. It must be close to thirty years since I've set foot on the new bridge. It's amazing how it's possible to hate something like a bridge.

Now that Route 70 has cut the Island in half, you can drive across the northern panhandle of West Virginia without paying the least bit of attention to it. The great Ohio River will be just something you go zipping over—some water you see beneath you for a minute or two—and then you'll be on your way to

Columbus. It's early evening, the beginning of twilight, and there's a steady flow of traffic going both ways. "What are we doing up here?" Cynthia says.

"I just wanted to see it."

We've walked onto the bridge far enough to be over the river. We're looking toward the tunnel they've cut through Raysburg Hill. "Johnny and I walked across here before there was any floor in it."

I don't think she's heard me. "We walked across on the girders— or whatever the hell they were. Big steel beams. They were, I don't know, maybe a foot and a half wide."

Still she doesn't say anything. "I can't remember how old I was exactly. About Patrick's age. Maybe a little older."

"What do you mean, there was no floor in it?" Her voice is flat and wary.

I shrug. "You know, like *no floor*—just the beams."

I look directly at her. She's looking at me. "Larry, you can't even stand on a kitchen chair."

"Yeah. It's amazing, isn't it?"

We both look out to the center of the bridge. "God, if you'd fallen off—" she says in that same flat, careful voice.

"Oh, yeah. Game over. You can see it's a hell of a drop, and neither of us could swim."

"Why did you do it?"

"I don't know. We dared each other. We walked over to town, and then we messed around over there for a while, and then we walked back over the goddamned thing. All the time I was over in town, I was dreading walking back, but we had to. I had on my Academy shoes—you know, slick leather soles—and it was really slippery on those steel beams. I was so scared—I can't even remember it I was so scared. The actual... The time when I was actually walking on the beams is... it's just a blank. No memory. I just know I did it."

She's shivering. I put my arm around her. "Well, I'm glad you didn't slip," she says.

We start back to the car. "What do you mean, you had to?" she says.

"I don't know what I mean."

"Did you talk to Jessie about this?"

"Oh, sure," I say, and I don't know why I'm lying to her. I kept meaning to talk about Johnny, but I never quite got around to it. I even knew I was avoiding it, and still I never quite got around to it.

We get into the car. "The door is ajar," it says. "Fuck off," I say to it and close the door.

I put the key in the ignition, turn on the engine, and I'm afraid of driving. I feel a blast of heat just like I did in the building with the tile floor. I start to sweat, and I feel dizzy, and this time I'm afraid it *is* my heart. I press my forehead into the steering wheel and take two or three big breaths, and I suddenly remember driving with Johnny over the s-bridge out the pike in Bud's old Chevy, and it's so vivid it could have happened just minutes ago.

It took every ounce of nerve I had not to take my foot off the accelerator. The bridge was coming up hideously fast, and I was still booting it down, and Johnny was howling with laughter. I whipped the wheel, kicked the brake once, hard, and we went into a skid. I stomped her down again. We were sliding sideways across the bridge; the abutment whipped by in front of my eyes as I whipped the wheel over—missed by less than a foot—and I stood up on the accelerator, rose out of the seat, screaming like the car was screaming, my foot on the accelerator, and we went burning on down the road. "Ninety," Johnny was yelling, "Jesus Christ, it was ninety." I let the speed drop off, and he passed me the quart of beer.

I'm feeling all the feelings that would be exactly right if I'd just done what I remembered. I'm sweating, and my legs are shaking, and the fear's so strong it's like a coppery taste in my mouth.

"Larry," Cynthia says, and I feel her hand on my arm. I sit up. "What's the matter?" she says. "Are you all right?"

The steering wheel's so slippery it feels like somebody's greased it, and then I realize it's my own sweat. "Larry. Please say something. You're scaring me."

I look over at her, and I don't want to scare her. "I'm all right. Everything's all right." I put the car in gear and ease out onto Front Street.

We walk into my mother's apartment, and I start to cry. I didn't even feel it coming. One moment I'm walking into the clean, stripped living room and it hits me that this really isn't my mother's apartment any more, and the next moment I'm bent over, hugging myself, crying. I hear myself making a sound like "Oh, oh, oh," and I walk from room to room. I don't know what I'm looking for, and then I understand that I'm looking for my mother. There's absolutely nothing left of her. I'm not aware of Cynthia untll I feel her put her arms around me. We're out on the sun porch. She's crying too. We hang on to each other and cry.

It's comforting to cry with her. Because she's crying too, I don't have to feel embarrassed or creepy about it; neither of us tries to stop, so we just stand there and cry till we run down. Through the windows I can see the river and the twinkling yellow lights of downtown Raysburg and the twilight sky above.

"Oh, God," Cynthia says, fishes a little package of tissues of out her purse, blows her nose, throws me the package. We sink down into chairs we're leaving for Mrs. Campbell. It's as though there was a big, huge pile of sludge sitting on us, and now it's dissolved. We can both feel that it's dissolved. "Oh, God, Larry," she says.

"One more night," I say. If I still smoked, this would be an absolutely dandy time to have a cigarette.

"Oh, Larry, I'm sorry. I drank too much. I'm about half pissed."

"So what? We'll go to Jeff and Linda's and get really pissed. How's that?"

"Great." But neither of us make a move.

I look at her, and for the first time today, I see her as beautiful. "You want to call the kids?" I say.

"Oh, sure." But then she looks at her watch. "Allie will be in bed—at least she damn well better be."

"We could talk to Patrick."

"We'll be home tomorrow, hon."

"Yeah, okay."

She's looking at me as though I'm a map she's reading. I wonder what she's seeing. "It's bringing it all back for you, isn't it?" she says. "You know, like your mother dying is bringing back Johnny dying."

Is that what's happening? Of course that's what's happening. Why haven't I thought of it that way? "I guess that's right."

"He was really a big person in your life, wasn't he? You've never talked about him all that much, and I hadn't realized it."

"I suppose he must have been. He was, I don't know. Of course he was a big person in my life." Why do I find it so hard to admit that?

"God, the thought of you guys up there on that bridge. It's amazing that both of you aren't dead. What on earth were you thinking about?"

"Cynthia, I honest to God don't know what we were thinking about." But one thing I do know is that I don't want to talk about Johnny. Yes, it is amazing that both of us aren't dead.

I want to get her focused somewhere else, so I say, "What were *you* crying about? I mean other than out of deep, natural wifely sympathy?"

She laughs. "Oh, it's just silly. God, was I mad at you."

"I know. I'm sorry."

"I wouldn't have got so mad if you hadn't really hit a sore point. I've said to myself a million times, Cynthia, it would have been so *easy*—you asshole."

"And you still get so excited by all that stuff."

"Yeah, I know. And I was—" Her eyes spring full of tears again. "Oh, fuck, this is ridiculous."

"What?"

"The last time I saw Ruth Collins—that's Mrs. Epping's daughter, and she was ninety-two—she said, 'Oh, I do hope I get to see your book about Mother—' Oh, shit, I thought I was finished with this."

I take her hand. Alison sometimes cries so hard you can't understand a word she's trying to say, and now that's what's happening to Cynthia. She takes a few deep breaths; then she can manage to get the words to come out in little gasps. "Nobody understood that—a Ph.D. thesis—isn't a book. They thought—I was writing—a book. The Thompsons said to me, 'Please let us know—when the book comes out.' And there's no book. There's never going to be any book."

She takes a few more breaths. "God, what a ridiculous thing to be crying about. It was so many years ago."

"It's not ridiculous."

"Well, it isn't like somebody died, is it? But it just feels so sad when I think about it. It feels like... a little stillborn baby. Oh, God, Larry," she says, sobbing, "I'm so sorry."

"Don't be sorry. You're allowed to feel bad."

"Fuck off with the therapy shit."

"Okay, sure. But you *are* allowed to feel bad."

She stands up, pushes her hair back with both hands. She walks to one side of the sun porch and then back to the other side. "Oh, fuck," she says. "You know Milicent Kaufmann?"

That stops me. She might as well have picked a name at random out of the phone book for all I know about any Milicent Kaufmann. "Who the hell is Milicent Kaufmann?"

"Oh, for Christ's sake, you know. The big survey. She ferreted out every obscure woman writer in the history of American letters—"

Then I get it. "Oh. Right. *The* Kaufmann. That big, thick maroon thing that weighs about twenty-five pounds." The Kaufmann is a publisher's dream—a book that comes out and immediately establishes itself as the *one* authoritative text, goes through edition after edition, and keeps on selling year after year because it's required reading in colleges and universities from the Mexican border to Tuktoyaktuk. We, unfortunately, didn't publish it. "Sure, I know it. Phyllis was always quoting from it. What about it?"

"Have you read it?" Cynthia says.

"Of course I haven't read it. It's not a geography text."

"Well, she's got a chapter on Mrs. Epping."

"I thought you said nobody had written about Mrs. Epping."

"Nobody had until Kaufmann did."

"You haven't told me this."

"I know I haven't told you this. I haven't told anybody. I bought the goddamned book, and I waited till Patrick was asleep and Danny was out of the apartment, and I shut myself in my room and read the chapter in one big gulp. I felt like somebody had kicked me in the stomach, and that was the end of my thesis."

"So she scooped you, huh?"

"Oh, no. By then I was"—and she tries to laugh when she says this—"the world's leading authority on Mrs. Epping. It was that I thought I was wrong. I actually thought, oh, thank God this came out before I did my thesis so I didn't get caught in public saying all those wrong things. That's how hyped I was on authority. It actually took me a couple months before I could go back and read it again and admit that, well, it wasn't *me* who was wrong."

I haven't got it yet, but I can feel it's important. I look at her and wait.

"You know what would have happened to me if I'd come out in public and disagreed with Milicent Kaufmann? The girls would have torn me to shreds."

Now that Cynthia's decided to tell me this story she hasn't told anybody, she can't get the words out fast enough. When Cynthia's mad—I mean burning hot, furiously angry—she always cries. She's pacing up and down the sun porch, and tears keep running down her cheeks. "The most horrible, ironic thing," she says, "is that I adored Milicent Kaufmann. Everybody did. And I still adore her." She pokes at her face with a tissue, and the tears keep coming.

When Cynthia met her at a conference, Dr. Kaufmann was just a few years away from retirement. "There were damn few role models for women academics in those days, and she was one of the big ones. She was one of the first feminist critics, and she'd had to fight her way for everything she'd got, and put up with all the shit the boys dumped on her. They'd actually let her go at... I forget where she was. You know, they never fire you at a university, they just don't renew your contract—and she went someplace else, and then it took her years and years to get tenure. She founded one of the first women's studies departments in the country.

"She was just wonderful. A big, solid woman—she looked kind of like the Red Queen in *Alice*—and she was really kind and helpful to all of us coming up. There must be hundreds of women in universities she's helped out. When I applied for my grant, she wrote me a letter, and she hardly even knew me."

So of course Cynthia thought that Milicent Kaufmann had to be right. The chapter on Mrs. Epping started out saying all the right things, "exactly what I would have said—that Mrs. Epping should be considered an important writer, she should have a small but secure place in the canon—but the boys ignored her because she wrote about women, and for women. And her books are filled with all these details of women's lives—clothes and manners and cooking and courting and families—and the boys thought it was trivial because they thought women were trivial. And that's all true, damn it. It really is."

Then, after the introduction, the chapter started to go off the rails. "She says it was really a shame that Mrs. Epping married because marriage destroyed her work. Well, eleven more novels, and a book of memoirs, and a weekly newspaper column doesn't exactly look like destroyed work to me. She goes on and on about how hard it must have been for Mrs. Epping to fit in her writing around the demands of a husband and children. Well, it *was* demanding to run a household in those days, but Mrs. Epping— like all women of her class—had servants, and she got up every morning at six and wrote till noon every damn day but Sunday, and that's a goddamn thirty-six-hour week, but I guess Dr. Kaufmann didn't know about that.

"She has this pathetic passage about how disappointed Mrs. Epping must have been when the charm of her 'literary courtship' wore off to find herself living with a dull merchant in a little back-water town—and Kaufmann must have invented that, because it's based on no evidence whatsoever. It was hard to live up to, but the Eppings actually did achieve something like the ideal nineteenth-century marriage—and Mrs. Epping loved Massillon. And I thought, how on earth could Kaufmann be coming up with this stuff? And then it finally dawned on me that she hadn't done her homework. She'd read *Redemption* very carefully, but she'd skimmed the other novels, and she'd obviously never read Mrs. Epping's letters or her newspaper columns—and I had all that stuff to go on, and she didn't.

"The main thrust of her criticism is that Mrs. Epping was a great storyteller but not much of a feminist, that marriage had obviously blunted her critical faculties, that she never wrote another book that came up to *Redemption*. Well, she never wrote a book as *angry* as *Redemption*, but the books out of her late middle period are a hell of a lot better than *Redemption*—more complex, better written.

"And Kaufmann implies that Mrs. Epping would have been a hell of a lot better feminist *if she'd only known better*. She quotes a lot of feminist writers, and says things like 'at the time Clarissa was writing her highly sentimentalized portraits of domestic life with their obligatory happy endings, so-and-so was writing...,' and Kaufmann obviously doesn't know that Mrs. Epping had met these people socially, and had certainly read them, and had commented on their ideas in her newspaper columns. She doesn't even allow Mrs. Epping the dignity of holding her own goddamn opinions.

"I just couldn't do it, Larry. I'm not a combative person. I've got a big mouth, but I don't intentionally go out looking to get in a fight, and, well, not only was I going to have to try to write old-fashioned literary biography at a time when everybody was into deconstruction and talking about the death of the author, but if I'd said what I really thought—God, it would have been just terrible. The funny thing is that I didn't think Milicent Kaufmann would hold it against me that I disagreed with her. She's a genuine scholar, and given the scope of her book, she couldn't have been expected to get everything right. But, God, all the young feminist critics would have gone after me like wolves. They don't leave you any middle ground. You're either for them or against them, and if you disagree with them, you're against them, and then you get lumped with the boys—and a lot of the boys really are wretched, patriarchal pigs, and there's no way in hell I wanted to get lumped with *the boys*."

As weird as it is, I'm glad that Cynthia's so upset because it's taken me totally out of myself, and the inside of myself was getting to be a fairly grim and tedious place. We've left a table lamp for Mrs. Campbell; it's dark by now, but neither of us bothers to light it.

"Things aren't as doctrinaire now as they used to be," I say.

"How the hell would *you* know?"

I've got to laugh at that. "I don't. I'm just repeating what I heard from Phyllis."

"Oh, *Phyllis*. Fuck Phyllis."

"Look, hon, maybe you're right to forget the Ph.D. But why don't you write the book anyway? If it's not a Ph.D. thesis, you wouldn't have to take on Milicent Kaufmann. You wouldn't even have to refer to her."

"For Christ's sake, Larry. I barely have time to brush my teeth."

"Quit your job."

She looks at me a moment, and then she tries to laugh. "That's ridiculous."

"No, it's not. We're really close to being able to live on my salary. The mortgage payments are going to stay constant, but my salary's going to go up. Eventually you're going to inherit money from your parents. We could go into debt for a couple years, and as long as we were careful, we'd get back out."

"Shit, I wouldn't be able to— I'd have Alison—"

"Leave her in daycare. She loves her daycare."

"Oh, no, Larry. Come on. I couldn't do that. Just for a book?"

"Why not?"

"I worked really hard to get that job, and it's easy money—"

"What? You like crunching numbers in a computer eight hours a day?"

"Nobody bothers me. It's actually kind of relaxing. I'd never get another job, not with the recession—"

"So it's not a bad job. So what? My job's secure, and you're wasting your goddamned time. And your time is the only thing you've got."

I can see that she's thinking about it. She looks out the window at the river. "Shit," she says. I wait.

"No fucking way," she says, but I don't believe her.

7

FOR THE FIRST TIME TODAY, I feel all right—not brimming over with joy, you understand, but like a reasonable facsimile of my usual adult self, and for the moment a reasonable facsimile is plenty good enough. Most of the lamps are gone, so all we've got left are the nasty, glaring overhead lights. The rugs are gone too, and when we walk, our footsteps echo. Despite the fact that the apartment's lost all its personality—all the years of accumulated stuff that made it an extension of my mother—I can't seem to get myself ready to leave it. I keep wandering around looking at the bare walls, the bare floors. I keep looking out the windows.

"You know," Cynthia says, "this might have been the worst day we've had since we got married."

"You know," I say, "it just might." Being able to say it means it's over. "God, I'm glad you came down here with me. I don't know what I would have done if you hadn't."

"Oh, you would have coped."

"Sure I would have *coped*. But it would have been a fairly terrible way to have to cope. You've been just terrific."

"Oh, right. I sure was a big help today, wasn't I?" It's not a particularly funny line, but it's got us laughing like a couple loons, and then my wife, the eternal optimist, says, "Human beings aren't designed to stay depressed longer than a few hours."

That sets me off again. I'm laughing so hard I'm doubled over. "Oh, is that right?" I say. "Maybe you ought to explain that one to me some time."

I wander around some more—out to the sun porch, out to the back porch. I don't know what I expect to find; anything of my mother's that would mean anything to me is on its way to Sharon. I walk back into the bedroom. The last time I'd been in there, Cynthia had almost finished packing her suitcase, but now it looks like she's *un*packing it. Her clothes are spread out on the bare mattress. "Just looking for an alternative," she says, "and there isn't one. It's too late to buy anything, and the problem with Linda is, well, her taste isn't exactly what you'd call muted. What do you think the chances are of her having even one black dress with a high neckline and a long skirt, let alone two?"

"Do you have to wear black?"

"Of course you have to wear black," she says in the voice of a mom speaking the eternal truth. "It's a shame I didn't bring it, but why the hell would I? The perfect thing would have been, you know, that long black skirt with the pleats and that little black jacket that has kind of a period look."

"Everything you own has kind of a period look."

"Oh, come on, that's not true," she says automatically, her mind somewhere else. Then she turns and grins at me. "God, how ridiculous. I'm worrying about how I'm going to look at the funeral."

"Wear your business suit. You know, the one you wore on the plane."

"It's gray."

"Big deal."

"Oh, well, maybe Linda will have something. Are you ready to go?"

"I don't think so." I don't know why I'm not ready to go, but I'm not.

"It's all right. Take your time. I feel all right."

I do the circuit of the apartment again, and then I go out onto the back porch and sit down on one of the pieces of lawn furniture we're leaving behind. It's nowhere near high summer yet so the night has brought the temperature down. There's a good breeze. Cynthia comes out and sits down with me.

"Larry? What kind of arrangements do you want me to make if... when you're gone."

The question has never arisen before. I have to think before I answer it. "Whatever will make you and the kids feel better. I won't care. And seeing as we're considering this— It's probably not something I'll have to worry about, but how about you?"

She answers so quickly she must have decided a long time ago. "I'd want to be buried with you. I hope you want to be buried in Massachusetts, because I do. I'd want you to see me, but after that, I'd want the casket closed—I don't think the kids would need to see me, but maybe they'd want to. You decide. I'd want an old-fashioned service, with, you know, 'ashes to ashes.'"

I'm so touched I can't say anything. I reach out and take her hand. "Do you think there's anything left afterward?" she says.

"No."

She sighs. "I don't know whether I do or not. I guess I do, although it doesn't make any sense, does it? It must be kind of bleak to think there's nothing left."

"Yeah. I guess it is."

"I'd like to think we'll be together forever."

"Just the way Mrs. Epping thought?"

"Oh, yeah. Just exactly the way Mrs. Epping thought."

We sit holding hands in the dark. "Are you trying to say goodbye?" she says.

"Yeah, I suppose that's what I'm doing."

"Well, talk about her then."

That makes perfect sense to me. That's exactly what you're supposed to do, isn't it? But I can't think of much to say. I lean back and close my eyes.

"The earliest memories I've got of her," I say, "are working in the garden down on the river bank in the evening. The war was still on. She loved gardening."

Then there's another memory—something I hadn't been looking for, something I'd forgotten. My mother and I were alone in her car, the brown Dodge. It was night, and we were coming in from out the pike. I was twelve or thirteen. "I can't remember where we'd been," I say to Cynthia, "and I don't know why Johnny wasn't with us."

My mother hadn't spoken for a long time. When she did, what she said was related to absolutely nothing we'd been talking about. "Larry, there are times when I'd like to get in the car and drive away and never come back. I'd like to drive and drive and drive until I was a thousand miles away and never come back."

What she'd said was so unlike my mother that I didn't know what to do with her statement. If somebody had told me she could say something like that—and in such a hard, angry voice that it'd be impossible not to believe her—I would have laughed. Even though she'd called me by my name, I wasn't sure she'd really been talking to me, and there was nothing in what she'd said that seemed to require a response. I'd always thought of her as a timid person, but all of a sudden I was trying to imagine her as someone who could get in her car one day and decide to drive a thousand miles away and never come back. She hadn't said so, but I had the feeling that she wasn't including me in the trip. So what would happen to me and Johnny and Bud and my grandmother?

We'd just come over the top of Raysburg Hill, and we were winding our way down the other side toward the Suspension Bridge. "Do you think you'll ever do it?" I said.

"Do what?"

"Get in the car and drive away and never come back."

She laughed. "Don't be silly."

"Up until then," I say to Cynthia, "it had never occurred to me that she wasn't— I don't know how I would have put this, how I would have formulated it back then, but I remember the feeling. I was surprised, shocked. I'd always thought she was, well, I knew she wasn't perfectly happy, but always I'd thought she was content. It'd never occurred to me that she'd want to do anything other than, you know, go to work every day and pay the bills. And that's what she did, year after year. There was a kind of fatalism about her—"

"A Depression kid," Cynthia says, "a whole generation like that. Any job is better than no job, and you keep the job you've got. It's sad when you think about it. She must have gradually felt all her hopes and dreams slipping away from her—first the Depression, and then she must have invested a lot in the relationship with your father, and that didn't work, and then along comes good old Bud."

"Yep, good old Bud."

The day that's ending has begun to feel to me like a big, splashy soap opera jammed end to end with conflict and tears, and passionately felt speeches, and lots of intense, heavy emotions. Not that any of it was false, or even overblown—not that there was anything *wrong* with any of it, you understand—but where we've arrived feels so peaceful, just so damned *ordinary*, that it's an enormous relief. It's great just to sit and chat and feel some detachment again.

"When I first met Patrick," I say, "he was so much like me— like the way I was as a kid—it used to give me an odd feeling of things repeating. Gee, haven't I seen this movie before?"

Patrick's favorite character was She-Ra. Mine was a young female Tarzan in a comic book ("and I'm really digging for this," I tell Cynthia) named, the best I can remember, Sheena the Jungle Girl. Watching She-Ra was one of the first things Patrick and I did together. We watched her with religious regularity. She-Ra, like a lot of kids' cartoons, appears to have been drawn by a bunch of whack-off artists, and she's a pretty weird role model for little girls (hey, you too can look like a Barbie doll and also be strong enough to lift entire mountains), but for little boys, she's *really* weird. I'd pin a towel around Patrick's neck to make a cape, and he'd hold aloft his toy sword and yell his version of She-Ra's magical incantation—"For the honor of gray smoke!"

"God, was I glad when that phase ended," Cynthia says. "Remember, he kept asking me to get him a She-Ra suit."

"Yeah, and you'd always say the same thing: 'No way, you're a boy.' It used to amaze me you could be so clear."

"Well, Jesus, some things have *got* to be clear."

She's right, of course, and because of her, Patrick was never in the muddle I was in as a kid. Unlike me, he was used to seeing people naked, and the second or third time I stayed over at Cynthia's, I wandered into the bathroom in the morning, didn't bother to close the door, was standing there half asleep, peeing, and I looked over and saw Patrick staring at me. A huge, sunny smile spread across his face, and he said, "Hey, you've got a peenist *just like me!*"

I was in grade school before I'd figured out what Patrick already knew by four—that what distinguishes boys from girls isn't the length of their hair but what's in their pants. Nobody ever said to me, 'No way. You're a boy.' Nobody, when I was a kid, would ever have used language that simple and direct.

"I was a bit of a sissy, and so was Patrick"—I'm finding this surprisingly hard to say—"but I don't think it hurts a boy to dress up like She-Ra, or... I used to smear lipstick all over my mouth and walk around in one of my mother's slips— What I think does hurt a boy is if he can't find any way to fit into boy culture. It makes him feel creepy and bad—a total outsider—and I know, because I felt that way. Patrick's not much of a jock, but he does fit into boy culture, and if I've helped him to do that, I'm glad."

"You've been a wonderful father, Larry," Cynthia says.

"Wonderful? Who knows about wonderful, but I guess I'm not doing too badly, and, well, Johnny and Bud gave me a way into boy culture, and whatever else I might think, I've got to be grateful to them for that."

I get up and stretch. I'd thought I was just at the point of leaving, but it still doesn't feel quite right yet so I sit down again. "When's the first time you ever had an idea?" Cynthia asks me, taking me by surprise. "I mean a real one—something that wasn't just a rationalization for something else?"

It's an interesting question. "I don't know. Graduate school I guess. When I began to get a handle on human geography."

"Yeah," she says, "I was in my last year at the Cliff. We took classes at Harvard, and I had a prof—he was the one who liked my Kate Chopin paper, and I used to write these automatic things I thought I believed, received opinions, and he'd write me little notes in the margin, just asking me questions, and I used to get mad enough to kill him, but I guess some time in that year, he actually forced me into having an idea. It's funny isn't it? Because we certainly *thought* we had ideas."

I look at my watch and it's after ten. "We better get going. Jeff strikes me as a man who likes his sack time."

"Yeah," Cynthia says, but she doesn't move. "This is nice, Larry. Let's just sit here a few minutes more."

I can see a little slice of the river from where I'm sitting, and there's a good, steady, cool breeze blowing, and I'm perfectly content to sit here a few minutes more. My mind feels scattered in a million directions. I'm not thinking about anything in particular, and it's a good feeling. Then I remember how reluctant I was to talk about Johnny just a little while ago, and I'm surprised that I should have been so reluctant. As much as I've been thinking about him in the last few days—remembering things I'd thought I'd forgotten—why shouldn't I talk about him?

"I can still see Johnny's crazy apartment," I say to Cynthia. "Bud was never there, so Johnny could do exactly what he damned well pleased with it."

It was on the second floor of an old house down on the south end of the Island not far from Raysburg Downs. You could go in the front way, up the inside stairs, but neither Johnny nor I ever went in that way; we walked up the rickety wooden back steps to the door that led into Johnny's kitchen. Those back steps just hung there, sagging, tacked onto the back of the house, and they should have been condemned. Some hard-drinking types from the track rented the first-floor apartment, and whenever they had a wild party and started chucking bottles out the window, Johnny would say, "Hear that? Makes me feel right at home."

In the summer, the door to Johnny's kitchen was always open; there was a screen door on a spring in front of it, the kind that slams with a crack when you let go. Johnny wasn't big on washing dishes, so most of the time there'd be a week's accumulation of them. When all the dishes were dirty, he'd load them into a shopping cart he'd stolen from a supermarket, wheel them into the bathroom, and wash them in the bathtub.

That summer—the summer he died—was the first time he'd ever demonstrated much of an interest in the opposite sex. Bud's men's magazines—he bought both *Playboy* and the tackiest of low-rent pulps, the kind with drawings of half-naked girls being tortured by Nazis—were scattered all over the place, and Johnny and I thumbed through them because we thought we should, but they didn't interest us much, and when Johnny fell for an image, it wasn't any of the busty centerfolds or tied up victims, but a pretty little girl on the cover of an Acme Discount catalogue.

I spent a lot of time looking at Miss Acme Discount, as we called her (there was at least one catalogue cover taped to every wall in the place, so it would have been hard not to spend a lot of time looking at her), and I thought that if she'd miraculously appeared in the flesh, it would've been doubtful she'd have been old enough to go out with Johnny. She was a genuine carrot-top redhead with a spray of freckles and an enormous white bow in her hair; she might have been as old as fourteen but was probably closer to twelve. She was cute in a Norman Rockwell, kid-next-door way, but I had trouble imagining her as the object of a grand passion, and what Johnny thought about her I never knew, because it was a subject he didn't care to discuss.

Johnny used the living room as a workshop, so it was always full of gadgets under construction. He didn't try to put a pretty finish on anything, but whatever he made was always neatly and solidly constructed. One I remember very clearly. A clock and a rat trap were screwed down to a piece of wood. Johnny had removed the second hand from the clock; the minute hand was soldered with fine wire to the part of the trap where the bait goes. The part of the trap that's designed to squash the rat held a tight double row of kitchen matches; a wood block with coarse sandpaper glued to it was mounted where the matches would fall. You could have got the whole thing into a bread box. We watched, and eventually the minute hand sprang the trap. The matches went off with a gratifying whoosh and a big flash of flame.

I was impressed, but I said in my most off-hand voice, "Great. So where the hell are you going to set it off?"

Johnny always struck people as shy; I knew him better than anybody did, and shy wasn't what he was, but I could see how people thought that. He spoke in a very soft voice, and he'd look at you quickly and then look away. "Nowhere," he said. "I just wanted to see if it'd work."

When Bud went bankrupt, there hadn't been enough money for us to continue at the Academy, but I'd been an honors student and Johnny hadn't. It'd always been easy for me to learn what teachers wanted me to learn and then spit it back on tests just the way they wanted it spit. (That's how I got to W.V.U., and how I got to Harvard, and how I got out of the Valley.) So my mother went out to see Old Liniment and told him that unless they gave me some kind of scholarship, I couldn't stay at the Academy. I was the number three man in my class, so he waived the tuition.

Johnny went down to Raysburg High, and they tracked him into industrial arts. "That makes sense," my mother said. "He's always been good with his hands. Maybe he can learn some kind of trade." I thought it wasn't fair—although I didn't know why it shouldn't be—and I still felt guilty about it, but I never knew what Johnny thought because he never told me. I do know that he liked having all the facilities of Raysburg High available to him and took advantage of them. He was always "borrowing" things from the school. I walked into his place once and found him sitting on the living-room couch with an arc welder going. Sparks were flying everywhere. "You goddamn idiot," I yelled at him, "you're going to burn the place down."

He had a welder's mask on. He pushed it back and grinned at me. "I hadn't thought of that," he said.

One of the things Johnny had learned from Bud was that "clothes make the man," and he was always a snappy dresser. He wore those gawky black-framed glasses we had in the fifties—exactly like Buddy Holly's—and they looked good on him. He brought his shirts and pants back to my grandmother to be ironed, and the maddest I ever saw him was once when he wanted to go out and didn't have a clean, freshly ironed, white dress shirt with

French cuffs. At the Academy we had to keep our hair cut short, so as soon as Johnny was free, he grew himself an Elvis Presley DA complete with sideburns. I was jealous of that.

At Raysburg High he was "running with a rough crowd" as my mother put it, and I never met any of them until the funeral. One of the guys from that "rough crowd" bawled like a baby when he saw Johnny in his coffin, and I was touched that somebody who wasn't family had liked Johnny enough to cry for him.

"But why the hell shouldn't he have had his own friends?" I say to Cynthia. "I must have thought he didn't have any real life separate from me or something. I don't know what I thought. I haven't thought about this in years."

Johnny was good at acquiring things at a "five finger discount." He carried a pair of shears around with him and snipped speakers from the poles at drive-in theaters. He had his apartment wired end to end—he must have had twenty speakers in there, the whole works controlled from a panel screwed onto the wall above the hi-fi (this was pre-stereo). He could flip a switch, and a speaker would go on in the bathroom, or the bedroom, or halfway down the front steps. When he had them all on at once, the whole building turned into one big speaker, and you could hear it from blocks away. When he wanted to bug the neighbors, he put on bagpipe music.

Johnny was fascinated by a woman he could see though a window while he was riding the bus from the Island down to Raysburg High. She was in a second-floor apartment in an old building, and she was always sitting in the window when the bus went by. "Is she pretty?" I said.

"No— Well, sort of— It doesn't really matter if she's pretty or not."

"Is she young, old, what?"

"I don't know. Middle-aged I guess. Or maybe a little younger than that. She looks tired. She looks like she doesn't want to be up that early. She's got something on that looks like a nightgown, but maybe it isn't."

She seemed—the best he could tell—to be sitting at a desk in the window, and there was a strange object on the desk. "It looks like a Coke bottle covered with rubber bands—or something like that, I don't know what, or maybe with glue, with glue and rubber bands. I can't imagine what it's for, what she's doing with it. I never see her do anything with it."

"Can you see what she's doing at the desk?"

"No. She's always looking down at the desk—I think it's a desk—but I don't know what's she's doing. No, she isn't always looking down. Once she was looking out the window. She looks so *tired*. I keep thinking, what is she doing there? Why is she there every morning? What is that thing next to her on the desk? Why does she look so tired? I mean, what is she *doing* there?"

He looked directly at me and then away. He really cared about this strange woman he saw for a few seconds every weekday morning. Maybe, I thought, it was the most he'd ever cared about anything—but, for the life of me, I couldn't figure out why. "Was the window woman there this morning?" I'd ask him sometimes when I hadn't heard about her for a while.

"Yeah, sure. She was rubbing her forehead."

"Why don't you get off the bus and go knock on the door?"

"I've thought of that, but what the hell would I say?"

"That's really strange," Cynthia says. "What was it about the woman? What did he want? Did he know what he wanted?"

"He tried to tell me, but I could never understand it."

I can remember him sitting in his living room with all his junk around him—screws, nuts, bolts, wires, pieces of wood, pieces of scrap metal, clamps, glue, a soldering iron—and he's saying, "It was raining, really cold and raining. It was still dark. Her light was the only light in the house, and she was sitting at the desk. I just can't figure out what she's doing. *Why is she there?*"

The summer he died, I'd just graduated from high school, and Johnny had a year to go. We surely must have talked about the future—what we planned to do with our lives—or maybe we didn't, because I can't remember anything serious we said. That spring we stole a couple beer kegs from behind a bar; Johnny washed them out and fitted them with air locks. He had read that potatoes fermented quickly—and they did—and produced a foul, whitish fluid thick with sediment. The only way we could drink it was mixed with 7-Up, and it did get us drunk, but it also made us throw up and left us with sick, throbbing headaches. So, using glassware from the Raysburg High chemistry lab, he built a small distillation apparatus, and by summer it was producing— painfully slowly, a drop at a time—a fiery liquid, clear as water. It must have been close to pure alcohol, and two or three shot glasses of the stuff would practically lay us out on the floor. I'd turned eighteen and could buy beer, so we'd take a few quarts of beer and a pint of homemade vodka and get in Bud's old Chevy and go for a drive. We took turns seeing how fast we could power-slide the old s-bridge out the pike—

As I'm telling Cynthia this, I'm beginning to feel something almost like an electrical charge passing through my body. My skin's prickling all over. It's not a good feeling. "Are you all right?" she says.

I can't figure out how she knew there was something wrong with me. "Yeah, I'm okay. I just remembered something. That spring we climbed a water tower. I can remember standing at the bottom looking up, and it was, God, just enormously high, and I thought, I don't want to do this. And I looked over at Johnny, and he looked at me, and he said, 'I bet there'd be a hell of a view from up there.'

"I just had to keep breathing deeply and go up one rung at a time. I knew if I looked down, it'd be game over. We got up on the top, and I'd never been so high up on anything in my life. I'd never been so scared of anything in my life. But we sat up there and pretended everything was perfectly normal. And then, of course, we had to come down again—"

"Oh, God," Cynthia says, "*boys*. I'll never understand boys."

"He went down a mine shaft over in Ohio with some guys from Raysburg High," I say. "There was supposed to be an old body in there, but they didn't find it. When I heard about it, I thought, Jesus, what are you trying to do, one-up me, you little shit?"

My mouth feels as though it's suddenly been filled up with tiny cotton balls. When I talk, I'm making a nasty clicking sound. I keep sucking on the inside of my mouth, but I can't seem to get rid of it.

"Larry, are you all right?" Cynthia says.

"Yeah, I'm all right. We never found any old body. Down at the bottom it opened into a system of caves. There were... I swear to God, they came in levels, like floors. We found three levels. At the very bottom there was water in one of them, like a little underground lake."

I can't sit still any longer. I get up and walk to the side of the porch that looks out over Front Street. I can feel my knees shaking. "We kept going back to that mine shaft," I say. "We kept trying to see how far down we could get. I used to have nightmares that I was still down in there somewhere, that I'd forgotten to come back up again, that I'd fallen asleep and my light had gone out."

I walk back across the porch and sit down. Now it isn't just my knees; I'm shaking all over. "I didn't want to go into those goddamned caves, but—shit. That little prick wasn't going to do anything I wasn't doing, by God. He wasn't going to one-up *me*, by God."

"Jesus, Larry," Cynthia says, "you're so angry. I can feel it just crackling off you."

Anger? Is that what it is? I can feel it burning all the way through me. No, I can't possibly sit still. I jump up and start pacing. "The little prick. Jesus."

I see Cynthia looking at me with a quiet, expectant face—some detached part of me thinks that she's probably exhausted by all we've gone through today, poor kid—but I see that she's waiting for whatever's coming, and I don't know what's coming.

"Why the fuck would he go in the water if he couldn't swim?" I ask her just as though she might know the answer. The moment it's out of my mouth, I know what a dumb question it is.

I just heard myself cry out, and I can't figure out how the hell I could have done that without deciding to do it first. I'm standing there frozen, scared, trying to figure it all out. Cynthia reaches out to me, and I take her hand.

"I was out with Bobby Cotter one night," I say, crying, "and he drove me back to the Island. 'You ever swim in the river?' I asked him, and he never had. So we went down to the bank and stripped our clothes off and went in the river. We didn't go out very far, and I'd learned how to tread water, so that was pretty much what I did, and he was the best fucking swimmer in the Ohio Valley, so I knew I was safe. It was, I don't know. It was kind of magical. And so I said to Johnny, 'A buddy of mine and I went for a swim in the river. It's really kind of nice, you know.' And he looked right at me, and he looked away, and he said, 'Yeah. Was it nice?'"

I boot Bud's old Chevy up the drive to Bobby Cotter's place, get it going fast enough so I can sail around the house with the clutch in and the engine off. I lean back in the seat as though I've fallen asleep, my left arm trailing out the window. "Hey, hey, hey," I hear the boys call at me as I go by. I jerk the emergency brake hard, and the old heap of tin practically stands on its nose. In my honor, the

boys are doing "the cafeteria mutter"; it's a good old Academy tra-
dition—you pitch your voice as low as you can, and you try not to
move your lips at all, and you fall into unison with everybody else,
and you chant "Hey, hey, hey, hey, hey, hey, hey," until an officer
gets so annoyed he calls the whole damn room to attention. I'm out
of the car; I kick the door shut with my heel. The sun's high and
hot, and the boys are lying around the pool—"Hey, hey, hey."

"Armbruster, you old load," somebody says.

"Gentlemen, gentlemen," I say and sink down onto a lawn chair.
"My God," I say, "if it ain't the Academy mermen in the flesh."

"Who's this guy?" Uncle Ken Higgs intones. He's called
"Uncle" because he's tall and gaunt and he looks like a vulture.

"Uno cargo grando," Tom McFee says.

"Hey, hey, hey, hey, hey—"

"At ease, gentlemen," Bobby Cotter says.

Most of us have graduated, but there are a few younger boys
with a year or two to go—Russel Anderson, Franky Gavin, Jeffy
Snyder. For those of us who are leaving, this summer is the last
time we'll all be together, and we're all thinking about that
although we don't talk about it much. The Polish lady who works
for Bobby's mom has set out some sandwiches, and I help myself
to one. I lie back in the sun, happy, and I think the same thing I've
been thinking for weeks now—where the hell did it go?

My senior year. Down the tube. Over and done with. I was the
captain of C company—the biggest bunch of loads in the
school—and I liked being the captain of C company. "The jerk-
off boys," we were called, and I'd march my company to the far
side of the field where the staff couldn't hear us, and then we'd
swing along singing, "I got a gal in Sistersville, she won't do it but
her sister will, honey, oh baby, mine."

I wonder if I'll ever be with a bunch of guys I feel as easy with
as this bunch of guys from the swimming team. In September

we're scattering in all directions. Uncle Ken and I are going down to Morgantown. Bobby Cotter's going to Princeton. There are guys going to W. & J., Raysburg College, Yale, Ohio State, Purdue... "Where you going to flunk out?" is what we ask each other. I don't think I'm going to flunk out, but I'm scared anyhow. I was at the Academy seven years, and I'm not ready to leave it. Maybe I'll be ready in September.

Now we can still tell each other how much we hate Old Liniment, and imitate Captain Penny's rants—"Gentlemen, you are the most miserable collection of worthless pieces of cow dung I've ever had the misfortune to encounter in all my years of teaching"—and tell stories about Pete, our fat coach—"God, did you see what he ordered? Two whole goddamned chicken dinners is what he ordered." I'm never going to forget this, I tell myself—never. Most of the boys are in the pool now; I'm lying back with the sun on my face, and I can hear the splash of the water. Everything smells like chlorine.

I used to wake up in the winter and think that nothing—absolutely nothing—was worth the effort. All I wanted to do was go back to sleep, and I couldn't go back to sleep, and my senior year would last forever. There'd be essays to write, and tests to take, and College Boards, and it was all just an endless, impossible pile of shit. Now it's over, and I can sleep as much as I want, and I can't believe it. Swimming season is over, and we were undefeated. Exams are over, and final drills is over, and the big round of parties is over—Jesus, the Cotters sure threw one hell of a party for Bobby, a four-course dinner served by maids—and the Military Ball is over.

I took Dougy Moore's little sister to the ball because I didn't know anybody else and I thought she was cute enough and I thought she'd like to go. The best I could tell she did like it; she never said much of anything to me beyond "Hi," but she got a new dress for it, and when we parked out at Rock Point, she grabbed me hard and shoved her tongue in my mouth. We made out for an hour, and she still didn't say anything. I thought she was sweet, and I'd like to see her again, but she's only a sophomore at Canden High, and I'm going down to the university, so forget that.

I graduated number three in my class, and maybe I could have been number one if I'd tried, but number three without doing dick shit is pretty damned good. No matter how you slice it, *life* is pretty damned good. Bobby Cotter is sitting next to me looking out over the pool, and I wonder why he's not in the water, and I wonder if he's worried about going to Princeton. "I'm happy," I say to him. He's one of the few guys I could say something like that to.

"Is that right?" he says as though he's astonished. "Happy? Seems to me I've heard that word somewhere or other. Well, I'm glad to hear that, Lawrence."

"You know," I say—and I'm surprised I'm saying it—"most of the time when you're happy, you remember it. You look back and say, oh, I was really happy. It's good to know you're happy when you *are* happy."

"Yeah," he says without smiling, "that's right. That's absolutely right."

When I leave that afternoon, the boys chant "Hey, hey, hey" for me as I coast the car down the driveway. I kick in the ignition, and it coughs and bangs—and starts. I hear them give me a cheer. I beep the horn and roll on down the hill. I don't know what I want from life, but however it turns out, it's got to be something like the boys hacking around Bobby Cotter's swimming pool on a sunny day in July.

I park in my usual spot by our apartment, and I'm in plenty of time for dinner. I walk in, and I know something's wrong; I can feel it in the air before I see anybody. Maybe it's because my mother and grandmother are talking in such weird, quiet voices. I walk into the kitchen and they both look straight at me. They've been crying.

"Sit down, Larry," my mother says.

I don't want to sit down, so I don't. "What's the matter?" I say. "Come on, tell me."

"Johnny's been drowned in the river."

I look at them, and I think how silly it is that they could believe something like that. I've never heard anything more ridiculous in my life. "Oh, come on," I say.

"It's true, honey. The police were here. Some people saw him go down. They haven't found him yet."

I look at both of their faces, and I see how much they've been crying, and I imagine how happy and relieved they'll be when they find out that's it's all been a mistake. "They haven't found him yet?" I say, and I feel infinitely superior to them—I know I have to be gentle with them—because they believe that something terrible's happened and I know it hasn't.

"Who saw him?" I say patiently. "What happened?" If we talk about it, I'm sure the truth will come out.

My mother's crying too hard to talk. My grandmother says, "He was with some boys—you know, that rough crowd from Raysburg High—and they went down to the river." She's talking very slowly.

"Somewhere up North Front," my grandmother says, "I guess that's where it was. They just went in the river. And they went out too far. I guess they must have got out in the channel. He got swept away from them. He started yelling for help—I guess none of them could swim very well. The other boys got back to the bank, and they saw him go on down the river. And then they saw him go under."

"Go under?" I say.

My grandmother takes my hand. "They saw him go under,

honey. They didn't see him come back up again. They went and got the police. They're out there searching for him now."

She makes it sound so goddamned real that if I didn't know better, I could almost believe it. "He's probably on the bank somewhere," I say, "on down the river on the bank somewhere. They just haven't found him yet."

"Honey," she says slowly, squeezing my hand for emphasis, "the boys saw him go under. Some people over in town saw him go under too. He got out there in the channel, honey, and he got swept on down the river. And he went under. And nobody saw him come up again."

I'm so mad at my grandmother I could kill her. I can't understand why she's working so hard to make me believe this. I pull away from her. "It's not true," I say. "It's a mistake. He's all right somewhere. He's on the bank somewhere, and he's all right."

I won't listen to any more of this crap. I turn and walk out. I walk down the hall. I'm breathing hard, panting. My knees are buckling under me. I reach out to steady myself on the wall. I can hear my mother crying back in the kitchen.

Oh shit, I think, he can't swim.

I take a deep breath, and I turn, and I walk carefully, just as though I'm in a parade, back into the kitchen. I sit down on a kitchen chair. "Maybe he got to the bank somewhere," I say.

"Honey," my grandmother says, "that channel out there in the front river moves along like a freight train."

I start to cry. It's like somebody else has started to cry. As soon as I know it's me crying, I stop. I've got to understand this. "When did it happen?" I say.

"A couple hours ago."

"Who saw him?"

"The boys he was with saw him. There were some people over on the wharf who saw him. There were some people on the bridge who saw him. It was all too quick, and nobody could do anything."

"What happened?"

Then, just as though she hasn't said it before, she says it again, and this time, as she says it, I can see it. "He got swept out into the channel. And he was going faster and faster. And he called out for help. And he went under. And nobody saw him come up again."

"Don't worry about me," I say. "I'm all right, and I'll be right back. I promise, I'll be right back."

"No, honey, wait a minute," my mother says, but I don't pay any attention to her.

I walk out of the apartment and down to the river bank. The sun is shining. Squinting against the sun, I look down the river. I can see boats, lots of boats, down the river. Is it because it's a week-end? They couldn't be looking for Johnny, could they?

Why now? I think. After everything we did, why is it now? Why is it him and not me?

God, he must have been so scared. What did he think? Did he think that he was going to get out of it just the way he'd got out of everything else? Was there a moment when he knew he wasn't going to get out of it? What did he feel when he went under? Did it hurt when the water went in his lungs? How could he have done something like that—gone through something like that—and how could it all be over by now?

There's something dizzying, sickening, about what I'm thinking. Maybe he doesn't know anything at all now, and I've still got to find out that you don't know anything at all—but if that's the truth, then how the hell will you ever know it? What do you think just before the end, and what do you know afterward, and does it matter? If you don't know anything afterward, then what does anything you do when you're alive matter? And why was it him and not me?

It can't be true. Not really. He's got to be on the bank somewhere on down the river.

I walk back to the apartment. "We should eat something," my grandmother says.

"I'm not hungry," my mother says.

"I'm not either," I say.

"Eat anyway," my grandmother says. "You've got to keep your strength up."

They've been trying to get Bud, but they can't find him. He's due to go on night shift at the hotel later tonight, but nobody's seen him yet. They've left a message for him to call. "He's probably sleeping it off somewhere," my grandmother says. "Do you know where he goes, Dorothy?"

"No," my mother says. "I don't know where he goes. I never did. He could be anywhere."

My grandmother made fried chicken and mashed potatoes, and I try, but I can't eat much of anything. I'm surprised. Before this, I couldn't have imagined feeling so bad I wouldn't want to eat. The phone rings, and we all jump like we've been shocked. My mother answers; we stare at her until she shakes her head. No, it's not Bud; no, they haven't found Johnny's body—I can't believe that, his *body*—it's a friend of my mother's calling up to say she heard about it, to say how bad she feels about it. When my mother gets off the phone, she says, "Oh, God, I hope we can get to Bud before somebody else tells him."

That doesn't make any sense to me. What difference could it possibly make? "I want to go down to the river," I say. "I want to look for him."

"Oh, please, honey, don't do that," my mother says.

"No, Larry," my grandmother says. "There's dozens of people looking for him. We need you here now."

Need me? What on earth for?

"Oh, God," my mother says. "Poor Bud. Oh, God."

My grandmother, just as she always does when she's cooking, is wearing an apron. She stands at the kitchen window looking out; she was drying her hands on her apron, and now she's stopped like she forgot what she was doing. She stands at the kitchen window, holding her apron in her hands, looking out at the river.

"Uncle Dave drowned in the river," she says, "and Grandpaw never got over it. Uncle Dave drowned in a boating accident—it was a terrible accident, one of the worst ones we ever had on the river. Lots of people drowned that time. Grandpaw told all the boys, 'I don't want you to go on the river,' but they all did, every one of them. They all went on the river. My dad worked his whole life on the river."

She turns back and looks at me and my mother. "We were big for each other," she says. "We always counted on each other in the old days."

My grandmother has never been one to say clearly what's on her mind, but I know that she's just said to me, "We need to count on you, Larry." I'm willing to be counted on, but I don't know what it is I'm supposed to do. I wish there was something to do—anything at all—except sit around and wait.

I'm an occasional, weekend smoker, but neither my mother nor grandmother has ever seen me smoke. I pick up my mother's pack of Chesterfields and say, "Do you mind?"

"What difference would it make if I did?" she says, and then in a moment, "Go ahead. Thanks for asking, anyway."

My mother and I sit and smoke. About an hour later, Bud shows up. He hasn't heard about it yet. He's only a little drunk; he's got a suit and tie on, his hair's slicked back, and he looks pretty damned good. He comes in grinning. "What's going on anyway? They said at the hotel I should come over here." Nobody says anything, and he says, "Hey, what the hell's going on?"

My mother takes Bud into the front bedroom and shuts the

door. After a moment he lets out a huge groan. Then he starts to cry; it's an awful hacking sound. The crying stops, and then, suddenly, he howls. It's just like an animal that's been hurt, and he does it just once. Then he yells, "No."

My mother comes running out of the bedroom. "Larry. Call Charlie Schwab. Tell him to get a bottle and get over here fast."

I feel so sick I'm afraid I'm going to throw up, but I'm glad to have something to do. Charlie's in the phone book, and he's already heard—it's on the news, he says—and he'll be right over. I stand out on the sun porch and wait for him. I believe it now, and I wonder why I'm not crying. When Charlie shows up, he's got a nearly full bottle of Four Roses. My mother takes him straight into the bedroom, and then she leaves him alone in there with Bud.

My mother and grandmother and I sit on the sun porch. The sun's gone down, and it's getting dark. "I'm going to call the police again," my mother says.

"No, Dorothy," my grandmother says. "Let them alone. Let them do their job. They'll call you when they find him."

After a couple hours, Bud and Charlie come out of the bedroom. Bud's so drunk Charlie's got to hold him up. "He's going to be okay," Charlie says to us. "Aren't you, old fellow?"

Bud rests his hand on my shoulder. I can feel the weight of him. "Oh, God," he says—his eyes look blind, and I don't know whether he's talking to me or not—"I can't stop thinking about Johnny rolling around out there in the river."

"Come on, old boy," Charlie says, "let's get you somewhere you can lie down," and he slips an arm around Bud's shoulders. From where we are on the sun porch, we can see Charlie help Bud into the car. He helps him into the back, and Bud falls right over on the seat. My mother starts to cry. My grandmother walks back into the kitchen, and I can hear her start to wash the dishes.

"Oh, this is going to kill him," my mother says, crying. "He's a weak man, and this will just kill him. Oh, God, why does anybody have to have so much misfortune? They operated on Agnes eight times, did you know that?" Agnes was Bud's first wife.

"Before they were through, they cut both her breasts off. Oh, God, he told me all about it, and he cried like a baby. The doctor told him, 'Bud, you just have normal relations with her. That'll make her feel a whole hell of a lot better.' But he couldn't do it. He told me, 'Dorothy, I tried, and I just couldn't do it.'"

I know my mother wouldn't have told me that if she hadn't been feeling so bad, and I wish the hell she hadn't told me. I leave her there crying in the dark, and I go into my room and lie down on the bed. I don't plan to fall asleep, but I do.

I wake up at dawn, and I haven't even taken my clothes off. I know I've got to go down to the river. I walk along the bank all the way from Belle Isle to the south end, and I keep imagining what it'd be like to find him. I imagine him alive, sitting under a tree, saying, "Christ, Larry, it took you long enough. I thought you'd find me last night." And I imagine him dead, floating in the water. I didn't think I was going to find him, but the world feels very mysterious to me now, and I knew I had to look.

I walk over to Johnny's apartment, and I see Charlie Schwab's car outside. I'm a little surprised, but where else was Bud going to go? I don't know whether I want to see Bud or not; a big part of me wants to just get the hell out of there, but something in me says I should go up and talk to Bud. I don't understand this.

Very quickly, I climb the back stairs. I've got sneakers on, and I'm being quiet, but I don't understand why I should want to be quiet. I get up to the top step outside the kitchen, and I sit down on it. Through the screen door I can see one of Charlie Schwab's arms resting on the table—at least I think it's Charlie's—it's a big, muscular arm covered with hair. I sit on the top step without moving, and I can hear the men inside shifting their weight on the kitchen chairs. I hear liquid pouring from a bottle, and I hear the bottle being set down on the table, and I hear somebody drink. Then somebody groans, and it's probably Bud.

I don't know what I'm doing here. I should either go in and talk to them, or I should sneak back down the stairs and leave, but I don't do either of those things. I sit on the top step for what must be over an hour, listening to the shifting of weight on the chairs, to the sound of liquid being poured, to the sound of somebody drinking it. Every once in a while Bud groans, and Charlie—I think it's Charlie, who else would it be?—says, "I know, old fellow. Yeah, I know."

When Bud first turned up in my life, I didn't like him at all. Over the years I did my best to like him, and sometimes I did. Johnny and I had fun with him sometimes, and I can remember Bud being kind to us sometimes, and I ask myself if I like him now, and I don't have any clear answer to that.

So maybe Bud is one of the biggest assholes in the universe, he's still the closest thing to a father I've ever had, and what I'm thinking now is that I'm the only son he's got. I'm thinking that it wouldn't hurt me to go inside and sit with him for a while, to give him a pat on the shoulder and let him know that he can count on me. To let him know that he's still got me—or something like that. And maybe it'd help, maybe he wouldn't feel quite as terrible as he does. I can't quite bring myself to do it, but I can't bring myself to sneak away either. I feel stuck there on the top step, and the sun's getting higher.

"Oh, Jesus," Bud says. "Oh, Jesus, Charlie. Why did it have to be my boy? Why couldn't it have been that rotten Larry?"

"That son of a bitch," I yell. I grab up the chair I've been sitting on and smash it against the wall. "That fucking—worthless—god-damned—shit," I yell, smashing the chair against the wall. It's old lawn furniture, and it's flying in all directions.

Cynthia has jumped up and backed away, and I keep hammering the wall until all I've got left in my hands is one piece of wood. I throw that one piece of wood off the porch and down onto Front Street.

I'm crying so hard I can't see, and I sink to my knees. I feel Cynthia put her arm around me. I grope for her hand; I grab it and hold onto it. She kneels down with me, and I can hear that she's crying too. "Larry," she says, "you don't think— After all these years you don't still think you killed him, do you?"

"No. I don't still think that. I'm not sure I ever really thought that. I mean I don't think I ever entirely believed it. But I did *something*. The horrible thing is, it's all so goddamned complicated."

After I heard what Bud had said, I sneaked down the back steps and took off running. I didn't know where I was going. I didn't know what to do next. I went down to the river, and I sat by the river, and I didn't know what to do. I can't remember any more what I was feeling; all I can remember was a big blank— absolutely nothing meant anything. I somehow knew that what I had to do was find the next thing, whatever it was. It could be really simple, like going home and taking a bath. Anything at all like that, and then that next thing would lead to another next thing, and then another next thing after that. But I couldn't find the next thing.

Walk, I told myself, so I stood up and walked. I thought I'd like to go see Pete Saunders, our coach, and then I thought, Jesus, is that ever a dumb idea. What do you want to see him for? But I couldn't think of anything else, so I walked over to his house and knocked on the back door.

Pete was sitting at the kitchen table eating breakfast. He had on a bathrobe, and it seemed like a strange thing for him to be wearing; he was so fat it looked like it was ten sizes too small for him, and his enormous gut stuck out from the front of it. "Come on in," he said. He didn't seem the least bit surprised to see me. His wife was there. I'd never met her. "Make him some pancakes," he said.

I sat down at the kitchen table. "Couldn't sleep, huh?" he said.

"I guess not."

"That's not surprising."

I hadn't mentioned Johnny. "They'll find him today," he said.

"You think so?"

"Oh, yeah. Sure, they will. There'll be dozens of boats out looking for him, and one of them's sure to find him. What was he doing out there? Do you know?"

"I don't know. Hacking around, I guess."

"Yeah. Hacking around, huh? Was he much of a swimmer?"

"No. Not much."

"Yeah, it's a real shame. A real shame. These things happen every few years, and it's always real sad. You get out in that channel, you don't know what's hit you. Even put Bobby Cotter out there, he'd have a bit of a fight, you know."

"It's really bad out there, huh?" I knew he'd swum the river plenty of times.

"Yeah," he said. "You're always surprised at the current out there. It looks so peaceful if you're standing on the bank."

He told me about the old days when they'd fire the cannons to bring the bodies up. "It didn't work, you know," he said, "but they thought it did because the bodies always come up."

"Why do they come up?" I said. He was the Sheriff, and he ought to know.

"When they've been in the water, they bloat up with gas after a while, and then they come up of their own accord."

"Oh, Pete, don't tell him that," his wife said.

"Why shouldn't I tell him? He wants to know. Yeah, son, your brother will come back up today, and we'll find him. Don't worry about that. We'll find him all right."

I didn't stay in Pete's kitchen much longer than an hour, but it changed things for me. Before that, I'd been—I don't know how to put this—hanging by a thread, but after that, it was better. I don't know what I would have done if I hadn't gone to see Pete, the Sheriff of Ohio County, that good man.

I've stopped talking, and Cynthia says, "Did they find him that day?"

"Oh, yeah. It was just like Pete said. That afternoon they found him. Some people in a little motorboat found him. He was floating gently in the water down south of the Island."

It's dawn. The birds are staking out their territories for the day, and there's a cool pewter light filtering across the river. Cynthia and I are sitting together on the floor with our backs to the wall. There's bits of broken chair lying all around us. We haven't said anything for a long time—it feels like over an hour. I've cried so much I feel hollow and exhausted. "Well, I guess we're not going to get to Jeff and Linda's," I say.

"I guess not." It's just light enough for me to see her face. "Should we try to get some sleep?"

"I don't know. Maybe."

All the bedding's gone. We fold up sweaters for pillows and lie down together on the bare mattress. "I love you, Cynthia Ann."

"I love you too, Larry."

I don't feel the least bit sleepy, but my eyes are burning. I close them, and there's a vague scattering of things moving in my mind—not quite thoughts, more like blurry images, folding and refolding into each other. It's just that old, familiar drift to sleep, I say to myself, surprised—it's just that funny state that happens once every day. That's all it is. Sometimes it frightens me so much I yank myself back out of it; sometimes I do that over and over again before I let myself go down into it. Now I'm thinking that it's strange for me to do that—kind of pointless. It doesn't matter whether I do it or not, I still have to sleep.

I wake with a jerk, grab for something, feel my hands grip the mattress. "Sorry," Cynthia says. I can feel the tingle on my cheek where she's kissed me. The sun's up, and it's going to be another hot one. "We've got to get going, hon," she says. "It's after nine."

She must have had a bath; her hair's still damp. She's wearing her gray business suit, and she looks crisp and fresh. "Do you want to get breakfast somewhere? We'd have to leave right now."

"No, we'll eat something later. Is that okay? Did you sleep?"

"A little bit. Enough."

I shave, put on my suit and tie. I clean up the broken wood on the back porch. I leave the keys in the middle of the table for Mrs. Campbell and carry the suitcases down to the car. I don't have any desire at all to go back and walk through the apartment one last time.

The funeral is in the little chapel at the cemetery. Although my mother hadn't set foot in a church in thirty years, she was nominally a Presbyterian; early in the week when I was so out to lunch I wasn't paying much attention, Cynthia called the church and arranged for a minister. I heard her on the phone saying, "I know it must be hard for you—you didn't know her. We just want something short and simple."

We're a few minutes early, and so is the minister. If I'd had any choice in the matter, I would have preferred an older man; he's a young fellow with a big horsey face and big hands and feet. He offers his condolences, and there's a homely gravity to him that seems okay to me. Cynthia pays him, and all of us are faintly embarrassed by the transaction. He's got an old, battered Bible with him, and he raises it to Cynthia in an odd gesture that looks like a salute.

"What was that all about?" I ask her.

"Oh. I told him to use the King James—none of this Revised Standard garbage." I've got to laugh at that.

My mother is in her little polished wooden box at the front of the chapel. People have sent flowers, and I dutifully read the cards. "Don't lose them," Cynthia says. "We'll have to send notes."

We step out of the chapel and into the sunshine; Jeff and Linda are walking down the path from the parking lot. "How nice of them," Cynthia says, "they didn't have to come." Linda has managed to locate a simple black dress, and I look at Cynthia to see if she's noticed, and of course she has.

"Sorry we didn't make it last night," I say.

"No problem," Jeff says. "We didn't do anything special. Just sat around in front of the tube."

Funerals make most people stiff and awkward, and I can see that Jeff and Linda won't allow themselves to talk. "Sure is a pretty day," I say.

"Oh, you bet," Jeff says. "Couldn't ask for a nicer one."

Other people are arriving now, and I've got to search my mind to remember who some of them are. I haven't seen most of them in twenty or thirty years—most of them are old people—and they kindly introduce themselves. There's not more than a dozen, but it's enough to suit me.

We sit down on the folding chairs, and the minister says a few words about my mother; he's obviously had some help from Cynthia, and once again I'm grateful to her. He talks about my mother's years of service, her kindness and her steadfastness, and it isn't exactly what I would have said, but it's okay. "In the sweat of thy face shalt thou eat bread," he reads from his old Bible, "till thou return unto the ground; for out of it wast thou taken: for dust thou art, and unto dust shalt thou return." I wonder if Cynthia picked that passage, and I look at her, but she's looking straight ahead.

"Naked came I out of my mother's womb, and naked shall I return thither: the Lord gave, and the Lord hath taken away; blessed be the name of the Lord."

"Amen," one of the old people says, but I can't see which one it was. I'd thought I was finished with crying, but my eyes sting.

The minister manages a relatively smooth segue into the life everlasting; Jesus makes a brief, ghostly appearance promising us the Resurrection, and we're dispatched with a psalm: "Surely goodness and mercy shall follow me all the days of my life..." Short and simple, Cynthia said, and that's what it was, and there's nothing about it I would have changed.

It's been years since I've been at a funeral—the last one was my grandmother's—and the protocol must be different now; they used to lower the coffin into the ground—or at least I think they did—but my mother's little box will go in some time later. Linda, who never met my mother in her life, has been crying; she's still dabbing her eyes. She manages a smile. "My mom died just last year," she says as though she needs to explain herself.

"You guys feel like having brunch?" Jeff asks me in a quiet, self-conscious voice.

"Oh, sure. Isn't that exactly what you're supposed to do after funerals—eat?"

I want to see my mother's grave, so they follow along behind me until I find it. She bought the plot years ago; it's right next to my grandmother, and that seems right. The grave's been dug. I suppose it doesn't matter who puts her in it.

"You got anybody buried here?" I ask Jeff.

"Are you kidding? There's Snyders all over this damn place."

"You know where that big monument to Karl Eberhardt is?"

"Yeah," he says, pointing, "it's right over there."

The way I orient myself in the cemetery is by Karl Eberhardt's monument. He was one of Raysburg's old-time robber barons, and he had a life-sized sculpture made of himself. He's wearing a frock coat, and he's standing solidly on his pedestal staring angrily out toward the National Road; on each side of him is a kneeling, weeping woman with wings. "What wonderful, splendidly rotten taste," Cynthia says.

"Isn't it though?" I say. "The old joke I heard from my mother is that it's Karl with his wife and mistress."

The Armbruster plot is down to the right. I see Bud first. Then, next to him, the flat stone that says: John Henry Armbruster, 1943–1960. The moment I see the stone, I know that I won't find what I want here at his grave, but I stand for a moment looking at it anyway.

"He was in my class for a couple years," Jeff says.

"Yeah, he was only at the Academy a couple years."

"It's a shame for somebody to die that young—I didn't know him very well." What I'm thinking is that nobody knew him very well, but I don't want to say that.

Jeff and Linda take us to Raysburg's answer to a yuppie restaurant—it's replaced the old hole-in-the-wall where Johnny and I used to eat spaghetti at four in the morning—and we have eggs benedict and cappuccinos. We actually manage to be fairly cheery. Our wives swap addresses and phone numbers and vow to keep in touch; it's an easy thing to say, but I have a feeling they both mean it.

"I'm sorry you didn't meet our kids," Linda says.

"You guys have to come up," Cynthia says, "bring your kids. Any time. Come on, let's make a date or you won't do it."

We talk about the Labor Day weekend; Jeff can always take some extra time off, he says, if he plans ahead. "Yeah, do it," I say. "It's not that long a drive, really." He'll have to see. He'll give us a call.

Jeff and I fight for the bill; Jeff got the huge tab on the *Belle of Raysburg*, so I make sure I win this one. In the parking lot, Linda and Cynthia hug. Jeff offers me his hand, and I take it. I look right at him, and I think he probably looks just about as old as I do. "It was sure great to see you again," I say.

"Oh, hell," he says and wraps his arms around me. We give each other big bear hugs, then stand back, embarrassed and grinning. "How do you like that, Lar?" he says. "See what a couple sensitive New Age guys we turned out to be."

We've still got plenty of time, and when I turn west on the National Road, Cynthia doesn't ask me where we're going. She must know that I'd have to go down to the river. I drive over Raysburg Hill and over the Suspension Bridge to the Island. I park halfway up Front Street. I lead her across someone's lawn, down between two old houses, to the river bank. She doesn't say a word. We're faced directly toward downtown Raysburg; off to our right is the goddamned new bridge. It almost—but not quite— obscures our view of the Suspension Bridge.

"I never knew where he went in exactly," I say to her, "but I think it was around here."

From here it would be easy enough to go down to the river. The land slopes gently right down to the bank. I don't remember if all these trees were growing then, or if they were as high as they are now, but if they had been, they would have cut off the view from the houses. Nobody would have seen the boys going down into the river. The sun is almost directly overhead now, and the glare off the water is terrific. I can't remember the last time I saw things look so sharp and clearly defined.

"I'm not sure," I say to Cynthia. "I'm not sure exactly where he went in."

The longer I look at it, the less sure I am. Maybe this isn't where he went in at all. Maybe it's farther up the Island. Cynthia doesn't say a word. She seems content to stand next to me and let me think whatever I'm thinking. "It's been thirty-two years," I say. "I'm not sure I remember exactly. I'm not sure I ever knew exactly."

I look down at the river. We always lived in apartments by the river. I think about my grandmother telling me over and over again, "Our people always went on the river." When my mother was considering moving to Sharon, she used to say, "I'd miss the river."

"God, it's been a long time," I say to Cynthia, and the minute I've said it, I feel something change in me. I've remembered all I have to, and it doesn't matter whether or not I know exactly where he went in. I'm finished with it. I don't want to stand around any longer looking at the Ohio River. I want to go home to Massachusetts and be with my kids.

If I'd known when I was eighteen that it would take me thirty-two years before I'd feel entirely whole and at home in myself again, I might not have had the strength to make it all the way here—and that would have been a shame, to have stopped at any time before I got all the way here. I want to say that to Cynthia, but I can't find a way to say it that doesn't sound self-pitying, and that's not what I'm feeling.

"I'm ready to go," I say.

"Okay," she says, but she doesn't move. She's looking up toward the hills above Raysburg.

"Did you know that Mrs. Epping went up in a balloon?" she says.

I'm so startled it takes me a few seconds to absorb what she's just said. Then I turn toward her. She's still looking up. "No," I say. "You've never told me that."

"Didn't I? I forget what I've told you and what I haven't. Well, she did, isn't that amazing? It was a couple years before the first war. A balloonist came through—you know, doing the county fairs—and he said he would be honored if Mrs. Epping would go up with him. Nobody expected her to. She was an old lady by then—in her seventies. Her husband had been dead for years. But she did it, and wrote it up in the *Massillon Register*—'My Trip in a Balloon.'"

We find little kids so touching because they can be astonished and delighted by things we take for granted. "Oh, Daddy!" Alison said to me once, "Come quick. I show you. The spider made her web again." Now Cynthia's face is exactly the way Alison's was when she said that.

Cynthia is looking up into the sky above downtown Raysburg, and I follow her gaze up into the empty sky. She's staring with such concentration that, for a moment, I can almost see it too—the fat balloon floating up there high above the hills.

I've never seen a picture of Mrs. Epping when she was old, so I imagine her as looking something like my grandmother. Then, suddenly, it's my grandmother up there above the river. She's wearing gloves and a hat and a dark purple dress, and she's sitting upright—perfectly unafraid—in the basket of the balloon with her hands folded in her lap as she gazes down upon her world.

ACKNOWLEDGMENTS

Horace Bixby's advice to the young Mark Twain is found in *Life on the Mississippi;* in the Penguin Classics edition (1984), James M. Cox uses the same quotation in his introduction (p. 19). I have borrowed the line spoken to Mrs. Epping—"We might yet succeed if we could only have three generations of single women"—from Constance Cary Harrison's 1893 novel, *A Bachelor Maid.*

Except for public figures mentioned in passing (George Bush, Ross Perot, etc.), all the characters in this novel (including Mrs. Epping) are fictitious.